Sand

and

Ash

Sand

and

Ash

D. Moonfire

Broken Typewriter Press • Cedar Rapids

Broken Typewriter Press
5001 1st Ave SE
Ste 105 #243
Cedar Rapids, IA 52402

Broken Typewriter Press
https://broken.typewriter.press/

ISBN 978-1-940509-16-7

Version 1.1.0

To Jon

Miwāfu

This novel is set in the Mifuno Desert where the native language is Miwāfu. Names in this language are significantly different from English, so here is a short guide on pronunciation and usage.

The biggest difference is that every name is gendered, which is identified by the accent on the penultimate syllable. There are three types of accents:

- *Grave* (as in hèru for stallion) is a tiny tick that goes down to the right. The grave accent indicates a masculine aspect, either in physical gender, size, or power. Names with grave accents either end in a lower pitch or the entire word is spoken in a lower tone.
- *Macron* (for example, hēru for colt) is a bar over the vowel. This is a neuter term, used for many gender-free words or expressions within the language. It is also used for mechanical devices, abstract concepts, and children —both human and beast. Macrons are spoken as a long vowel or drawing out the word just a beat longer than normal.

- *Acute* (héru for mare) is a tiny tick that goes to the upper right. The acute indicates feminine aspects of the word. It can represent control without power or precision. These words end on a high note or the entire word is spoken in a higher pitch.

The only instances where accents aren't used is adjectives or indication of ownership. So, if a valley is owned by the clan Shimusògo, it is known as Shimusogo Valley.

The names themselves are phonetic. A syllable is always from a consonant cluster to the vowel. For examples: Mi.wā.fu (IPA /mi.waː.ɸɥ̊/), Shi.mu.sò.go (/ɕi.mɯ.↓so.go/), and De.sò.chu (/de.↓so.tɕɥ̊/). The only exception is the letter "n" which is considered part of the syllable before it when not followed by a vowel. For example, ga.n.ré.ko (/ga.ŋ↑re.ko/) and ka.né.ko (/ka.↑ne.ko/).

Miwāfu has no capital letters, they are added to satisfy English conventions.

Previously

Sand and Blood started with Shimusogo Rutejìmo trying to sneak into the clan's shrine to steal his great-grandfather's ashes in an effort to prove himself capable of the act. He was caught by Hyonèku and forced to tell his grandmother, Tejíko.

When Tejíko found out about his failed attempt, she beat him until Gemènyo interrupted. Tejíko stops beating Rutejìmo and lets Gemènyo talk to Rutejìmo. Gemènyo's talk points out that Rutejìmo has never applied himself and most of the clan considered him to be too weak to amount to anything.

Despite this, he was sent on a rite of passage to let the desert determine his future with the clan and to see if Shimusògo would grant him magic. The other four teenagers near his age were included Chimípu, Pidòhu, Tsubàyo, and Karawàbi.

After traveling for almost two weeks, the elders of the clan abandoned Rutejìmo and the others in the middle of the night. The revelation split the group in two, with Tsubàyo and Karawàbi leaving and Rutejìmo joining them. Chimípu stayed behind to care for Pidòhu who had broken his leg after falling.

It wasn't long before Rutejìmo struggled with Tsubàyo's commands and Karawàbi's brutality. After a brief incident where Tsubàyo tried to steal a horse, Rutejìmo returned to Chimípu after experiencing his first touch of Shimusògo, the ability to run faster than normal.

Reunited with Chimípu and Pidòhu, the three decided to take Pidòhu home. They traveled with a handmade stretcher. Along the way, they encountered Mikáryo who was hunting the murderer of her sister and the thief of her horses. Mikáryo realized they were on their rites of passage and withdrew, but swore that she would have one of them if the murderer, Tsubàyo, was not presented to her.

The trio continued along the way, growing in power and also closer together. Rutejìmo found that some of his knowledge was wrong and struggled with jealousy of Chimípu's power which quickly outpaced his own. Pidòhu was also experiencing his own epiphany of Tateshyúso.

Eventually, they encountered Tsubàyo who tried to kill them repeatedly. Pidòhu was kidnapped and Rutejìmo encouraged Chimípu to go after him, leaving him alone. That night, Mikáryo returned to watch over him as he slept despite being a clan of the night.

The next day, encouraged by Mikáryo, Chimípu and Rutejìmo went to rescue Pidòhu. Tsubàyo managed to defend himself and Rutejìmo was captured while freeing Pidòhu. That night, Mikáryo returned and indicated that she would only accept Tsubàyo as her sacrifice.

When morning came, there was a final encounter where Rutejìmo was able to save Pidòhu from falling and all of their powers emerged and grew. At the end, when the rest of the Shimusògo clan showed up, there was a standoff with Mikáryo who claimed Tsubàyo as her own. Rutejìmo stopped the potential fight by calling a vote to save her.

Chapter 1

Running Alone

In Miwāfu, only the last part of a name is accented. This creates a confusing situation for outsiders when a member of the Beporómu clan is named Beporomu Fusóki.

—Jyomiku Komishímu, *Words of the Desert*

Shimusogo Rutejìmo ran alone across the desert, chasing after a bird, a dépa, he could never catch and only he could see. No matter where he ran, his feet struck solid ground. As his bare foot lifted from the ground, the rock crumbled back into shifting sands before being sucked into the plume of dust and rock that billowed out behind him. Despite running faster than most horses, his heartbeat was a steady rhythm that matched the impacts of his bare feet against the sun-burned ground. On a good day, he could cover thirty miles in less than an hour for as long as the sun hung in the sky.

The small bird was Shimusògo, his clan spirit. Only a foot tall, it always raced a heartbeat in front of him no matter how fast he sprinted. If he slowed, it would disappear and the heat and exhaustion would bear down on him. But when he chased Shimusògo, Rutejìmo felt the euphoria of magic pulsing through his veins and beating underneath his feet.

For the first time in months, he ran for the sake of running instead of racing from one end of the Mifuno Desert to the other while delivering documents and decrees. For a few days, he didn't have to worry about recording legal contracts in Wamifuko City or the constant back and forth between Kidorisi Valley and Mafimara Ridge during tense negotiations for trade rights.

The last job, the one involving the Kidorīsi and Mafimára clans, still haunted his thoughts. More than a few times he had to circle around an ambush or sneak into the valleys to avoid being attacked by those opposed to the treaty. The wound on his leg still itched from his brush with a sniper's arrow.

Rutejìmo tore his thoughts away from the previous job. The two clans signed their treaty, and Rutejìmo personally delivered it to the archives in Wamifuko City. It was the end of three months of hard running, and he was ready to spend a few days doing nothing but relaxing.

The desert air beat against his bare chest and tickled the dark hairs that dusted his chest. It tugged at his red trousers with sharp snaps of fluttering fabric. Motes of bright energy slipped out from Shimusògo's wings and joined in with the wind to buffet his skin. The energy streamed around his body before joining in with the vortex of air created by his passage.

Rutejìmo smiled and pushed himself to run as fast as he could. Despite his speed, he was still the slowest runner in the clan. But alone on the sands, he didn't have to worry about anything besides running in a lazy circle around Shimusogo Valley, his ancestral home. He kept the valley in the periphery of his vision and strayed no more than five leagues away before coming back around. Even close to home, there was always danger.

The sun touched the horizon. The dépa turned sharply and headed for the valley. He followed without question, submitting himself to the spirit's will. The route brought him in line with the entrance of the valley, and he raced across a patch of sharp rocks before coming up to the familiar trail that would bring him home before the sun's light faded.

Like all spirits of the sun, Shimusògo gained power from the light, and Rutejìmo gained his power from the spirit. When darkness descended across the world Rutejìmo's speed would fade, and he would feel every ache, pain, and guilty thought in his head. He would be just another man in the desert, slow and plodding.

Too soon, he was coming up to the two pillars that marked the entrance of the clan's valley. He slowed down and cringed. He hated that moment when he ceased to run. In front of him, the dépa grew closer with his slowing. When he smoothly shifted from a run to a jog, the bird disappeared from sight.

The magic stopped with the dépa's disappearance. Without power fueling his speed, Rutejìmo sank into the sand. The peace and joy of running slipped away, and the aches of his month-long missions seeped back into his joints.

He jogged past the pillars, gasping for breath. Two red and orange cloths embroidered with the Shimusògo name billowed from each side. The right banner had signs of being recently patched, and he wondered which child had managed to rip it.

"Good run?" asked Gemènyo. As always, a cloud of pipe smoke swirled behind him and marked his passage. His short black hair had a fringe of white on the temples. The older man strolled down stairs carved into the rock behind one pillar. The stairs led to a guard post where someone could see anyone approaching the valley.

Rutejìmo nodded and stopped. The world spun around him for a few seconds before he adjusted to being still. "Yes, I just needed to..." He gave up trying to find a word and shrugged, running his hand through his own short-cropped black hair before shaking the sweat from his palm.

Gemènyo chuckled. "Shimusògo run." It was the clan's motto.

"Shimusògo run."

They both headed into the valley. Their bare feet slapped against the stone, but Rutejìmo could barely feel the impact. His feet were heavily callused from constant running on sands and rock. Only during the rapid slowing, when he dug his feet and hands into the ground, did he feel the drag of the earth against his soles.

They passed a pair of teenage boys dragging a box of supplies to the guard post. They left behind a trail of dirt and Rutejìmo followed it back with his eyes until he spotted where the two cut through the fields to shave a few minutes from their route between the cooking area and the entrance.

Gemènyo pulled his pipe out and clicked his tongue in disapproval.

One of the boys looked up and blushed before grabbing the box and dragging it faster.

Rutejìmo chuckled and shook his head. It wasn't that long ago when he did the same thing. He had no doubt the punishment would be the same, planting the next round of crops underneath the watchful eye of one of the clan's elders.

"Hey, Jìmo?"

Rutejìmo smiled at the familiar use of his name. "Yeah?"

"Want to play cards tonight?" He gestured up to the side of the valley to where their homes were carved into the rock. All of the cave entrances where simple holes in the stone with the occupied ones covered by a red or orange blanket with the owner's names. Gemènyo's home was a few rods, just under thirty feet, past Rutejìmo's bachelor cave.

"Are your wife and mother joining in?"

"Probably not. Faríhyo is cooking, and her mother is on cleanup," Gemènyo gestured to the large cooking area in the center of the valley, "so both will be out chatting until lights out."

He took a long, dramatic deep breath. "I can smell her lovely cooking even from here."

"I doubt you can smell anything with that pipe burning."

Gemènyo hefted the pipe in his hand and swished it around, tracing lines in the air.

Rutejìmo could tell he was writing something obscene. With a grin, he slashed his hand through the smoke. "Old men like you shouldn't use words like that."

"Old men like me and Hyonèku shouldn't have to invite young men like you over for cards."

Hyonèku was Gemènyo's best friend. They grew up together and were comfortable enough to share everything with each other. They also treated Rutejìmo as a treasured younger sibling, something he didn't get from his own brother.

Rutejìmo shrugged to cover the brief moment of discomfort. They headed up along the narrow paths leading to the family caves. "What am I going to do? Sit in my cave alone for the night?"

"No, but there are other things you can do. Things most young men do."

Rutejìmo rolled his eyes. "I'm not into chasing around the girls, if that is what you mean. Most of them run faster than me."

"Oh no," Gemènyo chuckled, "I would never suggest the young courier try to actually find some companionship on his own. These old bones," he began to limp, "need the company in case I fall."

With a chuckle, Rutejìmo smacked him on the shoulder. "Well, Mènyo, if you need some help I'll ask Tejíko. I'm sure she'll..." He grinned at the mock horror Gemènyo displayed at the mention of Rutejìmo's grandmother.

Gemènyo shuddered. "Fine, fine. I won't mention it again."

"Yes, you will. And if it isn't you, Nèku will say something. I'm just not," a guilty memory rose up, a dark-skinned woman with horse tattoos across her back, and he struggled to complete his sentence. "... not ready yet, I guess."

"You're thinking about Pabinkue Mikáryo again."

Rutejìmo looked up with a start and cringed at Gemènyo. "What?"

Gemènyo smirked and gestured to a necklace Rutejìmo wore around his neck. "I can tell when you play with that." The black leather was snug around his throat, and a large, chipped-off tooth hung from it. Mikáryo had broken it off a large snake that would have killed him. A lesson, she told him, but one that Rutejìmo still struggled to understand.

With a blush burning on his cheeks, Rutejìmo snatched his hand away. He looked across the valley. "I don't know what you're talking about."

Gemènyo stepped closer and patted Rutejìmo on the shoulder.

Rutejìmo's shoulders and back tensed, but he nodded and continued walking along the trail. They passed the lanterns that would light the trails at night. At the moment, the crystals were dark while they soaked up the sun.

"Jìmo," Gemènyo said in a softer voice.

His stomach twisted, but Rutejìmo looked back over to his friend.

Gemènyo finished tapping more weed into his pipe. "I'm not saying give up on Pabinkue Mikáryo; just realize that you will probably never see her again. It has been ten years."

Images of Mikáryo drifted across his mind—the tattoos on her back, the black fabric wrapped around her body, the way her loincloth hung from her hips when she knelt in front of a fire—until he tore his thoughts away. "I know."

"Though," he glanced at Rutejìmo with a smirk, "she clearly made some impression. Sure she didn't crawl into your sleeping roll when we weren't watching?"

Rutejìmo groaned and rolled his eyes. "No, she was threatening to kill me the entire time."

"Not what we saw," Gemènyo said with a smirk.

Stepping back, Rutejìmo punched Gemènyo in the shoulder. It was supposed to be a playful hit, but it impacted harder than he intended.

Gemènyo stepped back, his feet scraping the edge of the path before he regained his balance. He drew deep from his pipe before blowing the smoke in a cloud around him. "Come on. Throw your stuff in your cave, and I'll meet you down at the fires."

Rutejìmo nodded.

Gemènyo disappeared in a blast of air and sparkles of fading sunlight. The smoke from his pipe flew after him, swirling in a vortex to mark his travel along the narrow path up to his own home. He stopped at the entrance to wave at someone, and the wind brought the cloud of pipe smoke into a haze around his head.

Rutejìmo pushed aside the blanket covering the entrance of his own home and ducked into the darkness. He lived in one of the smaller caves in the valley with only one common room and a hall leading into two smaller rooms. Inside the door was his travel pack, sitting where he had dropped it off before running. Bracing it on his shoulder, he walked past the nearly empty main room and into his bedroom.

He spilled the contents of his pack out on the bed and sorted through the mess. He didn't use his travel rations, but he had to refill one of his water skins. He returned items to his pack after checking them, so he would be ready to run on a moment's notice. He had a roll for sleeping, a small tent, and an alchemical gel for cooking. A trio of travel lights, small globes with a clockwork mechanism, settled into their customary place inside his bag.

Outside of survival gear, he had a book of poetry and his voting stones. Each of the black rocks with white ridges represented one year of being an adult in the clan. Another thirty rocks were secreted underneath his bed, but he was still a year away from pulling out the next one.

It took him only a few minutes to clean up from months of travel and prepare for the next trip. He knew that Gemènyo would be at least another hour—he had a wife and two children to regale with his adventures on the sands. Normally his wife would have run the Kidorīsi and Mafimára route, but she was pregnant with their third child. Rutejìmo had taken her place for the last five months while she succumbed to the care of retired couriers in the valley.

After twenty minutes of stalling, hunger finally evicted Rutejìmo from his cave. He set his full pack right inside the entrance before leaving. As the blanket slid into place, a girl's voice interrupted his thoughts.

"Great Shimusogo Rutejìmo?"

He turned to the speaker as she stepped out of the darkness. It was Mapábyo, Hyonèku's adopted daughter. The teenager was right at the cusp of womanhood, and everyone wondered when Tejíko, the clan elder and Rutejìmo's grandmother, would send her on her right of passage.

Unlike the rest of the clan, her skin wasn't the warm brown of the northern clans but the deep black of the south. She and her parents were part of a six-month caravan trip that Hyonèku had joined when Mapábyo was four. Her parents died during a raid and no one stepped up to take care of the young girl. Hyonèku, who had already fallen for the girl, carried her back across the desert to join the clan.

She wasn't born into the clan, but she had the body of a clan runner. She was thin and muscular, with little fat to grace her curves or chest. Her bare feet were heavily calloused. She wore a white tunic with a red skirt wrapped around her waist; it was an outfit that Rutejìmo hadn't seen before, but the skirt used to be her adoptive mother's. Her bare ankle sparkled with a steel bracelet that rested on the ridge across her foot.

He smiled and gave a low bow. "Good evening, Mapábyo. You look nice."

She held her arms behind her back and inched into the light of the lantern. Her eyes, a deep green flecked with lighter lines of emerald, flashed in the light. "Could I bother the Great Shimusogo Rutejìmo with a question?"

He chuckled. "Of course, but call me Rutejìmo at least."

She smiled and inched closer to him. Her long, black hair had been braided into a thick line down her back. Twisting her foot on the ground, she peeked up at him. "Sorry... Rutejìmo."

Rutejìmo stepped into his cave and grabbed two stools from inside the entrance. Turning around, he almost bumped into her. For a moment, he stared into her green eyes, and an uncomfortable feeling twisted his gut. "Um, out here would be best. That way no one would get any ideas."

"Oh," she stepped back.

Rutejìmo set the stool on the ground.

She watched until he stopped moving, then sat down on it. Twisting her hands in her lap, she struggled for a moment then said, "It's about... the rite of passage."

He sat down heavily. "You know I can't tell you anything. Part of the rites is not knowing what will happen; otherwise you might not hear Shimusògo when he calls."

She gave him a pleading look. "I know, but I was hoping you... might be willing to break the rules. I remember when you came back from yours. You had this," she waved her hand as she paused, "haunted look on your face when you didn't think anyone was watching. And ever since, you've run just a few steps away from the others."

Rutejìmo thought back to his own rite of passage. The clan had abandoned him and others in the middle of the desert to find their true character. Rutejìmo, to his dismay, almost didn't survive it. He only lived because of friendship from the other teenagers in the clan. It also introduced him to Pabinkue Mikáryo, the woman who haunted his dreams.

Mapábyo held up her hands. "Anything? Please, Great Shimusogo Rutejìmo?"

He chuckled softly. "Pábyo, I can't tell you what's going to happen because I don't know. What I went through was nothing like what your father or even Gemènyo experienced. You probably won't even realize you are in it until..." He realized he was saying too much. "Well, until you're in the middle of it."

She sighed and tugged on her braid.

He glanced out into the valley where night was descending. Crystal lanterns were flickering to life, bathing the trails in hazy blue light. The one outside his cave hummed before coming to life. With a flicker, both Rutejìmo and Mapábyo were cast in a harsh, painful light.

"It's been years since I've been old enough," she said on the edge of tears. "Why haven't they taken me by now? Is it because I wasn't born a Shimusògo?"

With a shake, he pointed to the shrine. "You got in trouble trying to break into the shrine during Shimusògo's birthday festival. And you should be glad it was Chimípu who caught you instead of your father. He wouldn't have stopped at the entrance."

She giggled softly and ducked her head. "I thought Chimípu was going to kill me."

"So did all of us. Though," he grinned, "I had four pyābi that you would have made it to at least the pillars."

Mapábyo looked up with a gasp. "You did?"

Gemènyo stepped into the light and said, "Yes and I had ten that she would beat your ass before you made it past the cooking area. Of course," he grinned and exhaled, "I won."

Ducking her head, she stood up and gestured to the chair. "Good evening, Great Shimusogo Gemènyo."

Gemènyo shook his head and gestured back to the chair. "Don't you know better than to ask about the rites?"

"Yes, Great Shimusogo Gemènyo." She spoke in a quiet, deferential voice.

"Go on, your papa's probably asking for you down by the fires."

She ran down the trail toward the fire, not with the magic of the clan, but with the energy of a teenage girl. She wouldn't be able to chase the dépa until after her rites, when the stress would lay her soul bare to the spirit of the clan.

Rutejìmo stood up, grabbed the two stools, and replaced them inside the cave.

When he stepped out, Gemènyo was watching him with a smirk on his face.

"What?"

"Oh, nothing... Great Shimusogo Rutejìmo."

Chapter 2

Decisions Made

Certain rituals in one's life are carefully planned behind the scenes.
—Ryochisomi Kadèfu, *Introduction to Kyōti Society*

"Three of snakes in the north, one point." Rutejìmo tapped his card against one of the four piles before picking up the top card from the other three piles on the table.

"Damn, that was my three of scorpions." Gemènyo sat with one leg in a crook and his pipe balanced on his knee. He groaned and pulled out a six of snakes and set it on the east pile. "Your turn."

Rutejìmo glanced down at his cards. He only had two left, but neither would help him get another trick out of the cards on the table. Hissing through his teeth, he plucked out the card with an illustration of two rocks sticking out of a sand dune.

Gemènyo grinned.

Rutejìmo placed it on the south pile. He shuffled through the stack looking for another snake. He got through the pile before he realized he picked the wrong one. "Damn." He grabbed a random card, the five of birds, and set it down on top of the rocks. "Your turn."

"So," Gemènyo said, "you think Mapábyo is going to have her rites soon?"

Rutejìmo glanced up. "Probably. Why?"

"Oh, just curious." Gemènyo set down a three of horses on the north pile. "I heard her asking you about it."

Rutejìmo had only one card left. He set it down on a nine of birds. "I'm out. She was just curious. Don't worry, I didn't say anything to ruin the surprise. Not like there is anything I could do to ruin the joy of being abandoned in the middle of the desert to die."

"Ha!" Gemènyo slapped down his card on top of Rutejìmo. It was a four of scorpions.

Rutejìmo looked at the cards and groaned.

"A broken chain!" Gemènyo plucked the sequential cards from the four piles. "That gets me eight points. I win!"

Rutejìmo shoved his three pyābi across the table. Sitting back, he picked up his mug and watched the mist rising from the almost frozen bichíru, a fermented drink made from sweet plants. "At least I won the last game."

"And you're going to lose the next one. Deal."

As Rutejìmo shuffled the cards, he heard footsteps outside of the cave. With a nod to Gemènyo, he cut the deck and shuffled again. "Go on, old man, it's your home."

"Yeah, yeah." Gemènyo groaned. He stood up and headed for the entrance. He stuck his head out and then pulled it back in. "It's Hyonèku and Desòchu."

Rutejìmo froze at his brother's name. Afraid to make a scene, he cut the deck and shuffled it again.

Gemènyo held aside the blanket and the two men came inside.

Hyonèku was a friend to both Gemènyo and Rutejìmo. He was a tall, thin man with short black hair and a neat beard. He wore cotton trousers, dyed orange with red cuffs, and a white belt. Rutejìmo could see gray hairs ghosting across his bare chest.

Behind him stood Desòchu, Rutejìmo's older brother by almost a decade. He was powerfully built, with hard lines of muscles and battle scars. He had a closely cropped beard, barely a black shadow along his throat and chin. He wore a loose-cut, white jacket with orange trousers. Both top and bottom were trimmed in red.

Desòchu clapped hands with Gemènyo and glanced over. "You didn't stay long at the fire, Jìmo. Something wrong?"

Rutejìmo tensed and forced himself to shrug. "Wanted to play cards with Gemènyo."

"Great Shimusogo Tejíko was looking for you. And," his green eyes narrowed, "I heard that you were talking to Mapábyo."

Setting down his cards, Rutejìmo said, "She wanted to ask some questions."

"You didn't tell her anything, did you?" Desòchu's voice was tense, and Rutejìmo could see the muscles in his jaw tensing.

"No," Gemènyo said, "your little brother didn't say anything. I was listening the whole time."

Desòchu stared at Gemènyo, his lips pressed into a thin line.

"I brought something to drink." Hyonèku slipped past him and set down a bottle of spirits. "Deal me in."

Gemènyo sank down and tapped his pipe out into a wooden bucket. "Sure you have time for a game, Sòchu?"

His brother hesitated for a moment. "Yeah, deal me in."

"Three pyābi for the couriers, but Great Shimusogo Desòchu has to pay six because he won the last four games."

Desòchu gave a mock glare and sat down heavily. "How about I just bring these instead?" He dug into his belt and pulled out a small bag. He tossed it on the table and candied nuts spilled out.

"You're in," announced Gemènyo.

Rutejìmo dealt all the cards to the four players. When he went to pick up his own, he hesitated. The desire to stand up and leave rose inside him, and he struggled to fight it. It would just further ostracize himself from the others, and Desòchu had repeatedly criticized him for doing that. He bit his lip and then scooped up the cards.

None of the four men said anything for the first few minutes. The fire in the corner of the cave sparked and popped while they set down cards on one of the four piles. Occasionally, Desòchu or Gemènyo would finish a trick and pick up a card from each pile. Rutejìmo played conservatively, making no effort to draw attention to himself or trying to beat his brother.

Desòchu broke the silence. "Kidorīsi and Mafimára asked for a courier."

Rutejìmo groaned, and Gemènyo laughed.

"Those two..." Hyonèku shook his head sadly before setting down his next card.

Shrugging, Desòchu plucked a nut from the table before setting down his hand. His fighting bola thumped against the side of the table. "They pay annually and pay well, despite their fighting. Rutejìmo, I want you to do the hand-off. They know you."

Rutejìmo nodded and watched Gemènyo play his card before setting down his two of snakes on one of the piles.

"Hyonèku," Desòchu turned to the other man, "do you want to go with Rutejìmo?"

Rutejìmo hesitated, his fingers pressed against the rough card before he pulled his hand back. Desòchu never gave Rutejìmo a chance when it came to assigning jobs.

"Why?" asked Hyonèku.

"We're going to start Mapábyo's rites tomorrow."

Hyonèku grunted and nodded. "Yeah, I'll run with Rutejìmo. I don't think I could take watching her fumble around."

He smirked and kicked Rutejìmo playfully in the shin. "One thing to see Jìmo running aimlessly on the sand."

Rutejìmo grinned and glanced over to Gemènyo who winked back.

"But my own daughter?" Hyonèku snorted. "No, I'd rather steal one of Tejíko's maps and tear it in half."

"No," Desòchu said with a smirk, "watching your daughter's rites won't kill you. And we won't hear you screaming from here. Or have to clean up the blood."

Everyone laughed and the tension broke, but only for a moment. As soon as it ended, the cave grew quiet again.

"Great Shimusogo Hyonèku, thank you," said Desòchu. "Will you leave at first light?"

Hyonèku tapped his card on the table. "Isn't that Great Shimusogo Rutejìmo's choice? He's handling the package."

Desòchu glanced at Rutejìmo. There was a hardness in his eyes, a reservation that Rutejìmo had seen many times. The warrior rested his hand on his blade, but only for a second before making a show of picking up one of the treats off the table. "Of course. Jìmo?"

The muscles along Rutejìmo's spine tightened before he managed to nod twice. "First light is fine. We'll be ready."

Chapter 3

Nightmares

... including allowing the so-called warriors to vent their lusts on the unmarried youth in the name of "preparing" them for marriage.
—Rolan Madranir, *Barbarians of the Desert*

Rutejìmo sat in the dark. Beneath him, the sand scraped at his buttocks and hands. A cold wind of night peppered his face with flecks of sharpness. He could see the sun, but the brilliant orb gave no heat or light to the world around him. He was alone and helpless.

Most of his dreams started that way. Just as all of them ended in nightmares.

He hated and feared the night. He still remembered the day when he sent Chimípu out to save Pidòhu, and he was left alone to fend for himself. It had been ten years and memories were hazy, but the dying flame had been burned into his memories. Only a single light source lit up his world, pushing back the horrors that waited for darkness.

Ten years ago, he would have the same nightmare every night. The years had passed and the nightmares faded with time. Now, clutching his muscular legs to his chest, he remembered the sick fear of helplessness clawing at his guts.

He glanced over his shoulder, expecting something to come out for him. He wouldn't hear it coming, he never did. It was the warriors who saved him, first Chimípu and then... her. Pabinkue Mikáryo. The warrior of night who haunted not only his nightmares but also his fantasies.

Struggling to remember the confidence of a runner, he looked around. He searched for some light or a hint of what was coming for him: a mizonekima chyòre, the same type of giant snake that had almost killed him years ago; the bandits that preyed on the routes he ran between cities; or even some other unspeakable horror. Mifúno, in all of her glory as the desert herself, had secrets even on the beaten trails, and Rutejìmo knew he hadn't seen them all.

He whispered a prayer to Tachìra, begging the sun spirit to bring light, but there was nothing other than cold wind and sand.

Something brushed against his arm, and he jumped. Turning around, he clamped down on the muscles between his legs in fear of urinating on himself. There was nothing but darkness.

Letting his breath out, he turned back.

Mikáryo was right there, her face less than an inch from his nose.

Rutejìmo screamed and dove back. His heart slammed into his chest with a ceaseless drumming. He could see her bright as day, but he couldn't stop the fear that drove him to crawl away.

"You're pathetic," she said. She leaned forward to land on her hands, crawling after him on her knees. He could barely remember her anymore, just a memory glossed over by years of nightmares and dreams. He strained to recall the details that had faded with time.

Her black hair flowed down her chest, along the dark brown skin and over the black tattoos that covered almost every inch of her body. There were swirls of horses which trailed along her curves and beneath her clothing. She was almost naked, just like the day he saw her preparing to leave, with only a black cloth over her breasts and a matching loincloth.

Rutejìmo's heart pounded in his chest and he slumped to the ground. He couldn't breathe.

She crawled up to him, dragging her body along his legs. He could feel her arms, breasts, and hips with her movement. Her heat was a stark contrast to the icy wind streaming around them.

"Adorably pathetic, actually." And then there was that smile, a mixture of pity and affection.

Rutejìmo whimpered and reached out for her, afraid to touch her but desperate to feel her.

A flash of sunlight burst across his eyes and two dépas bounded over his chest. Before he could exhale, two bodies slammed into Mikáryo and threw her into the darkness. Rutejìmo knew it would be Desòchu and Chimípu, but he couldn't see anything but the sunlight glowing around their bodies.

The sound of fighting filled the air. They were attacking each other, bare fists against flesh. With each impact, a flash of sunlight or moonlight would burst out to highlight the blow before the darkness would rush back in. It left stars across his vision.

Rutejìmo clamped his hands over his ears and closed his eyes tightly. He hated the violence. He hated watching the clan warriors defend him, even when his life was in danger. He screwed his face in desperation to keep his senses shut, but the sounds and lights kept intruding despite his best efforts.

And then Mikáryo's scream, shrill and angry, slashed through the darkness. It rose to a high pitch and then there was a heavy thud. Her scream ended abruptly.

Rutejìmo sat up in his bed, gasping for breath. Sweat prickled his skin. He stared around, terrified to see a body draped across his bed or smell blood in the air. A pounding in his ears thumped with the rapid beats of his heart, drumming against his senses.

Gulping, he reached out and grabbed a travel light from his pack. The fist-sized globe felt comforting. He rolled it over and found the metal key on the bottom. Twisting it a few times, he released it and set it down on his lap. Inside, a clockwork mechanism began to rapidly tap against a crystal. Each impact against the crystal brought to life a few blue sparks which flowed inside the globe. After a few seconds, the entire thing shone brightly and filled the room with pale blue light.

He inspected the room, thankful when he didn't see bodies or blood. Every death had burned a mark across his nightmares. The first was seeing a boy he grew up with lying against a rock with his throat cut. The second was sitting across from Yutsupazéso, the clan elder before his grandmother, when she had a seizure during dinner. The latest happened a year ago when he walked into his grandmother's cave for dinner only to find her bowed over the body of her husband. The last was the first and only time he had ever seen his grandmother, Tejíko, cry.

Trembling, he pushed himself out of the bed. He felt drained and sick. He pulled on a pair of cotton shorts, a gift to himself on his twentieth birthday, and leaned against the wall. The cool stone felt good against his heated skin. With a groan, he grabbed the snake tooth around his neck.

Images of his dream drifted up, and he pictured Mikáryo kneeling above him. He could never forget the smoldering green eyes when she looked at him over the fire. Everyone in the desert had green eyes, but hers were almost pure emerald, and looking into them was like looking into a crystal-clear moon.

His heart began to quicken, and his manhood twitched. With a groan, he dug his fingers into his palms until the pain tore his thoughts away. Every time he thought about her eyes, he felt guilty. There was a flame there that haunted him as much as anything else, a childish fantasy over a decade old.

Mikáryo's clan spirit, Pabinkúe, gained power from the moon and night. Shimusògo, like all clans of the day, received their powers from Tachìra, the sun spirit. The two, sun and moon, were enemies since the beginning of time over the affections of Mifúno.

Rutejìmo staggered out of his sleeping area and into the main room. It was dark except for a thin sliver of orange light that speared from the entrance. He padded to the heavy blanket covering the opening, moving by rote memory around his few possessions. At the entrance, he could feel the cool air slipping by the blanket. He steeled himself and pushed it aside, stepping out into the night.

At night, the valley was dark except for crystal lanterns at the entrance of each cave. The crystals gathered energy from the sun during the day and then glowed orange and blue throughout the night. Judging from the faded light coming from his lantern, it was well into the night and few people would be up.

He let out a long breath and watched it fog in the air. Across the valley, he spotted Pidòhu's home with two lanterns on each side. The yellow banner with Pidòhu's name could be read from clear across the valley; the shades of yellow complemented Shimusògo's red and orange colors. Smoke billowed out of a vent in the cave and rose up into the night sky, flickering with red embers before fading into gray and then black. Pidòhu was up and working, probably fixing one of the steam-powered dogs the clan used for hauling loads from one end of the valley to the other.

Pidòhu lived in Shimusogo Valley with the other two members of the Tateshyúso clan. The two clan spirits were bound together, much like husband and wife, but in ways that only spirits could intertwine their energies and their families. But where Shimusògo was the dépa, Tateshyúso manifested as a shadow of a giant raptor sailing across the sky. She was powerful and silent, demanding more from Pidòhu than Shimusògo ever asked of Rutejìmo.

Rutejìmo considered heading over, then changed his mind. It would have only been a few seconds to sprint across the valley, but he kept Pidòhu up all night the last time they were both home. Rutejìmo stepped to the side and leaned back against the rock framing the entrance to his home. The cool air tickled the hairs on his chest and dried the sweat. He welcomed the prickle of his skin and the shivers that came from the cold seeping in through his back.

Memories of Mikáryo drifted through his mind, and he tugged on the snake tooth hanging from his throat. He struggled with the guilt that came of thinking about her black tattoos or the way she looked at him.

Someone raced the length of the valley bottom and a plume of dust rose behind them. Usually, everyone lost their power of speed when the sun dipped below the horizon, but being close to the shrine gave some measure of power to accelerate fast enough to race. He traced the curls of dust with his eyes until it stopped at the inner entrance of the valley.

Two women stood talking to each other with dust swirling around them. The older one, Kiramíro, was in her mid-thirties and heavily scarred from an ambush from a scorpion clan. She limped but still ran faster than anyone but Desòchu and the woman she was talking to, Chimípu.

He watched Chimípu speak, unable to hear her words. A year older than him, Chimípu's poise and talent came naturally. Even after years of fighting, her lithe figure showed only a few signs of her violent life, mostly with the healed scars along her shoulders, hands, and forearms. As she spoke to Kiramíro, she made an exaggerated bow which showed off her lithe form. Both of them laughed loudly and Rutejìmo wondered what joke Chimípu had just told. He wished he had her ease in talking to everyone, old and young.

Both Kiramíro and Chimípu were warriors for the clan. Not only could they run faster than Rutejìmo, Shimusògo gave them powers to defend the couriers and the valley from the other clans of the desert. He had seen Chimípu glow with golden fire, fight off a herd of telepathically-controlled horses, and use a slingshot to turn stones into flaming missiles that shattered rock.

There was a price for her powers though, a curse that Rutejìmo couldn't even comprehend living with. She was sterile, like all warriors, and she would never marry. The remainder of her life would focus on the clan as a whole, to protect and guide, to be a comforting shoulder, a stern teacher, and the hand of punishment. She would never retire either. It was only a matter of when she died in battle, not if.

His thoughts grew darker. During his rite of passage, he abandoned Chimípu and Pidòhu to the desert. He almost died, not by exposure or enemy, but by his own brother, Desòchu, who would have cut his throat to ensure that Rutejìmo didn't poison the Shimusògo clan with his disloyalty and need for isolation.

He sighed and thumped his head against the rock. He felt alone in the dark, haunted by memories, guilt, and death.

A blast of air slammed into him. He tensed and turned away before the sand bounced off his body. It took only a second for the wind to die down around him and he watched a few golden feathers flutter past him. He looked back to where Kiramíro and Chimípu stood, but only trails of dust marked them going separate ways. Silently, he followed the one trail of kicked up dust as it made its way toward him and stopped behind the faintly glowing woman approaching him. Flickers of heat and sparks rose up from her body, lighting up her hair in a halo of flame.

"You're up late, Jìmo," Chimípu walked the last few feet between them. She stopped on the opposite side of the entrance, leaning her shoulder against the rock. Her knife tapped against the rock, and the letters engraved on the blade flashed.

"Couldn't sleep."

"Because of Desòchu sending you out tomorrow?"

He chuckled, and then sighed. "No, nightmares."

"About Pabinkue Mikáryo?"

Rutejìmo realized he was holding the tooth. He pulled his hand away. "Am I that obvious?"

With a shrug, she rolled on her back and stared out across the valley. "Yes, but in your defense, it has been ten years. Most of us know about that," she gestured toward the necklace. "But I saw how you looked at her. You were smitten."

With a groan, he slid down the rock. "Why hasn't anyone told me I was that obvious?"

She laughed. "Because it was innocent."

"Why are people telling me now?"

"You've held a shikāfu flame for her just like Obepáryo pining for Hidòshi."

Rutejìmo noticed she didn't answer the question. He gave her a mock glare. "Obepáryo died waiting for Hidòshi to come back. She killed herself because she couldn't survive without him."

"Well," she shrugged, "I wouldn't have let you get that far." She winked and smirked.

"Thanks. I'll try to keep the tear-filled wailing to a minimum." He chuckled. "Though, no promises about the whole wandering barefoot through the desert, clutching my pregnant belly as I search the night for my one true love."

Chimípu crouched down and balanced on her heels. Her body found a perfect balance before she rocked back and forth. Her weapons, her knife and bola, swayed with her movements.

Rutejìmo watched her for a moment. "What's wrong with me, Mípu?"

She said nothing for a long moment. Then she pulled her knife and flipped it in her hand. She tossed it high above her. Little sparks of light ran along the name on the blade before it came down. She caught it neatly. Tossing it back up, she said, "There is nothing wrong with you, little brother."

He blushed at the name. She only called him brother when they were alone. It was a private form of affection, almost forbidden from a warrior who had to sever all ties of her own family.

Chimípu caught the blade with her other hand. "You're just different. That day on the sand, when you saved Mikáryo's life? Something changed in you. I saw you." She smiled and flipped her knife hard, and it shot up into the sky in a streamer of golden flames. "You became a man that day, but not in a way that me, Desòchu, or anyone else thought you would."

"I still wonder if I did the right thing."

Chimípu stood up. "No, you did the only thing you could do. And that is why I stood behind you and why you will always be my little brother."

He smiled sheepishly. "Thank you, Chimípu."

She stepped away from the stone, swinging her foot in a wide sweep before heading down the stairs.

Rutejìmo pushed himself up along the rock, scraping his back on the sharp edges. "Going to Pidòhu's?"

Chimípu stopped and looked over her shoulder. There was a sad and hopeful look on her face. "Do you want me to stay?"

Warriors like Chimípu served the clan in many ways; one of them was to provide companionship for those who needed it.

It could be a shoulder to cry on, company over a meal, or warmth in a bed. It was rare that they had to spend a night alone.

He knew what she was offering. She and Pidòhu spent much of their time together, but Rutejìmo had seen her visit the other unmarried bachelors in the valley. All the warriors did. For those like Rutejìmo, who had never had a woman in his bed, it would be an educational night. It was also expected that he would spend the night with her before he got married to another woman.

But as he looked into her questioning eyes, all he could remember was the sound of her fist hitting Tsubàyo's face. She had beaten him to the edge of death because he dared to attack her clan. It didn't matter that Tsubàyo had grown up with Rutejìmo and her, when he became a threat to the Shimusògo, Chimípu had defended the clan without hesitation. The brutal, visceral sound haunted him like everything else from that day.

Chimípu turned and walked up to him with a sad look on her face. She stopped next to him and rested two fingers on his lips. Her fingertips were rough and calloused.

He froze, the pulse beating in his ears.

"No matter what anyone says, it will happen when it's ready. Don't worry about your brother," she lowered her fingers to tap against his snake tooth, "or Mikáryo. When you are ready, just ask. I'll be there."

Tears welled in his eyes. He smiled. "Thank you, Mípu."

Chimípu stepped away and headed down the trail. She didn't run like she always did, and he knew she was stalling.

He could just call out for her and ask her back. She would come back, not just because it was her duty to the clan, but because he needed her. However, as he watched her strolling down the trail, all he could think of was the sound of her fist striking her enemies.

Rutejìmo closed his eyes for a long time. He turned and walked back into his cave, not daring to open his eyes until he was once again in the comforting dark.

Corrupting Influence

Rutejìmo and Hyonèku chased Shimusògo across the desert, racing after the bird they could never catch. The dépa's magic solidified the shifting sand and their bare feet slapped against rock no matter what terrain they crossed. As soon as their feet picked up, the rock crumbled into a dust plume that stretched far behind them.

Home was only a mile away. Rutejìmo could see the two pillars with massive banners hanging from each one. In the middle, he spotted flashes of oranges, reds, and yellows. He didn't know why there were so many of the residents of the valley outside of the valley.

A massive shadow sailed out of the valley. It was a giant raptor, a bird of prey that stretched chains across. It didn't matter, but he still looked up into the clear blue sky. No natural bird could create the shadow, and nothing blocked the sky. It was a shadow without physical form, Tateshyúso.

Hyonèku laughed. "Pidòhu must have an announcement." Even though the wind whipped across their faces, they could easily hear each other while running.

Rutejìmo grunted and continued to run in a straight line. He didn't dare slow down, lest he lose both the speed from Shimusògo and the rapture that came with his closeness to the spirit.

The shadow circled around them and then came up behind them. As it did, the heat against their skin cooled in an instant. Cold winds buffeted them from all directions, disrupting the constant pressure against their faces. The plume of dust and sand broke apart, scattering in the shadow.

Rutejìmo almost stumbled without the constant pressure pushing him back. He caught himself and forced his feet forward. The power of Shimusògo remained strong in Tateshyúso's shadow, but without the wind and choking dust.

A mirage rippled in front of them. It looked like the shadows spun a humanoid form from the strands of darkness.

Both Hyonèku and Rutejìmo continued to run.

The shadow grew thicker and darker until it was a dark burn in the world. Peeling back, a translucent figure of a frail-looking man appeared in front of him. He remained in front of them, floating across the sands a respectful distance ahead of the Shimusògo.

"Great Shimusogo Rutejìmo." He bowed deeply before turning to Hyonèku. "And to you, Great Shimusogo Hyonèku."

Hyonèku laughed and shook his head. Proper etiquette demanded Pidòhu address Hyonèku first, but among friends, occasionally other relationships took precedence. And while Hyonèku was one of Rutejìmo's friends, Pidòhu shared a bond with Rutejìmo that was far closer.

The shadow of the frail man bowed again. "Just so you know, Great Shimusogo Mapábyo just arrived home."

The use of "Great Shimusogo" spoke volumes. Hyonèku stumbled and then laughed. "Yes! Bless the sands!"

"She is injured though, so be—"

"I don't care!" Hyonèku jumped and spun around before racing to catch up with Rutejìmo. There was a huge grin on his face.

"And, Jìmo?"

Rutejìmo looked at Pidòhu, his eyes trying to focus through the translucent man.

"Your brother is quite annoyed with you."

Rutejìmo frowned. "What? Why?"

Pidòhu bowed deeply with a smirk. His body wavered, and then Tateshyúso's shadow shot forward, taking Pidòhu with it. The sun bore down on them again, the wind buffeting Rutejìmo's face.

Rutejìmo glanced at Hyonèku. "What was that about?"

The dépa they were both chasing shimmered and split in two with a burst of golden feathers. One of them grew accelerated and headed straight for the entrance of the cave. It grew translucent and difficult to see; Rutejìmo knew that Hyonèku would follow it while the one in front of Rutejìmo would disappear from his sight.

Hyonèku raced forward, a broad grin on his face. His casual speed reminded Rutejìmo how quickly the rest of the clan could outpace their slowest runner.

Rutejìmo glanced at the rapidly approaching valley. In the few seconds of running, he could easily see dozens of folk running and dancing between the two pillars. Burning rocks launched into the air in random patterns, bouncing when someone caught the flaming shots and threw them back up. Each time the rocks were tossed, they glowed brighter. Even from his distance, he could identify some of the warriors because their rocks shot ten times higher and were brilliant stars that arced high above the valley entrance before plummeting.

The clan was celebrating.

Rutejìmo needed more time before he joined the celebration. The idea of everyone talking, dancing, and celebrating didn't appeal to him. Taking a deep breath, he slowed down and let Hyonèku shoot out ahead of him. The wind behind the older man slammed into Rutejìmo, peppering his face with sand and rocks.

He ran alone for a few minutes before coming to a stumbling stop.

Shimusògo faded from sight, and Rutejìmo's feet sank down in the gravel of a stretch of scree. The heat bore down on him and he took a deep breath to clear the searing sensation from his lungs. When he wasn't running, he felt the aches and pains that Shimusògo's magic pushed away. It was the price of walking when he could be running, but Rutejìmo couldn't bear to accelerate again. He headed up the ridge of a dune and then followed it while dark thoughts clouded his mind. Sooner or later, they would move the celebration into the valley.

By the time he reached the entrance of the valley a half hour later, there was no one waiting. He used the back of his arm to wipe the sweat from his forehead and padded inside. It was quiet in the narrow gap between the steep rocks, but the noise of a party echoed loudly when he reached the entrance.

He kept to the side and headed up one of the paths leading to the home caves. As he walked, he peered into the floor of the valley. Someone had built up a bonfire, and the flames burned green in celebration. Many of the younger folk were dancing around the flames. He noticed that Desòchu was right in the middle, swirling around everyone and keeping spirits high. For now, he had most of his clothes on, but there were others already stripped in celebration.

His brother inspired everyone but Rutejìmo. Everyone loved him, just as they loved Chimípu and the rest of the warriors. Coming around the fire, Desòchu pulled nervous children into a line dance with an easy smile and infectious enthusiasm. He was showing them the way of becoming part of the clan, not by lectures, but by example. He loved everyone in the clan and would protect them until the day he died.

Rutejìmo turned away and trudged up the trail. He made it to his cave when he realized there was a cloud of pipe smoke around the entrance. Slowing down, he called out for Gemènyo.

Gemènyo stood up from the side of the entrance, the smoke wafting around him. "I thought you'd be sulking."

"I'm not sulking, I'm just..."

"Avoiding your brother?"

"I'm not in the mood to get yelled at, and I don't even know why yet."

Gemènyo chuckled and gestured for Rutejìmo to approach the edge of the trail.

Rutejìmo stepped up to it and looked down at the celebration. Mapábyo stood on the platform with a smile larger than her father's. She wore her red ceremonial outfit, heavily embroidered and tight around her hips. Rutejìmo was surprised she could wear it with her shoulder bound up in white bandages from her elbow to her neck. Her left eye was swollen shut, and there was more gauze around her other hand and across her forehead. He noticed more bandages on her legs, barely visible with the swirls of her dress when she moved from one person congratulating her to another.

Gemènyo rested his free hand on Rutejìmo's shoulder. "We led her over to a Wind's Tooth and told her to run home."

Rutejìmo shook his head. "Is the answer to all of life's troubles to throw someone in the middle of the desert and see what happens?"

"Pretty much, though when Hyonèku and Kiríshi were having trouble with their marriage, we actually chained them together." Gemènyo's teeth were a shock of white when he smiled. "But Mapábyo here ran into a pack of wild figaki tòra."

Remembering his own encounter with the wild sand hounds, Rutejìmo cringed. They were nearly hairless dogs with large teeth. Mostly they traveled in large packs at dusk and dawn. They were tenacious and always hungry in their short, violent lives.

"She outran them pretty well, but then she missed the signs and fell into a mizonekima chyòre pit. It was a big snake too, a female. We were all lucky that she wasn't protecting any eggs, otherwise we'd be bringing back a corpse."

Rutejìmo stared at Mapábyo with shock. "And she only broke her shoulder?"

"Yeah, girl had some smarts to her. She used her trousers as a sling and was firing the bones around the pit into the chyóre's mouth." Gemènyo switched to the feminine accent to refer to the female snake. "And when the tòra joined in, they went after the snake. Normally, it would just leave the bodies, but Pábyo started throwing the bodies into its mouth until eventually," he laughed, "it choked."

"That's... better than me." Rutejìmo watched her celebrate. He smiled to himself. She earned it, both in finding a way to listen to Shimusògo but also proving herself in the clan's eyes. He never had a doubt that she would be able to listen to Shimusògo.

"No, Jìmo, it isn't better. Just different. You saved Pidòhu when he fell off a cliff, despite a broken arm and almost being killed by Tsubàyo. You found your strength too." Gemènyo patted him on the shoulder. "Don't belittle yourself. You found a path and so did she. Mapábyo won't be a warrior, but she's a good strong runner."

Rutejìmo nodded. He started to turn away, but Gemènyo's hand gripped his shoulder tighter. Frowning, he looked at the older man. "What?"

"Look at her neck."

He turned around, a strange feeling running along his skin. Desòchu was pulling her off the stage while being both gentle and excited. As he set her down, he pulled her toward the fire.

Around her neck was a leather thong with a broken-off tooth hanging at the center of her almost black throat. She ran up toward the fire and joined in with the circle of dancers, the necklace was a shock of white that bounced with her movements.

"W-Why?" Rutejìmo shook his head. "Why did she make a necklace out of that?"

"We're wondering about that ourselves. You know, because you're the only other person who wears a necklace. One might say," Gemènyo's voice grew quieter but deeper, "it is more of a night clan tradition instead of the Shimusogo Way."

He felt thin and drawn. "I-I didn't tell her that."

"Really."

Rutejìmo jerked at the strange tone from Gemènyo. He peeked over but the older man just smirked.

"Your brother thinks otherwise."

Rutejìmo glanced back down.

Down in the valley, Desòchu was looking up at Rutejìmo. There was a dark look in his green eyes and a frown furrowed his brow.

Rutejìmo stared into his brother's eyes and a ripple of fear ran down his spine. They were a hundred feet apart, but he could feel the icy gaze even from there.

Desòchu's hand slipped from around Mapábyo's waist and the older man stepped out of the ring of dancers. He slipped around a group of men and women chatting, moving more like a creature than a man. His eyes glowed for a moment before the darkness swallowed him.

"Jìmo," Gemènyo said in a soft voice, "do you want me to stay?"

Rutejìmo opened his mouth to speak, but then Desòchu ripped him from the edge of the trail and slammed him back against the stone wall. The impact drove the air out of his lungs, and sparks exploded across his vision.

"What did you say to her!?" Desòchu yelled, punctuating his words by slamming Rutejìmo against the stone. "What!?"

Rutejìmo gasped for air, unable to draw in a breath. His back burned from the impact against the rock, and he could barely focus on the furious face of his brother.

Desòchu's passing brought in the heat of day and a howling wind. It blew past quickly, and the sand draped over both of them in a thin blanket.

Gemènyo stepped up to the two brothers. "Great Shimusogo Desòchu, isn't that—"

"Choke on sands, old man!"

Gemènyo stopped with a surprised look on his face. And then, a flicker of a harder emotion ran across his face. "No."

Rutejìmo stared in shock at Gemènyo. The older man had never stood up like that before, not to Desòchu at least.

Desòchu's lip pulled back into a snarl. "What?"

"You heard me, Great Shimusogo Desòchu. If you are going to castigate Rutejìmo, then I'm going to have my say. You are angry—"

"Damn the spirits, of course I'm angry. Mapábyo wouldn't have come up with that foolish idea on her own! It had to be him!"

Desòchu slammed Rutejìmo against the wall, the impact cracking Rutejìmo's head against the rock. "Shimusògo don't wear hunks of our enemies on our bodies. We are runners, not hunters, and not sands-damned horse bitches from the night!" His bellow echoed against the walls.

With a wrenching sensation, Rutejìmo's lungs drew in air. He gasped for breath. His chest hurt where Desòchu was holding him against the stone.

Golden flame rippled along his older brother's body. It was thin and wispy, like a mirage, but the heat rose around both of them. Desòchu growled and thumped Rutejìmo against the stone. "Why!? Why are you trying to destroy this clan!"

"I-I—" Rutejìmo could barely speak. "I didn't tell her to do that."

"Sands!" Desòchu yanked Rutejìmo off the wall and slammed him back. Energy flared from his body, briefly lighting up the rocks.

Rutejìmo's head hit the rock hard, and more sparks of pain washed over his blurred vision. He slumped but Desòchu held him pinned to the stone.

A blast of air slammed into both sides of Rutejìmo. He wasn't sure if he was falling but rocks peppered against his chest and arms.

"Boy," snapped an older voice, drawing Rutejìmo's gaze to the speaker. It was Tejíko, their grandmother and clan leader. She ruled with a hard fist, and everyone was terrified of her but respected her commands. Her long, white hair cascaded down her back. It had broken loose of her braid and plastered against her wrinkled skin.

Desòchu snarled at Rutejìmo, not looking away from him.

Tejíko stepped up and grabbed Desòchu by the shoulder. Her fingernails dug into the muscular skin. She twisted and pulled him away. "I mean you, Desòchu!"

Desòchu stepped back. "You saw the necklace she was wearing!" He gestured down to the valley. "Shimusògo don't do that! Night clans do! Horse bitches do!"

Rutejìmo slid to the ground, clutching the back of his head. It was sticky and hot. He pulled back his hand and stared at the bright red on his fingertips.

Chimípu knelt down next to him, and he jumped when he noticed her. Without a word, she tilted him forward to look at his head. He could smell perfume and sweat from her.

"I know," Tejíko said in her cracked voice, "Shimusògo don't, but Shimusogo Rutejìmo does. He has—"

"He's been holding that shikāfu for ten years!"

Rutejìmo's grandmother lifted one hand, neither agreeing nor disagreeing. "Yes, but we all have our own path."

Desòchu balled his hands into fists. He glared at his grandmother; his flames flickered and wavered with his emotions. "He's a poison to this clan, Great Shimusogo Tejíko."

"You tolerated it for a decade."

"I can live with his obsession with that bitch, but when it starts to affect the others, I cannot. He brought night into this valley, and I," he thumped his chest, "can't allow that! None of us can! We are Tachìra's children, not Chobìre's!"

Chimípu slipped off her embroidered jacket and folded it twice. She rested it against the rock and gently pushed Rutejìmo back. "Hold it here, Jìmo," she whispered, "The scrapes are shallow, and it should be enough to stop the bleeding soon."

He looked up at her feeling helpless and humiliated. He knew his brother was angry about Rutejìmo's tooth, but he never guessed at the intensity of the response from a single necklace.

Tejíko bowed. "Then why don't we ask Great Shimusogo Mapábyo?"

"Ask her what?" snapped Desòchu.

"If she will take it off willingly."

"Why would she—"

"Because!" snapped Tejíko, "She is an adult in this clan now. And she has that choice."

Gemènyo bowed. "I'll get her, Great Shimusogo Tejíko." He stepped back and disappeared in a cloud of dust. Rutejìmo couldn't see the valley, and it was long moments before Hyonèku and Mapábyo appeared in blasts of wind and rocks.

Joining them was Kiríshi, Hyonèku's wife and Mapábyo's adopted mother. She wore her ceremonial outfit like her daughter, but the fabric had been sun-bleached to match her closely-cropped hair that had turned white in the last few years.

Mapábyo saw Rutejìmo, and her mouth opened in surprise. She gasped.

Tejíko stepped forward. "Mapábyo?"

"Y-Yes, Great Shimusògo Tejíko?" Mapábyo spoke in a low voice.

"Desòchu has taken offense at this," Tejíko, rested one finger on Mapábyo's collar, next to the white bone dangling at her throat. "Could you tell us why you did it?"

Mapábyo paled, though it was hard to see on her dark skin, and glanced at Rutejìmo. "I-I liked it. It was a sign that I made it, that I survived."

"Wh—" Desòchu stepped back when Tejíko glared at him.

"And did Rutejìmo tell you to do that?"

Mapábyo clutched the necklace, and she twisted her hips. "No, I thought..." She peeked up at him and then away sharply.

"Rutejìmo is..." His grandmother struggled with her words for a moment.

Rutejìmo tensed with growing fear.

"... slightly different than most of the clan. He is cherished and loved," she glared at Desòchu, "and is dedicated to all of us as we are to him, but he still runs his own path."

Mapábyo's green eyes shimmered. After a second, she nodded.

"That also means that he does things that aren't quite the Shimusogo Way."

Rutejìmo closed his eyes. He felt more alone than ever before, despite being surrounded by family and friends.

Chimípu's firm hand released him, but then she patted him on the shoulder.

"Yes," Mapábyo said, "I know, Great Shimusogo Tejíko."

"I know that you are very proud," Tejíko said, "and we are all very proud of you, but this," there was a soft tapping of Tejíko's finger against Mapábyo's collar, "isn't Shimusògo."

Rutejìmo opened his eyes and saw a tear running down Mapábyo's cheek. It tore his heart to see her in pain. He wished she would just take it off and throw it away.

The young woman nodded and drew in a shuddering breath. "I understand."

Sniffing, she reached up and wrapped her fingers around the tooth. Closing her eyes tightly, she yanked down and snapped it from her neck.

Rutejìmo jerked at the noise, his stomach twisting and the world spinning around him. He wanted to crawl into his cave and forget the world, but he couldn't flee.

Desòchu held out his hand.

Mapábyo reached out to drop the necklace in his hand, but then pulled back. "I-I can use them for my stones, right? To vote?"

Desòchu's face darkened into a glare, but Tejíko spoke first. "That would be a wonderful choice. It is personal and intimate, just like everyone's. And I'm sure that both Desòchu and Chimípu," she looked at both warriors, "will be honored to help you find more before your second year."

There were more tears running down Mapábyo's cheeks, but she nodded. "Thank you, Great Shimusògo Tejíko."

Tejíko pulled Mapábyo into a tight hug. "Now, go on a short run with Chimípu. Maybe around the outside of the valley? Your parents will be down at the fire when you come back. You don't have to tell anyone about this, if you don't want. And remember, we are very proud of you."

Chimípu stood up and gestured for Mapábyo.

Mapábyo gave Rutejìmo one last, tear-filled look. And then, to his surprise, she gave a short bow before racing away.

Chimípu disappeared after her in a blur of movement and wind blew past Rutejìmo.

Desòchu stepped forward. "Great—"

Tejíko held up her hand to interrupt him. "You, boy, got what you wanted. Now, be gracious and go on a run."

His body tight with anger, Desòchu bowed deeply. He straightened and glared at Rutejìmo. "I should have never stood with you when that bitch's life was in our hands." His voice was a growl that shook Rutejìmo.

He disappeared in an explosion of dust, the speed ripping the rocks and sands after him. Wind and sparks of sunlight flowed in the wake of his passing. A rumble echoed against the valley.

Tejíko nodded to Kiríshi and Hyonèku who both disappeared in a rush of air.

When they were gone, Tejíko limped over to Rutejìmo.

He shook his head. "I'm sorry, Great Shimusogo Tejíko. I didn't mean for her to," he gulped, "follow my path."

Tejíko leaned against the rock and tilted Rutejìmo's head forward to inspect his cuts. Her body smelled of spices and perfumes, a familiar smell that reminded him of growing up in her cave. After a moment, she clicked her tongue and eased him back against Chimípu's jacket. "You were always trouble, boy." She chuckled and patted him on the shoulder. "But we also let you get this far. I know that you still hold a shikāfu for the Pabinkúe. While I don't like it, it is not our place to dictate your heart. I can only hope that someday you'll set that aside and realize that your life is here in the valley, not out there chasing some horse."

He let his fingers slip from the necklace.

"How is your head?"

Rutejìmo felt the back of his head. It was tacky but not bloody. "I'm not bleeding anymore."

"Then it would be nice if you joined us at least for a little. You don't have to dance but be present. Just for an hour?"

He nodded. "Yes, Great Shimusogo Tejíko."

"And smile. Mapábyo seems to have a high opinion of you, and I would rather her have her attention entirely on her accomplishments instead of slyly looking at your cave in hopes you will join us."

Rutejìmo stared up at her in shock. A blush burned on his cheeks. "W-What?"

Tejíko smiled broadly. "I'm still proud of you, boy. You've grown up. And even though Desòchu doesn't always say it, we all love you."

Before he could respond, she was gone in a cloud of sand and a rush of air.

Chapter 5

Leaving the Cave

The clans of the desert don't need locks among friends. A door, opened or closed, is simply a barrier for sand and critters, not visitors.
—Gidon Wamifuko, *The Pride of the Desert*

Rutejìmo woke up screaming. As he sat up, his thin blanket clung to his sweat-soaked shoulders. He reached for one of the travel lights that he kept scattered on his bed. When he couldn't find it, he whimpered softly and used both hands to thump around the rough blankets with growing fear.

A clicking noise filled the dark. It was the familiar sound of someone winding one of the lights.

He froze, and his skin crawled. He stared into the darkness, and his nightmares welled up to paint the darkness with hidden corpses and blood. He reached out for his tazágu, his fighting spike.

The winding stopped. And then there was a tap of the metal striking the crystal. The flash burst through the darkness, too fast for him to focus on its source. Heart pounding in his chest, he held his breath and trembled while waiting for the worst.

When the clockwork mechanism began to strike rapidly against the crystal, a flash coming from every impact, he jumped again. His fingers caught the edge of his weapon, but it rolled away from his grip.

The soft blue glow spread out from Chimípu's fingers and speared across the room. It lit up her smile before reaching her eyes. The bright green of her eyes appeared almost black in the azure light. "You know, Jìmo, if you're this afraid of the dark, picking the deepest room in your cave might not be the best spot to sleep."

Rutejìmo blushed and stopped reaching for his weapon. He sighed and felt his necklace shift across his bare chest. "Sorry."

"For what, little brother?" Her whisper seemed to fill the room along with the light.

He gestured blindly at the tazágu.

"Oh, I wasn't worried about that." A golden glow spread out from her body, rising from her outline in a haze of sunlight and heat. Her smile took on a different appearance when the blue light faded. It was still playful, but there was a hardness in her green eyes.

The heat licked at Rutejìmo's skin and he shifted uncomfortably. The sweat dried and prickled his skin, adding to his discomfort. He shifted around on his blankets. The temperature in the room rapidly increased.

For a moment, her body seemed to blur with a haze of feathers. He felt her power beating at the air around him, a pulse of running and wind blowing against his face.

Chimípu chuckled, and the flames faded to a dim glow. It clung to her body, highlighting her muscular curves and reddish hair. She had one knee on the edge of his bed, her body perfectly still as if she readied herself to strike.

"Warriors get all the tricks," he muttered without feeling jealousy. The prices the warriors paid for their powers were ones that he could never accept himself. A long time ago, he wanted to be one, but now he was content to be nothing but a courier.

She grinned. "It just means I don't need a light to wake up." She gestured to a small pile of glow lights at the foot of his bed.

"It's dark and I don't want to stumble." Flashes of his dreams came back, of Desòchu and Chimípu slaughtering Mikáryo. He turned away to avoid betraying himself.

"It's bright outside." Chimípu beckoned with her finger. "Come on, you're having breakfast with the clan."

Rutejìmo frowned. "I'm just going to eat here, like I—"

Chimípu stood up, "You are coming to breakfast. In the bright, cheerful sun and among the others in the valley." She grabbed his blanket and yanked it down.

He flinched at the sudden cold. "Mípu—"

"Get out of bed," she ordered, "now."

Rutejìmo muttered under his breath. He crawled out of bed, thankful he wore sleeping shorts. His blanket peeled away from his skin, clinging to the last of his sweat.

"Still having nightmares?"

He nodded mutely before standing up. His skin prickled with the cooler air against his slick back. He wanted to dry his skin, but not with Chimípu watching him.

"About what?" Her voice softened.

Images of Mikáryo's corpse on the ground flashed before his eyes. "Nothing, really. Just... random terrors."

She stepped up to him and rested her hand on his shoulder. The scent of flowers clung to her skin. Their eyes met and he tensed. He knew what she was silently offering. His body wanted it, and he responded quickly to her scent, heat, and presence. But the images of blood and violence from his nightmares filtered through his thoughts. He whispered, "I-I'm sorry...."

For a moment, he thought that she would force him, but she just patted him on the shoulder. With a grin, she gestured down. "Might want to take care of that."

Rutejìmo flushed as he looked down. "It's morning!" He snapped his head up to retort. "I just have to—" But she was already gone with a rush of air and a swirl of translucent feathers.

He took a deep breath and shook his head. Rubbing his short, black hair with his hand, he cleaned up, got dressed, and made himself presentable to be seen by the others. Less than ten minutes later, he stood in the entrance of his cave and shielded his eyes from the bright sun.

Tilting his head up, he whispered a prayer to Tachìra, the sun spirit. Years ago, he used to rush through the morning ritual but, after feeling Shimusògo in his veins, he learned that daily prayer was his way of thanking the sun for his clan's powers. And even his small measure of power demanded at least thanks to the sun spirit.

He spoke the long-familiar words, feeling the warmth of the sun push back the last of his nightmares. He could almost picture Tachìra standing over him, a distant presence that had been the ultimate source of his power since the day he first heard Shimusògo.

When he finished, he let the fabric drape back over the entrance and padded down the path. He didn't use magic to rush to the bottom, not in the valley, but instead strolled and waved to those who called out to him. There weren't many who acknowledged his presence.

Every morning, the clan gathered at the bottom of the valley and spent an hour sharing food, company, and conversation. Rutejìmo remembered the days of standing behind the tables, usually next to a large pile of plates and pots that needed cleaning. Since he became a courier, however, he wasn't expected to cook or clean between jobs unless he was injured. Which happened more than he liked.

He fought back a smile as he looked at a miserable boy who handed him a bowl with a muttered greeting. He patted the boy's shoulder and got into the first line.

"Good morning, Great Shimusogo Rutejìmo," said Faríhyo. Gemènyo's wife was a thin woman with a long face. Her hair, dyed a bright red to match the clan colors, had been pulled back into a tail to keep it out of the food. Her belly, swollen with a child about to be born, stuck out over the table. She was normally a very thin runner, but with her pregnancy she looked like an overfull water skin attached to a stick.

"And to you, Great Shimusogo Faríhyo. You are looking lovely today."

"I look like I'm about to pop." She filled Rutejìmo's bowl with a thick stew of meat in an egg sauce.

"Only a few more days, right?"

Her eyes flickered to Rutejìmo's left. "Gemènyo's been saying that for a week now."

Rutejìmo took a deep breath and caught the scent of Gemènyo's pipe. "Yes," he said with a grin, "but what would he know about children? He still has to grow up himself."

Gemènyo clapped his hand on Rutejìmo's shoulder. "I can still outrun you, boy."

Rutejìmo leaned into him and said to Faríhyo. "I never need his trail markers. I can always smell the route."

Laughing, Gemènyo nudged Rutejìmo out of the way. "Smell this," and he pulled out the pipe long enough to kiss his wife over the table. As he did, he tilted his rear toward Rutejìmo who was already backing up. When Gemènyo farted, Rutejìmo was safely out of range and holding his breath.

Some others weren't so lucky, and Rutejìmo smirked at the cursing behind him. He balanced his bowls on his fingertips to avoid burning them and wound his way around the crowded tables near the cooking areas to the far side of the central fire. Near the cleaning areas, the tables were usually empty for those not willing to get embroiled in clan relationships. He usually ate alone at the furthest table.

He found an empty table and set the bowl in the middle. With a sigh, he turned around and headed back for some bread, cheese, and a mug of sharp tea.

Less than a minute later he headed back to his table—and found the benches full. Hyonèku and Kiríshi were both sitting in the middle, having an animated conversation about southern politics. A crowd surrounded the couple, joining in on sides and eating during the opposing arguments.

His bowl had been shoved to the corner of the table, balanced precariously on the edge.

Rutejìmo prickled with annoyance but grabbed his bowl and looked for another table. When he found none, he was surprised. He spotted the end of one bench and decided it was the best place besides going back to his cave, which was discouraged. He sat down heavily on it and bent over his bowl, focusing on it while he shoveled food into his mouth.

"Good morning," came a soft voice next to him, "Great Shimusogo Rutejìmo."

Rutejìmo turned and saw Mapábyo sitting next to him. She wore a red shift buckled around her waist. Dark and ridged with calluses, her bare feet rested underneath the table. Morning light peeked over the valley ridge and through the legs of the folk around them, the sun glinting on her steel ankle ring. He ducked his head. "Oh, good morning, Great Shimusogo Mapábyo. I didn't see you there."

She giggled. "It still sounds strange to be called that. I'm used to being called Pábyo or girl."

He almost said "I'll call you Pábyo," but the words caught his throat. He cleared it and peered down at his bowl. "Yeah, um, you get used to it. Takes a while, unless you keep getting in trouble. Then, they call you boy... girl, child, or worse."

Gemènyo walked up next to them, well within range of the conversation, and Rutejìmo tensed for the sarcastic reply. To Rutejìmo's surprise, the courier continued past and sat down on the next table over.

Rutejìmo frowned with confusion before shaking his head. "I wasn't exactly the best behaved of the children."

Mapábyo giggled. "I remember you sneaking into the shrine and Papa catching you."

"And I remember," he pointed his spoon at her, "catching you trying to sneak into the shrine during Shimusògo's celebration a year later."

Her dark cheeks darkened even further, almost to black, and she looked down at her bowl. Rutejìmo noticed that she was clenching her toes in the dirt.

"Sorry," he said.

"No, you're right. I... I heard almost everyone gets caught."

"At least, Tejíko only made you dance in front of everyone."

Mapábyo giggled.

"She used to beat me from one end of the valley to the other."

"I heard she beat Chimípu once."

Rutejìmo looked around the circle. Chimípu was perched on the end of a table, her skirt fluttering against her muscular shins as she brandished a knife toward Desòchu. Smiling broadly, she planted one foot on a large pile of pyābi between the two of them. The coins threatened to spill out from underneath her toes.

Desòchu had a knife in his hand, and his foot next to Chimípu's. It was a playful duel, judging from the lack of magic rolling off their bodies.

Seeing his brother brought a sour taste to Rutejìmo's mouth. He turned his back on the two warriors, which forced him to face Mapábyo.

She looked up at him and then ducked her head again.

The feeling in his stomach increased, and he felt sweat prickling his brow. "So, um, have they told you your first job?"

Mapábyo nodded.

"And it is...?" he prompted.

Her eyes widened and he noticed she had yellow-flecks in her dark green eyes. "Oh! I'm doing the mail run from Wamifuko City to the Monafuma Cliffs. I'm running with Great Shimusogo Desòchu and Mama, um, Great Shimusogo Kiríshi."

Rutejìmo nodded and turned back to eat.

"What is your next job, Great Shimusogo Rutejìmo?"

He smiled at her. "Oh, just call me Rutejìmo."

A ripple of laughter echoed over the fires. Rutejìmo looked up, but couldn't see what Gemènyo was doing to earn the laughs.

Mapábyo repeated herself. "What is your next job?"

"Probably treaty delivery; seems to be the only thing I do lately. Usually by myself or with Gemènyo."

"Do you like it? The same run over and over? It's a two day run. Doesn't it get boring?"

Rutejìmo looked up at the edge of the valley. "When you run along a path you know and with good friends at your side, everything feels right in the world. It's comfortable, you know, and helps the hours pass."

Mapábyo pushed the hair from her face as she beamed at him. "I hope to find that someday. Running with friends, that is."

He nodded as he picked up his spoon. "You will soon enough. I have no doubt about that."

Chapter 6

The Next Job

While it is expected that an individual focus on a limited number of abilities, the specialization at a clan level creates a dependency among other clans that would be unfeasible in modern society.

—Paladin Ruse, *Supremacy of Kormar*

Rutejìmo sat at the end of the cliff and watched birds gliding lazily on the thermal updrafts out across the sands. They were circling slowly a few miles away while they trailed after a wagon caravan that made its way along the many trails crossing the Mifuno Desert. The birds always followed after the richer clans.

As he tried to identify the clan, he dangled his feet over the edge of the sheer cliff. It was a hundred foot plummet to the sands below, interrupted only by a safety net a few yards below him. Decades ago, the Shimusògo clan had commissioned to have their mountain sheared off into defensible cliffs. The lookout that he sat on was part of the alterations made to the mountains.

When he was younger, he dreaded looking over the edge. As an adult, he still didn't like the cliff but he had enough courage to stand near the edge and kick rocks into the air.

"Say, Jìmo," Hyonèku knelt down next to Rutejìmo and pointed to the birds. "How far away do you think those birds are?"

"A few miles, maybe less."

"What about that one? Think it would make a good dinner?" He pointed to one of the birds that sailed in a wider circle from the others.

Faríhyo laughed from behind them. She stood well away from the edge of the cliff, cradling Nigímo while tweaking the one-year-old's nose with her other hand. She sat in a nest of blankets and a few rolls of maps that were brought up and promptly forgotten in favor of her daughter, her third child. Nigímo squealed happily and clapped her hands. She babbled and reached out for her mother's hand, batting at the fingers. Her bright green eyes shimmered in the sunlight.

Enjoying the joy of the little one, Rutejìmo looked back and mentally measured the distance to the bird. "A quarter mile, why?"

"Bet I can hit it?"

Rutejìmo shook his head. "No chance."

"Twenty pyābi."

He held out his hands. "Twenty to hit a bird?"

"I'm bored. Give me something to do."

"Fine, twenty says you clip it. Forty if you down it."

"Deal!" Jumping to his feet, Hyonèku backed away. He pulled a wabōryo, a hunting bola, from his belt. Grabbing the middle of the rope, he hefted it. He found a clear spot on the lookout well away from Rutejìmo and his family. He took a deep breath and spun on one bare foot. He slammed his other foot down and continued to spin, accelerating as he rotated.

Golden feathers blossomed into existence around him, swirling in a vortex. A wind tugged at Rutejìmo's shirt, fluttering the red fabric along his collar and sleeves. The two ends of the bola glowed brightly until they became a brilliant ring of power.

Dust crawled across the cut stone ground, dragging small rocks toward Hyonèku. He pushed himself and accelerated into a blur.

Faríhyo called out over the whistling winds, "Forty says he misses."

Rutejìmo smirked. "He's probably not even going to get it off the cliff."

"Really? Watch this!" snapped Hyonèku. He slammed his foot on the ground and brought the glowing bola in a wide swing, throwing it with his entire body, before launching it toward the bird.

Power exploded from his hand and the bola shot out with a crack.

The rush of air pushed Rutejìmo toward the cliff, and he clamped his hand down on the edge to avoid slipping off. He was thankful that he wasn't a young child; the force of the blow would have tossed him off.

The bola left a wake of wavering air. A cracking boom followed. It echoed off the cliffs and rocks, reverberating back with deafening sound.

Rutejìmo turned and shielded his gaze to watch the bright light sail across the sky. It rapidly dwindled into a tiny point.

And then the light blew past the bird, missing it by yards.

Rutejìmo smirked. "You owe me twenty."

"Damn," muttered Hyonèku. "Think you can do better?"

"No, not really."

"Come on, Jìmo. At least try. You shouldn't aspire to mediocrity."

Rutejìmo rolled his eyes and crawled to his feet. Taking his time, he strolled to Hyonèku and plucked a second wabōryo from his friend's waist. "Fine, I'll try."

"I'll give you two hundred if you clip it."

Hefting the bola, Rutejìmo shook his head. "No deal." Even on his best day, he could barely hit something a few hundred feet away. A quarter mile stood well out of his range, but with the others watching him, he had to try. Scanning the sky, he spotted another bird, a smaller one that fluttered frantically to keep up with the rest of its flock.

He took a deep breath and spun around. His bare feet smacked against the ground, and he leaned into the swing, spinning the bola around. He strained against his own limits until his muscles burned with the effort. He remained painfully slow with his efforts to move fast enough to summon Shimusògo.

The anticipation burned in his veins, and he pushed himself harder. Flickers of power rippled around his hands.

He managed to reach the point where Shimusògo appeared at his feet. The translucent dépa was a blur of movement just ahead of him. It left no trail despite the dust and sand that bloomed behind it.

Rutejìmo tried to catch Shimusògo, yanking the bola around in faster and faster circles but the tiny bird always remained ahead of him. He would never catch it, no matter how fast he spun.

Translucent feathers swirled in the dust and sand that formed a tornado around him. The heat pricked his skin, and the dust peppered him. He kept spinning.

The balls of the bola ignited into flames. The heat pricked the skin of his wrist and arms. The speed caused the fire to draw into a disk of brilliance.

He felt the power surge inside him. It reached a crest and then suddenly Shimusògo shot out toward the cliff.

Rutejìmo released the bola.

It shot away, whistling when it spun away from him.

Rutejìmo stumbled and fell to his knee. He looked up hopefully, praying that for once he was good enough to reach the bird.

When he saw the bola already descending in a long, wide arc, he shook his head sadly.

Hyonèku nodded approvingly. "I think that was your best throw."

Rutejìmo glared at his friend. "Go drown in sands."

"Yep, I will someday." Hyonèku ran his hands through his short beard. "Let me try again."

"Excuse me," said Faríhyo, "I think it's my turn."

Hyonèku stepped back with a bow.

Rutejìmo held out his hands. "Want me to hold the chick?"

Faríhyo shook her head and unhooked a bola from her waist. "No," she said with a grin, "Real women don't have to put down their babes to prove themselves."

Clutching her child to her thin waist, she began to spin around. A few heartbeats later, she was in a ring of golden flames. The wind ripped at Rutejìmo's face as the vortex of dust and rocks became a column that stretched high into the air. The rush of air couldn't mute out the squeal of a giggling baby.

Rutejìmo stood against the sand that peppered his face, watching her with a growing sense of jealousy at her ability to summon Shimusògo's power.

The bola exploded from her with a burst of light. It rocketed across the sky as a brilliant spear of light, sucking part of the vortex behind it. The bola flew long and flat with a wide wake of power and dust expanding behind it.

Almost a mile away, a bird exploded in a cloud of feathers. The bola continued to shoot past it, leaving behind a red-stained cloud.

Hyonèku clapped slowly and dramatically. His lip twisted with his efforts not to grin. "Not bad."

In her arm, Nigímo squealed with joy and flailed her tiny hands around. She babbled and tugged on her mother's arm.

Faríhyo came to a stop and pointed out over the desert.

Rutejìmo followed Faríhyo's gesture. Her glowing shot covered another quarter mile before slamming into a second, larger bird. The avian's cry was unheard as it and the bola plummeted to the ground.

"Ríhyo," muttered Hyonèku, "Now that's just showing off."

"Yes," Faríhyo smirked, "I was. And now you get to show off how fast you run by getting the wabōryo and our dinner."

Hyonèku pointed to Rutejìmo. "Let the boy get it. He missed the most."

Rutejìmo groaned and brushed the dust from his trousers. As the slowest courier, he was frequently the one who had to run errands in the cities, serve the rest of the travel groups, and do the valley chores that needed more than an unsteady teenager's hand.

"No," Faríhyo's sharp tone stopped Rutejìmo. He looked up to see her staring at Hyonèku, one eyebrow raised. "We both knew Jìmo would miss. That isn't fair to him."

Rutejìmo pressed his lips into a thin line. No matter how hard he pushed or how fast he ran, he was always the weakest and slowest.

"Go on, Hyonèku."

Fighting back the embarrassment, Rutejìmo looked back and forth between the two of them.

Suddenly, Hyonèku's eyes widened and then he bowed. He turned, gave Rutejìmo a salute, and then disappeared in a rush of air and dust.

"Rutejìmo?"

He looked up.

"Change little Nigímo." She gave him the same serious look that she had just focused on her husband. There was no chance of arguing with her.

He nodded and took the squealing baby. There was a small setup to the side of the path leading down. It included fresh cloth diapers and a covered bucket for the soiled ones. Even with the foul smells rising from her diaper, Rutejìmo cooed to Nigímo to calm her down before stripping her down. It was one of the many tasks that everyone in the clan did, regardless of age and rank.

"Sorry about that." Faríhyo sat down on a rock near Rutejìmo. The smell of milk and perfume drifted along the breeze around them.

He shrugged, not taking his eyes off the little one. "It's fair, I lost."

"No," she said in a soft, hesitant tone. "You're good with children."

Another shrug.

"Ever thought about having one of your own?"

Rutejìmo froze, his fingers holding the cloth to Nigímo who struggled to suck on her toes. He stared at the little one, trying to get his mind around the unexpected question. When his lungs began to ache, he realized he held his breath. He let it out and finished pinning the diaper in place. "Not really, Great Shimusogo Faríhyo."

She clicked her tongue. "Don't start the Great Shimusogo right now, Jìmo."

"Sorry."

Faríhyo slid to the ground and folded her legs underneath her. "Why not?"

Images of people rose up in his mind: Mikáryo, Chimípu, and Desòchu. And, he felt more alone than ever before.

The snake-tooth scraped against his hand. Realizing that he was clutching it, he yanked his hand back and peered over the baby to her.

Faríhyo watched him with her head tilted. "Jìmo?"

"I..." his throat ached but he forced the words. "I never found anyone."

She reached over and tapped his chest. "You never looked. It helps, you know."

A blush burning on his cheeks, he scooped Nigímo from the ground and slipped his hands to her tiny fingers. When she grabbed on, he held her up so she could take exaggerated steps that went nowhere.

"You don't have to stay with Shimusògo, you know. You will always be one of us even if you live among another spirit's clan."

Rutejìmo nodded, not trusting his ability to speak. He thought of Mikáryo, the dreams of the horse woman welling up with his attention. With all his might, he closed his eyes and shook his head to clear the image of her naked thighs and tattoo-covered body.

"It's about time—" Faríhyo stopped suddenly.

A scuff of bare feet alerted Rutejìmo that someone had come up the stairs.

Faríhyo smiled. "Oh, Great Shimusogo Kiríshi."

Kiríshi stepped up to him, swept Nigímo from his hands, and then sat down next to Faríhyo. She was a larger woman than Faríhyo, but not by much. They were all muscular and scarred from years of running barefoot across the desert.

Kiríshi beamed at them and pulled her long hair over her shoulder. She twisted it twice before releasing it. "Good afternoon, Faríhyo and Rutejìmo. Talking about anything interesting?"

Rutejìmo's cheeks burned. "N-No," he stammered, "nothing important."

"You two are very serious for only beating Nèku. You should be laughing your feet off at him, not just making him run across the sands."

Faríhyo chuckled. "He needed the exercise."

Kiríshi tossed Nigímo in the air and spun her around.

Nigímo flailed her short arms around and gurgled happily. She gave everyone a broad, toothless smile.

Kiríshi said, "Don't think it was that much of a punishment. I saw Mapábyo coming."

Rutejìmo looked up across the desert. A few miles out, he could see a cloud of dust that marked the runners of the Shimusògo. Another plume of dust marked a line from the valley to the others and it slowly dissipated in the lazy breeze that rippled across the desert.

When he looked back, both women were smirking.

"What?"

"Nothing, Great Shimusogo Rutejìmo," said Faríhyo.

Suddenly uncomfortable, Rutejìmo stood up. "I should go."

"Don't forget," said Kiríshi, "you have cooking duties tonight."

He nodded.

"And you're going out to Wamifuko City tomorrow morning."

Rutejìmo stopped. "I am?"

"Yes," Kiríshi said with a smile, "you are."

"Not another treaty run." He groaned and shook his head. "I'm tired of dodging arrows."

"No, we're sending Mapábyo back out for another round of mail runs, and you're running for a negotiation."

"An offer, actually," said Faríhyo with a grin before taking her daughter back.

D. Moonfire

Chapter 7

A Lending Hand

There are constant pressures to excel. The slowest and weakest are singled out to perform demeaning chores to encourage the strong and humiliate the weak.

—Funikogo Ganósho, *The Wait in the Valleys*

Six Shimusògo ran across the shifting sands of the desert. The ripples of power from the lead runners, Chimípu and Desòchu, spread out across the grains and solidified to give Hyonèku, Kiríshi, Mapábyo, and Rutejìmo a solid footing. It was exhausting to be the lead, but Rutejìmo always wished it were him in the front instead of being the one in the back.

Their speed created a plume of dust and rocks over a mile long. Flashes of golden feathers rolled in the cloud, bright as they streamed from the two warriors, but quickly fading as they passed Rutejìmo.

Chimípu and Desòchu could cross a hundred leagues in a day and then fight at the end. Rutejìmo, on the other hand, could barely run a tenth of that before falling over with exhaustion.

Even Mapábyo, who had found Shimusògo a year ago, raced a few yards in front of him. He strained to keep up, knowing they were running painfully slow simply to keep him near. A heartbeat of sprinting and they could have abandoned him. In ten years, they hadn't, but that didn't stop them from running ahead of him. The clan always ran at the speed of its slowest runner, Rutejìmo.

As much as he hated the constant back and forth between the Kidorīsi and Mafimára clans, it was a safe enough route that he could run it alone. While racing along the familiar route, there was no one else to remind him of his failures. He was just a courier there, faster than any mundane runner.

A set of Wind's Teeth, large towering rocks sticking out of the sands, rose along the horizon. Rutejìmo recognized the jagged shapes and his stomach twisted at the sight of them. Ten years before, the clan had taken him and four others to the rocks and had abandoned them to the desert to see if the stress and terror would open the gateway to Shimusògo's power. He survived, but he bore the scars.

Rutejìmo tripped on a hidden ridge and stumbled. With his speed, he pitched forward and slammed face-first into the sand. His impact left a long gouge across the ridge before he flipped over and bounced off the next dune to twist back onto his front. Small rocks cut at his face and hands until he landed hard on his stomach and face.

Humiliated, Rutejìmo remained on the ground and took a deep breath. The grains of sand tickled the back of his throat and the heat rolled over him. The ache of a day's run burned at his legs and back.

He exhaled, and the sand blew away from his face. He crawled to his knees. The searing heat burned his hands, and he brushed himself off to ease the discomfort.

Looking up from his landing, he saw that the rest of the clan members had reached the Wind's Teeth. The fluttering feathers of their run faded, and the plume of dust rushed forward, swirling around their bodies and the rocks before cascading to the ground.

He knew they would be waiting for him. He forced himself to his feet and started walking toward the rocks. Wincing from the burning sand, he crawled up to the top of a dune and then followed the ridge as it swept toward the rocks.

Ahead, he saw two people race off in separate directions, neither of them toward him. A few steps in, a large translucent bird appeared over both of their forms and faded away. Both runners accelerated with a crack of air. An explosion of sand rocketed out in all directions, but was quickly sucked into the wind behind the runners. Less than a minute later, they were a league away.

It was Chimípu and Desòchu, the only ones who could run fast enough to crack the air. Rutejìmo's speed wasn't enough for them to sate the euphoria of running at top speed. Like the rest of the clan, they ran to relax and to mediate, which meant they sprinted around the camp while waiting for Rutejìmo to catch up.

The sour twisting in his stomach increased. If he had more speed, they could run further. But after so many years, he couldn't get any faster even though he tried. No matter how hard he pushed and strained, he couldn't speed any faster. With dark thoughts, he trudged along the sands, cutting across the dunes to cut down on the time for others waiting on him.

He was a few chains away when a third runner sprinted away from the rocks. He frowned and glanced at the two other dust clouds. Chimípu and Desòchu were circling a few leagues away from the rocks. Their bodies were invisible in the plumes of sand and flashing feathers, but the brilliant light at the tip of the clouds marked their presence.

Rutejìmo turned back to the rocks with growing curiosity. When traveling with such a small group, they usually didn't let more than two runners relax at a time.

To his surprise, the runner was coming for him. He stopped in shock and stared until he could identify the figure. It was Mapábyo.

He was still staring when she slid to a halt next to him. The cloud of dust rolled over him, peppering his face with sand and wind, before blowing past. He blinked to clear his eyes and stared at the rod-length furrow that her braking created in the ground.

"Great Shimusogo Rutejìmo? Are you okay?" Mapábyo wore dark red trousers and a white top. Both the shirt and the pants were cut tight to her body to avoid resistance from the wind. It also revealed a generous amount of her dark skin from her wrists and ankles. Small triangles of sweat darkened the fabric underneath her arms and between her small breasts. She had left her travel pack behind and her slender body seemed to waver in the last of the dust cloud.

He wiped the grains clinging to his sweaty forehead and shrugged. "Yeah, just needed to walk a little."

"You fell," she said. She stepped out of her trench and up to him. "I saw you."

Rutejìmo gulped. "You were watching?"

She smiled and her teeth flashed. "Why wouldn't I? Aren't we supposed to watch out for our clan?"

"No one ever does."

She looked sharply down at the ground. "They should."

"They don't have to. I know the rules, last runner in serves everyone. It doesn't matter if I run or walk the last few chains."

"But, Jìmo... Great Shimusogo Rutejìmo," her voice cracked, "I know that I've never run with you before, but every night on this trip you come in last. We've been running for three days and no one questions why."

He nodded and sighed, his eyes rising to look at the jagged rocks ahead of them. He still could remember Pidòhu falling from the tallest of the Teeth.

"Why?"

Rutejìmo couldn't answer. He didn't want to tell her how slow he was or how weak. He shook his head and walked toward the rocks. His bare feet left a trail in the burning sands.

A few seconds later, Mapábyo rushed up and matched his pace. Her dark skin seemed to flow through the heat shimmers as she walked next to him. A loose part of her shirt fluttered against his arm, tickling his skin.

They walked in silence for a few minutes. Rutejìmo tried not to think about the twisting in his stomach or the sick feeling that rose up when he contemplated the rocks. He wanted to keep running past them, but being alone in the desert was suicide, and the others wouldn't follow.

"Why?" she asked again, breaking the silence.

He closed his eyes and slowly opened them. "I'm not the best or the fastest. I never will be. You, Chimípu, even Hyonèku will always outrun me. So I don't really worry about coming in last. It's a constant, like Tachìra rising in the east and Gemènyo teasing me."

"So? Generations ago, Great Shimusogo Tsudakìmo was the slowest. And then he had to outrun the sun to save Myobùshi's spirit from the scorpion clans." She smiled and tapped his shoulder. "Maybe someday you won't be the slowest?"

Rutejìmo shivered at the sudden electrical touch. He cleared his throat. "But that was his ryodifūne, his final run. When he stopped moving," he sighed, "he died."

He gave her a playful grin. "I'm pretty content with living slowly."

Her hopeful smile faded. She pulled her hand back, her fingers leaving trails in the dust clinging to his sweat. "I don't want you to die."

He bumped her. "Me either. Breathing is good."

She pushed him back with a soft giggle. Her hand was soft against his, though he knew she had a mean right hook when she needed it.

"Besides," he nodded toward the rocks, "have you had your father's cooking?"

Mapábyo pulled a face, the bridge of her nose wrinkling. "I think he poisons us on purpose. At least Mama is a good cook, though," she bumped him again. "You are too."

"I've been cooking out here for ten years." Rutejìmo reached the top of a dune and straightened. "I'm probably the best travel cook there is. I do it enough."

Mapábyo giggled and stopped next to him. She pushed her long hair from her face and behind her ear. "Then why don't I cook tonight?"

Rutejìmo stared at her with surprise. "Really?"

Her eyes twinkled. "Yeah, but you've to run to the camp."

He shrugged, but when she beckoned to him, he froze.

Mapábyo smiled and gestured to the camp. "You run, I cook."

"What?"

"Shimusògo run," she said in a whisper. And then she jogged down the far side of the dune. He held his breath while he waited for her to accelerate in a flash of air and dust, but it never came. Instead, she ran down the slope of the sand without magic or speed.

Rutejìmo let out his held breath with a rush. He swallowed to ease his dry throat and raced after her.

Chapter 8

Wamifuko City

The Wamifūko established Wamifuko City as a place of barter where the intricate dance of clan politics is encouraged but magic is forbidden. Wamifūko will defend their neutrality with brutal and unending violence.

—Wamifuko Gidorámi, *Chronicles of the Wamifūko*

Few remembered Wamifuko City for the rich architecture or feats of engineering, though the city had both. Instead, the oral tales passed down about the city focused on its stink. The smell of sweat, urine, and countless animals had stained the stone—and no amount of wind or magic could erase it from the senses or memories of those who visited the city. The twenty thousand people who called the city home were the lucky ones; the constant stench eroded their noses until they could no longer smell. Guests like Rutejìmo weren't so lucky when they were reintroduced to the odor of the great city.

The Shimusògo slowed when they reached the shadows of the city. Ahead of them, jagged walls of the mountain rose out of the rolling hills and towered over the surrounding lands. In the late afternoon sun, the tips of the walls cast claws of shadow across the haze that hung over the city inside. A low rumble shook the ground from the din contained within.

Walking toward the city, looking up at the jagged walls, Rutejìmo felt very small. Even rebuilt, Wamifuko City dwarfed anything inside Shimusogo Valley. Forgetting where he was, he sniffed and then gagged on the overwhelming smell of sewage and animal waste.

"It never gets better," said Mapábyo, "does it? The smell?"

Rutejìmo shook his head.

"I keep hoping that it rains, just to wash it away."

He grinned and leaned over to her, the heat of her skin brushing against his senses. "Me too."

"Quiet," snapped Desòchu.

Mapábyo gave Rutejìmo an exaggerated look of horror, but it dissolved into silent giggles.

They amused themselves by making faces at Desòchu's back while they joined the line heading into the nearest gate, but their entertainment faded quickly when the line came to a halt and he stopped moving. Running all day had sapped Rutejìmo's strength, and he could feel the throb of fatigue tugging at his joints. He wanted to crawl into a bed and sleep.

The closer the runners drew to the city, the more they began to fidget. It started with Chimípu and Desòchu when they scratched at their wrists and joints. A moment later, Chimípu tugged on her hair while Desòchu rubbed his side. Rutejìmo knew it wasn't the run that caused them discomfort, but the presence of the other clans. Resonance, it was called, and it affected those with the strongest magic first.

Rutejìmo rarely felt resonance, his powers were too weak, but it didn't take long until even Mapábyo scratched herself with every step. She gave Rutejìmo apologetic looks while digging into her wrist with her fingernails. In a few days, they would be raw and scabbed.

He had to look away briefly. They reached one of the inward gates to the city a few minutes later. Nestled between two of the jagged walls towering above them, the gates functioned as a choke-point for defense and a place to exact taxes and e-nforce laws.

Two Wamifūko guards stood at the entrance in their heavy steel armor. Rutejìmo recognized the guard on the right by his armor. The helm, shaped in the form of a snarling horse with wide-open muzzle, revealed a man with a strong jaw and a cro-oked nose. Rutejìmo grinned at the sight of him and then forced the smile from his face when he saw Desòchu turning to look around.

A few moments later, they were at the gate. To his surprise, the warrior faced Rutejìmo and bowed. "Good evening, Shimu-sogo Rutejìmo." He spoke in a rumbling voice, and Rutejìmo's stomach clenched with a reflexive fear. "I'm glad to see you safe once again."

Rutejìmo glanced at his brother, the leader of the group and the one who spoke for all of them. At the sight of Desòchu's scowl, Rutejìmo's stomach clenched and a burning sensation rose in his throat.

He looked at the others. Chimípu shook her head with a grin. Mapábyo looked back and forth between him and war-rior. There was a curious smile on her face.

Rutejìmo turned back to the Gichyòbi, bowed deeply and said, "Thank you, Great Wamifuko Gichyòbi. I'm glad to be back to your home."

The warrior stepped forward and bowed to the rest of the clan. "I am Gichyòbi. I speak for Wamifūko."

Desòchu stepped in front of Rutejìmo. He bowed to the war-rior. "I am Desòchu, and I," he almost spat out the word, "speak for Shimusògo."

"Welcome back to the city, runners of Shimusògo. Have all of you been to our city before?"

"Yes."

"Then I will just remind you of the more serious rules." The armored warrior's face didn't crack from its seriousness. "No magic of your clan is allowed within these walls. Reasons are unimportant, and your purpose is irrelevant. If you use magic, we will respond harshly and violently. Start a fight and we will simply kill every single one of you."

Rutejìmo's stomach twisted at the harsh threat. The last time he entered the city, he saw how violently the Wamifūko responded when the two men chasing him used magic within the walls. The sight of the eviscerated corpses burned themselves into his memories and nightmares.

"Jìmo," whispered Mapábyo, "are you okay? You just paled."

Rutejìmo clutched himself and nodded.

Desòchu shot a glare at both of them before returning his attention to Gichyòbi. "We understand."

Gichyòbi stepped aside and gestured for them to enter the city. "Welcome to Wamifuko City. May you enjoy yourself in safety." He winked as Rutejìmo passed him.

After they entered, Mapábyo leaned over and whispered, "What was that about?"

He ducked his head. "Nothing."

Chimípu came up on the other side and clapped his shoulder. "So, you only had a little trouble with that delivery, huh?" She smiled cheerfully, although her fingers gripped the joint of his shoulder and sparks of pain ran up his neck.

Rutejìmo blushed even hotter. "There... might have been a few problems."

"Boy," it was an insult not to use his name, "did someone try to kill you again?"

He almost lied but then nodded. "Yes, Great Shimusogo Chimípu." He kept his tone deferential, knowing his trouble.

"Did you at least..." Her hand tightened on his shoulder. "... thank Gichyòbi for saving your feet?"

Rutejìmo smiled and nodded. After the attack, he had treated Gichyòbi and his family to the best meal he could cook. The night started with him being deferential and humble, but after the third bottle of wine they were laughing together. The hours passed with slurred stories of epic failures on both of their parts. He focused on the present and looked at her. "Yes, Great Shimusogo Chimípu."

Chimípu's hand relaxed and she leaned into him. "It's important, little brother, that you stay safe."

Rutejìmo tensed and glanced over at Mapábyo who watched with a look of curiosity.

"I don't want to lose you, okay?"

He turned back and favored her with a smile. "Yes, big sister."

Chimípu smiled and stepped away. Rutejìmo followed her with his eyes then noticed both Hyonèku and Kiríshi watching him. The burn on his cheeks intensified, and he turned away almost running into Mapábyo.

Mapábyo giggled. "Careful."

"Sorry."

She smiled and shook her hair to knock out the sand and gravel. "It wasn't that bad." Her smile widened before her eyes lifted toward her parents. Then, she glanced away herself.

Desòchu stopped near a fountain in a square. He turned around, rubbing his neck. As the hours passed, the itching and rubbing would grow worse. The most Desòchu and Chimípu could remain in the city was a couple of days before the resonance grew too much to bear.

Rutejìmo didn't suffer in the city like the others. His feeble magic created little resonance. It also made him ideal for deliveries and the endless wait for treaties to be negotiated.

Desòchu pulled his two water-skins from his belt. "Boy, fill these and meet up with us at Higoryo Inn." He pointed to a large stone building a half block from the fountain. "Since you came in last, you're paying for dinner."

Rutejìmo tensed but kept the frown from his expression.

Mapábyo stepped forward. "I can help—"

"You," interrupted Desòchu, "can do what I say and let him do his job. Go with your parents and get our rooms." Desòchu glared at Rutejìmo. "Three will be sufficient. I'll share one with the sluggard."

Mapábyo's lips pressed into a thin line but she nodded.

Feeling sick to his stomach, Rutejìmo bowed. "Yes, Great Shimusogo Desòchu."

A heartbeat later, Mapábyo bowed herself and repeated Rutejìmo's words. As Desòchu walked away, she turned to Rutejìmo. "I'm sorry."

"No," Rutejìmo sighed and shook his head. "He's right. I was last."

Mapábyo rested her hand on his forearm. "Maybe, after dinner...?"

He looked into her dark green eyes, unable to read her expression from her face.

"... you'll tell me what happened? With the warrior at the gate? I'd like to know."

Rutejìmo felt a smile quirking his lip. He nodded.

With a soft giggle, Mapábyo reached up and pulled his pack from his shoulder. She hiked the bag over her arm and jogged after Desòchu, Hyonèku, and Chimípu.

He didn't know why he smiled.

"That was nice," said Kiríshi. She handed the rest of the skins over.

Rutejìmo's smile dropped instantly. He cleared his throat. "Yes."

"You might want to thank her, though."

"What? Why?"

"She stood up for you again. She seems to be doing that a lot, don't you think?"

He started to say something, then something heavy slipped off one of the water skins and into his palm. Another weight clinked on the first. Frowning, he freed his hand and held up his palm. It was pair of twenty pyābi coins.

"Ríshi?" Rutejìmo looked up with confusion. "What is...?"

Kiríshi was already walking away before he could finish his sentence.

He watched her disappear in the crowds. When she didn't come back, he looked down at the coins and tilted his palm so they shifted to the side. Forty pyābi was a lot of money just to hand someone, even someone in the same clan. Normally, they bought little trinkets as gifts for others, but he rarely spent more than ten on a single gift. But Kiríshi also mentioned Mapábyo. Rutejìmo smiled a little to himself. He could get something for the young woman, if anything to show his appreciation for coming back when he struggled to reach the camp. And for standing up to his brother.

Pocketing the coins, he set out to fill the skins as quickly as possible. He knew the perfect place to buy a gift, but they closed at sundown.

Chapter 9

Indecision

A difficult decision means there are more questions to ask.

—Kyōti proverb

Uncomfortably aware that he had been agonizing over the feathered combs for an hour, Rutejìmo couldn't walk away. He had gotten his choices down to three pieces, each one as beautiful as the others. They were arranged on a cheap white cloth spread out over a splintered board that made up the stall's counter. Unfortunately, despite staring at them for an hour he couldn't choose one or even two of them.

He tapped the cloth next to the first choice, a white comb with bright red feathers. He pictured Mapábyo wearing it, though he felt an uncomfortable pressure around his heart whenever he imagined her in any detail.

"A lovely choice," said the older woman behind the counter. Sitting on an old crate, she spoke in the same flowery tone that she greeted him an hour before and, somehow, that made him feel guiltier for taking so long. "It will look lovely in your pretty girl's hair."

Rutejìmo pulled back his hand. He didn't have a girl. He didn't even have a female friend beyond Chimípu and maybe

Mapábyo. He wasn't even sure why he was standing at the stall, trying to make a choice over jewelry. Kiríshi's words echoed in his mind and he shook his head to clear it.

The second comb, a plain-looking one with brown teeth and feathers that reminded him of Shimusògo, would have been the obvious choice for Chimípu. Over the years, he had given her little gifts to show his appreciation for saving his life or simply running slow enough for him to keep up. It was small and insignificant, but Chimípu kept every gift he had ever given her on the shelves in her cave.

His lips pressed into a thin line. Chimípu had become his big sister when Desòchu stopped treating Rutejìmo as a brother years ago. It still left a sour taste in the back of his mouth, a reminder that he wasn't good enough for his sibling. The event at the fountain was one more example of how Desòchu continued to pull away from Rutejìmo and treated him as a stranger instead of family.

He glanced at his last choice knowing he would never buy it. For three years now, he had seen it on the old lady's table. The dark colors of the comb contrasted sharply with the white cloth and the other combs. The black and blue swirls along the bone ended with a single feather tied at one end with horse hair. It was the colors of the night, which ensured that very few people would even consider purchasing it. Whenever he saw it, though, he thought of Mikáryo.

"Excuse me, Great Shimusògo."

Rutejìmo looked up.

"We are coming to sundown, and I need to pack up soon." She waved to the stalls around her, most of them already partially disassembled. There were only a few final shoppers left strolling through the lane. In less than an hour, the street would be empty and hollow.

He sighed. "How much again?"

Her hazy, green eyes narrowed for a moment before the smile came back with just enough tension he could tell it was faked. "Eighteen for one, two for thirty-four. Three for forty-eight. Same as it has been every time you ask and every time you've purchased from me before." He could tell she was talking through her smile from the way she hissed.

Returning his gaze to the combs, he ran his fingertips along the feathers of the black one. He couldn't choose because he didn't know why he was buying them. He should buy the red one for Mapábyo since Kiríshi gave him the coins, but when he had the choices before him, the answer wasn't obvious.

"If you tell me about your girl, maybe I can help?"

He shook his head. "I-I don't know."

"You don't know your girl?" He could hear the question in her voice and felt his cheeks warming. "You've always bought my pretties for her," she tapped the middle comb. "Though you keep staring at this one," her wrinkled finger waved over the darker comb. "A forbidden love? A girl of the moon?"

Rutejìmo never realized how observant the old woman was. He shivered in fear and struggled to speak. "I... I don't have one. A girl, that is."

The old woman tapped on the third comb. "You've been looking at this one for many seasons. Maybe if you give it to her, she will finally be yours?"

He felt a tear in his eyes. "I-I haven't seen her since..." He coughed to clear his throat. "Ten years."

"A long time for a shikāfu."

Rutejìmo nodded. "So Desòchu says."

"Maybe time for a new girl? I'm thinking," the woman clicked her tongue before tapping the red one. "This one, right? The new girl in your life?"

He snorted and shrugged. "I don't know. Her mother gave me some money to buy something, but..."

The old woman smirked and pushed the red comb toward him. "Then you should buy this one... and only this one."

Rutejìmo frowned and looked at her. She was right but somehow he resisted.

"Just trust an old woman, okay? Buy this, and I give it to you for sixteen."

He stared at her for a long moment, torn and indecisive. He dug his hand into his pocket and grabbed the two heavy coins. They scraped against each other. He toyed with them and stared at the red comb.

Just as he stared to pull out his money, he felt an icy presence wash past him. He looked at the old woman, but she was glaring over his shoulder, following some movement from his right to his left.

Rutejìmo spun around and caught a brief glimpse of a herd of black horses that had trotted by. Their hooves made no noise on the flagstones nor could he hear their breath or the whisk of their tails. The herd moved in a pool of silence, formed by the dying conversions. None of the clans who gained power from Tachìra would ride a black horse.

"Herds of the Chobìre," muttered the old woman.

His heart beat faster and watched the silent horses head up the street. It was a frantic pounding, matched by a sudden tightness in his chest. The last time he had seen black horses, Mikáryo stood next to him.

Sweat prickled on his brow. He leaned to the side for a better look down the street. Normally, desert clans worked their names into the reins, saddles, and sashes. He tried to spot any letters, but he only spotted a few flashes of dark blue fabric before the silent mares disappeared into the crowds.

Rutejìmo glanced down at his tazágu. It was original Mikáryo's weapon and it had a similar blue wrapped around the hilt.

Setting his jaw, he took a step after the horses.

A thin hand clamped down on his wrist. Rutejìmo jumped and stared down at it, trying to puzzle out the wrinkled fingers that griped him tightly.

"Great Shimusògo," said the old woman without a hint of humor, "you will buy something. For my time, if for no other reason."

He lifted his gaze to her face. He saw nothing but the predatory glare of a vendor who wasted time with a man who couldn't make a decision. Gulping, he looked away to see the horses disappearing in the crowds.

Frantic to catch up and see if it was Mikáryo, he dug into his pockets. Grabbing both coins, he threw one on the table and pawed at the combs. His fingers caught two of them, the black and the red one. He tried to separate them, but they were caught on each other. He tried to shake it free, but they wouldn't fall apart.

He looked up to see only one horse still visible through the press of people.

The woman's hand tightened on his grip.

Biting on his lip, he threw the other coin on the table.

She released his hand, and he shoved both combs into his pocket.

"A pleasure doing—" but her words were lost as Rutejìmo ran after the horses.

He didn't know if the horses were Mikáryo's or not, but something drew him down the street after the silent equines. The large creatures filled the narrow street, but they moved quickly and gracefully. They seemed to flow around the crowds while he struggled to force his way past every person.

By the time he reached the end of the street, only the rising din of conversation and haggling marked their passing.

Rutejìmo raced after the horses, ducking through the crowds. He wanted to accelerate fast enough to summon Shimusògo, but didn't dare use magic within city limits. While the death threat may have been for show, he didn't want to risk the Wamifūko's goodwill by pushing his luck.

At the next intersection, he almost missed the horses' passing.

At the one after that, he lost the trail.

Frustrated, he turned in a circle, looking for some hint of the dark herd. When he found none, his shoulders slumped. He considered returning to the other Shimusògo, to deliver the comb he accidentally grabbed to Mapábyo.

Rutejìmo pulled his purchases out and held them in his hand. The red one had tangled up with the black one. Now that he wasn't trying to catch the horses, it only took a second to pull them apart. With a sigh, he eased the red one into a pocket.

He started to put the other comb away, but ten years of dreaming stopped him. He clutched his hand around the tines. He could find Mikáryo, if it was her. It wouldn't take long. Just a quick visit to give her a gift and then head back to the others.

With a nod that felt only a little forced, he headed toward a family packing their wares into a wagon. One of them may have seen where the horses had gone.

------------ Chapter 10 ------------

A Late Encounter

A hidden alley leads to both danger and treasure.
—*The Bandit King's Daughter* (Act 2, Scene 1)

Night descended on Wamifuko City. The buzz of insects added to the din of animals and people. Rutejìmo jogged along a path that circled just outside the city wall but well within the gaze of the many Wamifūko warriors who stood at the gates between the pillars of rock.

The ban against magic ended one chain from the wall, and a sparkling haze spread out over the various clan camps and among their camp fires. Even running past them, Rutejìmo could feel the resonance gathering in pools around the more powerful clans. Arcs of unnatural lightning coursed along the tents and ropes, igniting both fires and fighting. In the distance, a plume of magenta fire marked where an artifact exploded.

He circled around the conflicts, but kept his eyes out for black horses or the Pabinkúe banner. With every step, he felt more foolish. It had been hours since he saw the herd, but he couldn't stop looking.

In the back of his mind, guilt burned brightly. He needed to turn around and return to the inn with the rest of his clan. Desòchu would be furious at him and Rutejìmo didn't look forward to the hours of screaming that would follow. After an hour of searching, Rutejìmo realized that Desòchu couldn't get any angrier and kept looking.

He had to find the horses. It didn't matter if they were Mikáryo's or not. He just needed to find the horses and then he would head back to the inn. He needed to see them once and then he could return to his life as a courier.

Bearing down, he pushed himself to his limits and the world blurred. He knew that his passing would add a little to the volatile resonance in the camps, but not enough to damage artifacts or cause others pain.

Along the south side of the city, he caught a familiar sight: three mechanical scorpions towered above the crowds. Each one stood at least a chain high, and the light of bonfires reflected off the bellies and legs of each one. Waves of heat rippled over the devices and he remembered how the massive fires at each foot of the scorpions would power the devices to walk across the earth.

The last time Rutejìmo saw one of the scorpions was the night that Tsubàyo, a former clan mate, stole one of Mikáryo's horses and killed her companion.

"It can't be a coincidence," muttered Rutejìmo. He slowed to a stop. Insects swarmed around him and he waved his hand to brush them away.

Every time he looked at the brass legs of the massive devices, he remembered seeing them years ago. A storm of exhilaration and hope beat against his chest. His heart thumping painfully in his chest, he made his way toward the scorpions, careful to avoid crossing the ropes that marked each clan's camping area. He noticed that most of the banners and colors were dark, but he didn't recognize the names as he passed.

The familiar whites, oranges, and reds were gone, replaced by dark greens, blues, and blacks. He was among the night clans, those who gained their power from the moon instead of the sun like Shimusògo did.

He felt vulnerable among the clans of the night. His red outfit and white shirt felt more out of place with every step. He noticed people glaring at him, much like the others had cursed the black horses.

Rutejìmo slowed down, peering carefully to avoid intruding into private areas. He didn't know what they would do, but the horror stories whispered over the years bubbled up in his mind. He was among the enemies of Tachìra, and he was the outsider here.

An itch spread across his skin and sank into his bones. He scratched the joint of his right hand idly. He couldn't reach the source, but it gave him something to focus on instead of the growing fear. It took him a moment to realize he had started to feel the contrast of magic between his own powers and others, the differences of sun and night managing to irritate even his own weak abilities.

Lost in thought, he almost stepped off the path when he came up to a dead end. He stopped with a scuff of bare feet on the rapidly cooling ground. Less than two chains away were the scorpions, but ropes for three separate camps blocked his path. He couldn't reach his goal without stepping over one of the ropes or backtracking.

To his right, a pair of slender women juggled knives over a camp fire. They had pulled back their black hoods to reveal they were twins except for mirrored tattoos on their faces. The campsite on his left was empty, and his skin crawled when he looked at the furs heaped up in a wagon. Something scraped against his nerves when he considered crossing the rope, and he had to look away.

The third and final camp looked small compared to the others, with only three tents and a small, banked fire. He could see across the camp and spotted no obvious occupants. The largest tent entrance faced him but he didn't recognize the clan name on the banner next to the entrance. The white thread on black, on the other hand, looked unnatural even among the other clan banners.

Rutejìmo leaned to the side and looked through the small camp. If he cut through it, it would only be a few feet and seconds before he could hop on a path beyond it. He worried his lips, deciding if he would risk insulting a clan.

A shadow loomed inside the tent he was peering around. He panicked and stumbled back before the occupant noticed him, but his feet caught on a rock and he fell back with a loud thump. Cheeks burning, he pawed at the ground for purchase.

"... to keep it clean for a few days and out of the sun," said a young man as he pulled back the entrance of the tent. In his early twenties, the speaker sported a long beard that reached his belly and a bald head covered in tattoos.

"That won't be a problem, Great Garyofina Kichìko."

Rutejìmo froze at the sound of the second speaker's voice, Pabinkue Tsubàyo. The memories punched their way into his head: years of bullying when they grew up together, when Tsubàyo tried to sacrifice Rutejìmo to save his own hide, and finally, the memory of Desòchu and Chimípu beating Tsubàyo into unconsciousness for his failed attempt at sacrificing Rutejìmo.

Tsubàyo had changed since Rutejìmo last saw him, but he still had his childhood burns along the side of his face and down his chest and shoulder. Tsubàyo held his shirt in his hand, revealing a muscular bare chest. The melted flesh reflected the light differently than Tsubàyo's brown skin. Now, black horse tattoos ran across his chest, following the curves of his muscles and his scars.

"I know, Great Pabinkue Tsubàyo, but you still have a week of travel before you reach your destination and one infection will ruin your stallion." The other man rested his hand on Tsubàyo's shoulder. "Treat my art with respect, young man."

Tsubàyo hugged the other man tightly. "I will. Safe journeys, Great Garyofina Kichìko.

"Safe journeys."

Tsubàyo turned away from the tent and started toward Rutejìmo.

Rutejìmo's stomach twisted in fear, but he struggled to keep it from his face. It took most of his strength to look down at the ground instead of whimpering.

Tsubàyo stopped and looked down with an unfamiliar expression before holding out his hand. "Here."

Compassion was something Rutejìmo would have never expected from the man who bullied him most of his life. The Tsubàyo he knew spent his days ordering others and fighting against the yoke of adults. When the Shimusògo abandoned them in the desert, it was Tsubàyo who drove the spike between Rutejìmo and the others. It was Tsubàyo who tried to kill Rutejìmo to pay for a blood price.

Unable to control himself, Rutejìmo took the offered hand.

Tsubàyo gripped him tightly and pulled him to his feet. "Here you go." He turned to look back at the tent. "Shìmi, looks like your next customer is here."

The man in the tent came out. "Wasn't expecting someone so late, but come on in." He held open the flap to reveal a simple interior with a padded bed and a tray of sharp needles and inks.

Rutejìmo shook his head sharply. "No, I wasn't here for that."

With a gasp, he realized he could be identified by his voice. He clamped a hand against his jaw. Guiltily, he looked back at Tsubàyo.

Tsubàyo's hand tightened around Rutejìmo's, and his eyes narrowed.

Fighting back the fear, Rutejìmo turned and looked into the face of the man who had tried to kill him. Their eyes met and Rutejìmo cringed at the sharpness in Tsubàyo's expression.

"I know you," Tsubàyo's voice lowered into a harsh whisper. He released Rutejìmo and stepped back. "What are you doing here, Shimusogo Rutejìmo?"

Rutejìmo's throat felt dry and tight. He nodded twice. "Well met, Pabinkue Tsubàyo." He was surprised his voice came out smoothly. Years of running had given him some fortitude.

When Tsubàyo dropped his hand to the black hilt of a tazágu, Rutejìmo stepped back. He held up his hands to show he was unharmed. His own tazágu bounced against his thigh, the black hilt almost a twin to Tsubàyo's weapon; they were both made for the Pabinkúe clan. "I-I was looking for...." The rest of the sentence stuck in his throat, and the words couldn't come.

"For...?"

Rutejìmo closed his mouth helplessly.

"You're pathetic," snarled Tsubàyo. He released his hilt and stepped back. "Go away, boy... runner..." His face twisted into a scowl, "whatever you became. Just go. Go away before you ruin what happiness I managed to wring out of life."

Someone's boot scuffed the ground. "I thought joy rode behind you, my little horse thief."

Rutejìmo stiffened.

It was Mikáryo.

He had dreamed of her voice for years. He had nightmares and fantasies of her, things he couldn't share with anyone in the world. And, now, she stood right behind him. Afraid to turn around, he stared helplessly at Tsubàyo.

Tsubàyo's scowl deepened, and his attention focused over Rutejìmo's right shoulder. "I am, Káryo. Happier than I could ever be." He shot a glare at Rutejìmo. "And I plan on staying that way."

He used the familiar form of Mikáryo's name, something that would normally be only said in whispers and private conversations. But Mikáryo had always insisted on the familiar tone, even with strangers. Years ago, she said she had no time or patience for the bowing or the formal terms. One reason she spent most of her days in the desert instead of cities.

"And," purred Mikáryo, "who is your friend?" She approached and her voice grew louder.

Tsubàyo stepped back. "He's no friend of mine!"

She said, "Obviously, he's Shimusògo." She stepped up even with Rutejìmo. He could feel the heat of her body against his shoulder and then the touch of a bare hand on his arm. "I'm betting I know him, don't I..." And then she whispered into his ear, a smile on her lips, "Jìmo?"

Rutejìmo jerked at his whispered name.

Mikáryo walked around him, and his heart skipped a beat. In the night, she had stripped down to a simple outfit of a black band over her breasts and a loin cloth over her hips. Her outfit left most of her body uncovered, and the black tattoos that covered every inch of her shimmered in the torch light. The endless trails of horses, hoof marks, and herds followed every curve of her body: around the ridge of her hips, over the swells of her breasts, and down into the valley of her legs before continuing along her thighs. He knew that only one spot would be free of tattoos, a horse's head of empty space between her shoulder blades.

The body underneath the tattoos had been the subject of Rutejìmo's fantasies for years, but his polished memories had drifted from the woman before him. Her breasts were smaller than he remembered but her hips wider. The lines of legs and arms, though, he remembered almost perfectly—as well as the crooked smile she favored him with.

Despite wearing only a few strips of cloth, she remained armed with a pair of tazágu. The fighting spikes reached her thighs. He followed the lines of her body, trying not to linger too long on her hips and groin, before focusing on the weapon on her right hip. It, like the one she had given to Chimípu years ago, remained nameless while the other had a name inscribed down the length of the blade. He shivered at the sight of it; no one carried a nameless weapon without a reason.

"I see the little warrior girl gave up the weapon I gifted her."

Rutejìmo gulped and nodded. He pushed the hilt of his weapon to reveal its name.

"Did she name it?" Mikáryo asked.

"I did."

"What was it? A rabbit?"

"A... lizard. It tried to bite me."

Mikáryo stepped forward until her chest bumped against his.

Rutejìmo struggled to look into her eyes.

"You're still pathetic, aren't you?" Her voice was low and sultry, stark against his faded memories.

Tsubàyo snorted.

Rutejìmo inhaled, drinking in the smell of her body. It was sweet and flowery, with a hint of spice, sweat, and horse. It brought back pangs of fantasies and his body responded. He stepped back and twisted his hip to avoid showing his sudden hardness.

The corner of Mikáryo's lip curled up. "Yes," she said, "you are."

She was too close. Rutejìmo gasped for breath and shook. He wanted to reach out and kiss her or turn and run away until the sun rose. His heart thumped in his chest. He panted for breath, but the air didn't seem to reach his lungs.

Mikáryo's eyes flickered down and he felt her taking him in. When her gaze came up, her smile broadened. "And what did I do to earn this visit? Or are you here for Bàyo? Wanting to finish what he started?"

Rutejìmo opened his mouth, but no words came out.

"Pathetic." Mikáryo stepped back still smiling and turned to Tsubàyo. "Let me see, thief."

Tsubàyo scowled but turned so she could see his bicep. One of his tattoos, black in a field of brown skin, puffed out from his flesh and a droplet of blood oozed at the horse's throat.

She ran her thumb over it lightly and then nodded with approval. "Good choice, Bàyo. A good strong horse."

With a smile, Tsubàyo bowed to her.

Mikáryo glanced over her shoulder at Rutejìmo.

He inhaled sharply, his body shaking with his inability to do or say anything.

"Do you have anywhere else to be, Jìmo?"

Rutejìmo thought about Desòchu and dinner. No doubt, Desòchu had worked himself into a fury when Rutejìmo didn't show up. Rutejìmo could already picture his brother pacing back and forth in a blur. No doubt the flames of his anger would burn around his body. Rutejìmo shivered at the thought and tore his thoughts away. "No, nothing."

"Good," she said and held out her arm. "Want some dinner? I'd love to hear what's happened in the last few years."

"Ten," grunted Tsubàyo, the scowl still on his face. "And too soon to ever see him."

"And," she continued smoothly, "maybe you'll hear about our own adventures. Your little friend has become quite a horse thief."

Tsubàyo snarled and turned on his heels.

Mikáryo turned and, walking backwards away from Rutejìmo, beckoned with her finger.

After a moment's hesitation, Rutejìmo followed.

Chapter 11

Good Tales

Because of their sterility, a warrior's duty is to guide their clan in the ways of the bedroom.

—Jacin Torabin, *The Noble Barbarian*

"And that is how Bàyo stole both Pabinkue Kishifín's and Pabinkue Makohūni's herds right from underneath them, may their bones bleach in the sun." Mikáryo's laugh ended with a gulp. She drained the last of her bottle of wine and slammed it down into the sand next to her bedroll.

Rutejìmo laughed with her, though he didn't understand half the story. He had known that Tsubàyo could control horses with his mind, that was how he attacked Chimípu and Rutejìmo years before; but the idea of controlling a hundred horses at once without a word was too much to understand.

Tsubàyo chuckled and ducked his head with humility. His own bottle rested against his side. He had only drunk a third of it, and the red liquid sloshed with his movement.

Rutejìmo glanced over at the man who tried to kill him. A day before, he would have never even considered he would be sitting next to Tsubàyo ever again, drinking and chatting as if they were friends. It felt strange and disturbing. When they grew up, they were always rivals. The haze of drink tempered his anxiousness.

Mikáryo leaned over and thumped Tsubàyo on his back. "My little horse thief." Her voice was slurred from the second bottle of wine.

Tsubàyo looked away. He used a clumsy hand to part the flaps of her tent. The dim, morning light streamed in through the opening. "Káryo, morning is here. I need to get some sleep before we head into the city for supplies."

Mikáryo snatched Tsubàyo's bottle, waved it toward him, and slumped back on her thin pillow and blankets.

Tsubàyo turned to Rutejìmo, who tensed at the intense gaze. "Jìmo."

"Tsu..." Rutejìmo gulped and blinked to clear his eyes. "Great Pabinkue Tsubàyo."

Tsubàyo's lips twisted in a scowl. He glanced over to Mikáryo and then back to Rutejìmo. With a nod, he crawled out of the tent and jerked the flap back into place.

"Jìmo, don't worry about him."

The muscles in Rutejìmo's back and shoulders tightened. He took a deep breath and leaned back against a thin pillow. The sand underneath the blanket shifted with his movement, and he twisted a few times until the contours molded to his body. "It's hard. He tried to sacrifice me. I thought he was a monster, but to hear him tonight, he seems... kind and generous. He was never that when we were growing up."

"Everything passes. Everything changes." Mikáryo stretched. "Though, he is right. I can feel the moon about to sleep."

As the sun rose above the horizon, Rutejìmo felt the morning himself with a quickening of his heart and a pulse beating in his ears. The moment, which never lasted long enough, rushed through him and everything felt possible.

"Hard to believe that Bàyo has three kids already."

Surprised by the sudden change in conversation, Rutejìmo stared at her. "W-What?"

"Yeah," said Mikáryo. She arched her back. Her nipples tented the thin black fabric covering her breasts. "Two boys and a girl. The two young ones are going to be Pabinkúe, no doubt about it."

"H-He's married?"

"To a grain singer, of all things. Rojikinomi Fimúchi is a good girl, no interest in traveling of course, none of the Rojikinòmi do. But they watch the homes, protect the crops, and feed the Pabinkúe's horses."

Rutejìmo shook his head, trying to imagine Tsubàyo married or even having children.

Mikáryo grinned. "What? You thought he would remain celibate his entire life? Doomed to wander the deserts alone with me? Not everyone pines for the woman they saw once over ten years ago."

A blush burned his cheeks and he glanced down at his hands. He didn't think his affection for Mikáryo was that obvious, though it seemed that everyone knew. "How... how did —?"

"You're in my tent in the middle of the night, blushing like a boy when you should be sleeping." She chuckled and got on her knees. Using her hands, she crawled a few steps away from her blankets toward him. His eyes were drawn to the sway of her hair and breasts. She looked like a beast, the way her body moved and her fingernails dug into the sand.

When the fabric pulled away from her nipples, he inhaled sharply at the sight of the hard, dark tips standing up between tattooed skin and black cloth. He tried to gracefully rest one arm to hide his growing hardness, but he was sure he failed. Sweat prickled his skin. He stared at her, trapped by her gaze.

"What about you?" she asked with a purr. "Is there a girl in the valley for you? Or one running around with your heart in her bag?"

He couldn't look into her eyes. Turning his head, he stared at the tent. "N-No."

"What about the little warrior girl at least? Someone warm for the long nights in the desert?"

Rutejìmo closed his eyes. His hands balled into fists, and he tightened them until his fingers ached. "No, Great Pabinkue Mikáryo. We've never done that."

Sand shifted underneath the blanket and he felt the ground shifting underneath him. A heartbeat later, the warmth of her body brushed against his skin.

At the touch of her breath on his neck, he shivered and struggled to breathe.

Mikáryo whispered in his ear, her breath hot against his lobe and neck. "We're beyond those formalities, don't you think?"

With her whispered voice came more warmth and a rapid beating of his heart. "Y-Yes."

A chuckle, the faintest of sounds, and then she pulled back. "Pathetic. Even all these years later, you're still the boy who peed his pants that night, aren't you?"

Rutejìmo crawled to his knees. Fumbling with the tent, he stammered, "I-I have to go."

The rustle of cloth stopped him. He could almost imagine it sliding along her tattooed skin. And then the soft, almost indiscernible sigh of it pooling on the blanket. "Are you sure?" Her voice was soft and wry, teasing him to turn around.

His fingers clenched the side of the tent flap. He had trouble focusing on the dim light spearing through the opening, but he couldn't tell if it was the drink or the pounding in his heart.

"Leave if you have to." She chuckled again. "Or stay and let me teach you a few things your little warrior girl should have done years ago."

Rutejìmo's knuckles cracked with his indecision. He wanted to run and turn around at the same time. Fear and excitement burned through his veins, screaming at him to surrender or fight, scream or moan, anything but kneel near the feet of the woman he had fantasized about for years.

Chimípu had offered to bed him many times, quietly making herself available without pressuring. Kiramíro, the other female Shimusògo warrior, had done the same. That was what the warriors did. They taught the ways of the clan even in the darkness in the bedroom caves. None of them could have children—it was the price they paid for protecting the entire clan—so they were the gateways for teaching the way among the others.

He panted with anticipation. For ten years, he never had an interest in any woman besides Mikáryo. Now that she was offering herself to him, he found it hard to think past the aching of his manhood and the painful thudding of his heart against his ribs.

As much as he wanted her, he also knew it was wrong. Mikáryo was from a clan of the night, a warrior that fought against all of the day clans including Shimusògo. Every story about the sun and moon said she should have tried to kill him, not bed him.

Slowly, he closed his eyes. He should have accepted Chimípu's or Kiramíro's offer. He could have spent the night with one of the many other warriors who saved him over the years. Then, he would have been ready for the woman of his dreams. Instead, he didn't know what to do.

"Come on, I'll show you," she said quietly.

The fabric of the tent slipped from his fingers and settled back into place. In the sudden darkness, he pulled back and turned around.

——————————— Chapter 12 ———————————

Speaking for Shimusògo

"I speak for" is a powerful phrase in the clans because it means the speaker's words have the full weight of the clan behind them.

—Rapinbun Finol, *Politics of the Desert*

Rutejìmo woke with the rising of the sun for the second time since he entered Mikáryo's tent. The power of Shimusògo and Tachìra woke inside him and his bones tingled from the energy. It seeped through his skin and he let out a soft sigh of pleasure. It didn't matter that he wasn't running or even jogging, but the feeling that magic was now possible sung to him.

The tent around him smelled of sex and sweat, a heady combination that had become as familiar as his own body's scent. He thought he would be a different man after losing his virginity, much like he once thought that finding Shimusògo would change him, but he remained the same man who left his home cave less than a week ago. He stretched, burrowing his hands through Mikáryo's black armored fabric. No, he did feel different. It wasn't magical; it wasn't a new body, or new powers. Just a sense of awareness, of a world he never imagined before Mikáryo.

"It is morning, and the moon is sleeping," said Mikáryo. She crawled into the tent. She wore nothing but her underwear, a black band of cloth over her breasts and her loincloth. Now, he intimately knew what lay underneath the fabric and the difference was like night and day.

He reached over to stroke her thigh.

She set down a tray of roasted meats and pushed his hand away. "Not now. Those damn scorpions are about ready to move, and we need to follow. I'll be glad when this trip is done; I'm tired of chasing after those things with wagons of wood. But we're leaving in an hour."

Rutejìmo sat up. "Now?"

"Yes, now." She sat heavily down next to him.

"You have to go?"

"Sooner or later, the jobs always call. I can't stand the cities." She scratched her ribs. "My joints always ache even this far away from those damned walls and their warriors."

It had been two days since he entered her tent. He only left briefly when nature called and each time he couldn't wait to return to find what new things Mikáryo would teach him. She was a humiliating teacher, one who berated him as much as she taught him, but every time she called him "pathetic," he found himself craving more of the her sharp words and soft body.

Mikáryo stuffed a hunk of meat into her mouth and smiled. "Time for you to go back to your world. I need to return to mine."

"W-What?"

Mikáryo pointed toward the entrance of her tent with her chin.

He scrambled to his knees, the blanket sliding off his naked lap. "Just like that?"

She reached over and kissed him. The taste of meat wafted around him. "Yes. I have a job to do."

Rutejìmo froze and struggled with the sudden change of emotions. He stared at her, working his mouth silently. He wanted to stay with her and even Tsubàyo. He hungered for the feel of her body and the warmth of her skin. He reached out for her, but she ducked her shoulder out of the way to pull her black cloth from underneath his other hand. The fabric scraped against his palm, the wires sewn into it tugged at his fingers until she yanked it free. He jerked back.

Unsure of what to do, he watched while she dressed and ate.

She didn't offer him her plate or water. Nor did she say anything else as she busied herself with packing up.

Rutejìmo glanced down to see his clothes scattered on her blankets, a stark reminder of the sudden withdrawal of her affection. Baffled and heartbroken by her coolness, Rutejìmo tugged his clothes on and crawled out of the tent. He hoped she would call him back, but there was nothing. He sniffed and stood up.

Tsubàyo stood a rod away, folding the last of his tent into a tight bundle. He stood up while Rutejìmo did the same. Tsubàyo's glare burned Rutejìmo with its intensity.

Rutejìmo looked around at the shifting patchwork of camps and tents. Every time he staggered out of Mikáryo's tent for food or to relieve himself, the layout changed. Along the south side were clans of the night, but it didn't look any different than those who followed the sun spirit. People came, people left, there were fights and laughter. It was the same as every other clan in the desert.

Over his shoulder, the air around the three mechanical scorpions wavered with heat from inside their hard shells, hotter than the wood fires that had burned at the base of each of their feet. A dozen horses, all black, stood still and silent next to a large wagon of wood.

He glanced at the tent, but Mikáryo remained inside. Clearing his throat, he looked up at Tsubàyo. "Um..."

"Time to leave, Jìmo," said Tsubàyo curtly.

Tears burned in Rutejìmo's eyes. He nodded and backed away. Before Tsubàyo could gloat, he turned and stumbled between the camps. He didn't know where to go, so he headed for the outer limits of the camps.

As soon as he was free of the crowds, he accelerated into a rush. Peace poured into him and displaced the sharpness of Mikáryo's rejection. He circled around the city, but not at his limit. It was the Shimusògo's version of a jog, a rate that would eat away a dozen miles in an hour. It felt good to have his feet pounding on the ground, and he marveled how he had forgotten it while in Mikáryo's arms.

Sooner or later, he had to stop. He had to face the fact he had blindly spent two days with Mikáryo. All without telling Desòchu or even Chimípu. His stomach burned and he slowed down to settle it. He imagined Desòchu screaming at him, tearing him down in public. It didn't matter if it was right or that Rutejìmo had abandoned him for Mikáryo without a second thought, the idea of being castigated soured his stomach.

He forced himself to stop dwelling on imagined punishments and focused on Mikáryo. The last two days were more intense than anything else in his life. He had been happy. The only reason she would have rejected him was her job and his obligations. He smiled grimly to himself. He should have offered to stay and help; maybe then she would have kept him.

A flash of movement caught his attention. He looked up to see a translucent dépa fading into the head of a plume of sand over a mile away. Power exploded inside the plume and it accelerated, arcing toward him. The runner came thundering toward him and the plume became a boiling cloud of sand and rocks. It spread out into two wings that were distinctively a bird's.

The sick feeling in Rutejìmo's guts intensified and he stumbled.

The runner covered the distance between them in less than a minute. He could feel the power rising up front of him, a threat of approaching magic. Along with it was anger, a palpable wave of emotion that bode poorly for him.

Desòchu appeared in front of him in a rush of magic. One moment, he was a black dot coursing over the hills and, in the next second, he was covering the last few feet between them. His two open palms caught Rutejìmo on the chest and the air blasted around them. The impact brought the full force of Desòchu's sprint into Rutejìmo's body, and his world exploded into white-hot pain.

The ground fell away from Rutejìmo. He tried to reach for the sand, but his left arm refused to work. The pressure in his chest intensified until he thought his lungs would pop.

He hit the ground with a crunch. His arm caught the force of his landing. Rocks tore at his skin and left gouges along his arm, face, and legs. He caught a taller rock along his hip and the burst of agony ripped a scream from him. He flipped over and landed on the far side. He felt a long gash along his stomach before he slumped on the rocks.

Rutejìmo struggled to push himself up. Droplets of crimson splattered the rocks underneath him. The splashes were painful to look at in the burning sunlight. The scrapes and bruises began to throb with sharp sparks of pain, but he was still too dazed to know how much damage Desòchu had just inflicted on him.

"You pile of festering shit!" Desòchu's yell was Rutejìmo's only warning before Desòchu's foot caught Rutejìmo in the ribs. The kick flipped Rutejìmo over, and he landed hard on his back. Sharp rocks pierced the thin shield of his shirt, opening up deep cuts along his shoulders and back.

Wind blasted against him, peppering him with gravel. He sobbed and tensed, ready for the strike, but none came.

Just as he relaxed, Desòchu kicked him again in the ribs. The force picked Rutejìmo off the ground in a flash of golden feathers, and he sailed through the air before landing hard again. His head cracked against the ground and stars burst across his vision.

Desòchu grabbed Rutejìmo by the front of his shirt and yanked him from the ground. "Do you know how frantically we were trying to find you!?"

Chimípu came to a halt in a blast of wind. Her reddish hair fluttered in the fading light of translucent feathers. "Great Shimusogo Desòchu—"

"What!?"

"I humbly ask for you to give Great Shimusogo Rutejìmo a chance to explain himself."

Rutejìmo's body burned from his scratches and injuries. He blinked to focus and stared into his brother's face, seeing the anger and fury burning his eyes.

Desòchu threw Rutejìmo down and stepped back.

Groaning from the impact, Rutejìmo slumped to the ground. Sharp rocks dug into his back, but he couldn't tear his eyes away from Desòchu.

The warrior stepped back. "Well, boy, who kidnapped you and chained you for two days? Where are the marks of your torture?" Desòchu's growl brought a fresh pang of fear, guilt, and sorrow ripping through Rutejìmo.

"Great Shimusogo Desòchu...." warned Chimípu.

Rutejìmo looked helplessly at Chimípu and then back to Desòchu. He heard the others of the clan stopping close by. The rush of wind of three runners rolled over him: Hyonèku, Kiríshi, and Mapábyo.

He closed his eyes and shook his head.

Chimípu stepped up to him. He opened his eyes to see her holding out her hand. "Stand up."

Rutejìmo jerked at the sudden tenseness in her voice. He squeezed his eyes tightly for a moment, but held up his hand.

She gripped it and pulled him to his feet. His fresh scratches sent sharp pains sparking along his senses.

He staggered until he found his balance.

"What happened?" Chimípu asked. She sounded concerned but wary.

Rutejìmo tried to pull his hand free of her grip, but she clamped down. He tried again until she squeezed tight enough to grind his joints. When he looked in her eyes, he saw the same anger, but hers was tightly contained, a knife about to strike instead of a furious beast like his brother. He shivered at the thought and again tried to pull his hand free, and again failed.

Unable to look into Chimípu's green eyes, he looked over at the others, his gaze drifting to Mapábyo.

"What happened?" Chimípu repeated. The pressure on his hand increased.

Turning to her, he cringed. "I-I'm sorry."

Her grip tightened, and her lips pressed into a thin line.

She took a deep breath before she pulled him closer.

"I... I met..." He tried to say the words, but the words froze and refused to escape.

When she exhaled, a glow spread out from her body. The heat rolled over her skin, and he felt it gathering in her palms. It licked at his skin, prickling it, but soon it turned into a sharp pain.

"... I," he gasped. The tears rolled down his cheeks. "I-I found Káryo."

Something flashed across her eyes. It wasn't compassion but sadness. When it turned into regret, he choked back a sob. He tensed, knowing that they were about to punish him.

"Did you choose to stay?" The quiet question almost dropped him to his knees.

He almost lied to her and said Mikáryo kidnapped him. But looking into Chimípu's eyes, he knew it was too late. Guilt tore through him, and he glanced at the ground.

When Chimípu cleared her throat, he forced himself to look into her hard eyes. He saw mercy but also anger boiling inside her gaze. He wanted to drop to his knees and beg for forgiveness, but his gut said that there was nothing he could say anymore. He had made his choice.

Rutejìmo closed his eyes tightly until the tears ran down his cheeks. "Y-Yes, Great Shimusogo Chimípu."

Desòchu stepped up, his bare feet crunching the gravel. The heat of his anger rolled over Rutejìmo. "Do you," he growled, "know how much we ran around this city looking for you!?"

Rutejìmo tensed with anticipation.

Desòchu's fist caught him in the stomach, and the pain folded him in half. He felt the wind blasting around him from the magic in Desòchu's strike.

"We were worried about you." Chimípu's voice almost cracked with her own tears, but that didn't stop her knee from catching him in the chin, throwing him back up.

"We didn't stop looking for you!" Desòchu's foot caught the back of Rutejìmo's shoulders, but before he could curl up to protect himself, he was thrown forward.

Chimípu punched him in the left shoulder, and a blast of heated power spun him around until he lost all sense of being. He wanted to open his eyes, to try dodging the attacks, but he knew he had no chance.

Desòchu and Chimípu rained punches and kicks against him. The air grew hot with their magic and his body screamed out in agony. Every time he thought he was going to fall, their attacks threw him back up. He bounced between their blows, unable to do anything but gasp for breath. The blows sent sparks of pain across his vision and the impacts wracked his body. He couldn't tell left from right, or even up from down.

One fist caught the ridge of his eye and blood splattered across his vision. He tried to collapse to protect himself, but a foot came up between his legs and drove him off the ground. A sharp explosion of agony radiated from his testicles. His feet left the ground before another blow spun him in the air.

The last time Rutejìmo had seen this form of punishment, it was Tsubàyo who staggered between the blows. Rutejìmo fled before the end came, but this time, there was no escape. They slammed into him, one side and then the other. Magic flashed around him, translucent feathers forming a vortex with him in the center.

And then, nothing.

Rutejìmo swayed for a moment before collapsing. The ground crashed into his body, and he felt a hundred bruises, cuts, and burns screaming out. Before he could cry out again, he heard a single heart-wrenching sob from Mapábyo.

The sound of the young woman's cry somehow made the agony even worse. He curled up into a fetal position and broke down himself.

Strong hands grabbed his arms and pulled them apart. A sharp kick knocked his leg to the side. Rutejìmo tried to raise his hands to protect himself, but Desòchu batted his hands away before yanking him to his feet. "Stand up, excrement of a maggot!"

Rutejìmo flinched and struggled to his feet. He sobbed and waited for the new round of blows.

Desòchu cleared his throat and stepped back. "I am Desòchu, and I speak for Shimusògo."

Shaking, Rutejìmo clutched his aching stomach and forced his eyes to focus on the double images of the glowing man in front of him. The air wavered around his brother, and the flames were so bright it looked like he was standing before the sun.

"Rutejìmo, you have betrayed the trust of your clan, and you are corrupting the purity of Shimusògo." Desòchu's voice was a growl. "For that, you are dead to us for one year." He turned away from Rutejìmo.

Rutejìmo dropped to his knees, his injuries forgotten in the sudden shock. He never heard of someone being ostracized from the clan for so long, a day or three usually, a month at most. He turned sharply to look at Chimípu, pleading with his eyes.

The other warrior bowed her head, the regret and sadness obvious even with his blurred vision. She turned away from him, her back muscles tense and shaking.

Rutejìmo looked to the other side, to the three others. Hyonèku and Kiríshi stood with their backs to him, but Mapábyo stared with a trembling lower lip and tears rolling down her cheeks.

Hyonèku tapped Mapábyo. "Turn around," he whispered loud enough for Rutejìmo to hear.

Mapábyo shook her head. "N-No, you can't—"

Kiríshi turned around enough to hold her daughter's shoulder. Her light brown skin was stark against Mapábyo's almost black. "Not now. Just turn around, you need to."

"Mama," Mapábyo cried, "you can't—"

Rutejìmo cleared his throat to interrupt her.

Mapábyo jumped and stared at him.

Closing his eyes, he whispered through his split lip. "Turn around, Great Shimusogo Mapábyo." He didn't know why he said anything, but it felt right that Mapábyo didn't make the same mistakes he managed to make himself.

"J-Jìmo?" Her voice cracked. She stared at him pleadingly.

"Turn around," he said.

Mapábyo sniffed before turning around. Her feet scuffed on the ground while she made a slow half circle. His eyes came into focus with her movement but it took all of his effort to remain still until her back was to him.

He stared at her shaking shoulders for a moment before turning back to Desòchu and then Chimípu. None of them were watching him now.

With a groan, Rutejìmo pushed himself up to his feet. Everything hurt. His right eye began to swell shut, the pain radiating across his face. He swayed to find his balance. He opened his mouth to say something, but realized there was nothing he could say. He closed his mouth. When his split lip throbbed, he winced. Staggering backwards, he watched all five of their backs. For all but Mapábyo, he hoped one would turn around and speak up for him. For her, he silently prayed to Shimusògo that she wouldn't follow his footsteps.

When he was far enough, he turned on his heels. Limping away, he pushed himself to run. Every step turned into a storm of agony, his legs not moving as fast as they used to. His breath came in a blood-flecked wheeze, but he strained to run faster. It didn't matter how much it hurt, he needed to know if Desòchu's proclamation also stole his powers away.

The dépa raced past him, and the rush of power burned in his veins. A bliss and peace spread out along his limbs, blending with the agony and humiliation.

Rutejìmo sobbed with relief. Shimusògo had not abandoned him.

Without any direction, he ran blindly after the clan's spirit.

Chapter 13

A Second Chance

No blade is sharpest but when it cuts directly to the heart.
—*Two Families, Two Children* (Act 3)

Rutejìmo ran without a hope or purpose. He was driven only by a desperate need to escape the tearing in his heart. The sight of his clan turning their backs on him flashed across his mind, adding a suffering that dwarfed his physical injuries. He knew he had done wrong, but he never thought his own brother and Chimípu would assault him.

His footsteps were unsteady and irregular. The familiar thud and rhythm had been replaced with an unsettling jerk when his right foot struck the ground. He had been injured before, but never as thoroughly. Shimusògo kept the pain away, but the longer he ran, the more he knew he furthered his injuries by moving. For a moment, he consider running until the end, the ryodifūne or the final run, but that wouldn't serve anyone.

He skidded to a halt. His tortured body struck the ground and a scream rose in his throat. Everything hurt, from the muscles clear down to the bones. His joints scraped with every movement and he could barely see out of his right eye. Gasping for breath, he stared at the ground and tried to forget Desòchu's words. Images of Chimípu turning her back on him brought another sob ripping out of his throat and he bowed down, crying in the middle of the sand.

It hurt to breathe. His throat scraped with every gasp and sob. Rutejìmo forced his jaw shut to avoid crying out, his breath irritating his split lip with every exhalation. The fingers of his left hand began to swell up from his bruising. He glanced at it and felt sick at the sight of the scrapes and drying blood.

A thud shook the ground.

Rutejìmo inhaled with a wheeze.

Another thud. Small rocks danced around his hand, rolling over his scraped thumb before clinging to the blood oozing from shallow cuts.

Panting for breath, he lifted his head. Over a rocky hill, he watched the three giant, metal scorpions making their way from the city. Their footsteps shook the ground, and the scrape of metal drifted over the wind with every ponderous step. Ripples of heat poured out from their tails, leaving a hazy cloud behind each one.

Rutejìmo pushed himself to his knees, groaning from the effort. His eyes never left the mechanical creatures walking away. Mikáryo would be near the scorpions. She had sent him away, but that was when Rutejìmo needed to return to his clan and she had to continue on her route.

He didn't have anywhere else to go. He knew she would accept him, if just for the year or only a month or two. He needed some way to survive if he couldn't count on his clan.

Staggering to his feet, Rutejìmo jogged after the scorpions. Rising hope held back the curtain of agony. Reaching the end of a short plain of rocks, he accelerated until Shimusògo raced past him and he followed.

A few minutes later, he ran up behind the caravan. The scorpions were in the middle, with scouts on horses spread out in a narrow fan. The lead horses appeared to be testing the route for the heavy mechanical devices by the way they stomped the ground with their front hooves. A trail of wagons followed behind the scorpions in a ragged line. Most of the wagons had Pabinkue horses pulling them, the pitch black equines moving gracefully in the shadows of the scorpions.

He followed a ridge of rocks to come up alongside to the caravan. His eyes focused on the horses, trying to pick out Mikáryo from the other riders.

When he came up to a short cliff with deep shadows, he caught sight of movement. He slowed down when the darkness bulged out toward him. The shadows peeled away from the wall, forming the shapes of a pair of horses and their riders.

Rutejìmo stumbled to a halt, dropping to his knees when his leg gave out from under him. He skidded along gravel a rod before stopping.

The shadows separated from the cliff and then peeled back in the sun to reveal Mikáryo and Tsubàyo. Both were covered head to toe in black cloth but he knew the eyes that focused on him.

The hooves of Mikáryo's horse struck the ground, but made no sound. Like a living shadow, the equine flowed over the ground to circle around him.

He looked up at her, trying to formulate words.

"Why are you back, boy?" Mikáryo asked.

Tsubàyo circled the other way. "What happened to you?"

"Yes..." Mikáryo's voice trailed off and she stared at him intently. "What happened to you?" She leaned over her horse to peer down at him.

"I," Rutejìmo gasped and looked up at her, "I got in trouble for staying with you." Even as he spoke, he felt useless and pathetic.

Tsubàyo snorted and continued to circle. He had no reins on his horse, but he rode smoothly.

Both horses wove around Rutejìmo in a tight circle.

Mikáryo's eyes narrowed. Her horse slowed, and she slipped off. On the ground, her feet scuffed against rocks. She walked over to him.

Rutejìmo staggered to his feet. He swayed to keep his balance.

"What happened?" she asked.

When she didn't insult him, Rutejìmo felt a brief moment of hope. "Desòchu kicked me out."

"Out of the job?"

"Of the clan—"

Tsubàyo snorted again, a smirk visible in the folds of his cloth.

Rutejìmo blushed hotly and shook his head. "—for a year."

"Why? Because you were with me?"

The scorn in her voice brought a blush to Rutejìmo's cheeks. He nodded once.

"Then why come back?" Mikáryo stepped back and pressed her palms against her hips.

"C-Can I come with you?"

"No."

Rutejìmo inhaled sharply. "What?"

Mikáryo shook her head firmly. "No. You can't."

His mouth opened in surprise.

"We are still on our separate paths, Jìmo, and you can't go where we're going."

"I can work for you. I don't have—"

She stepped forward. He saw her hand coming around and flinched. The back of her hand caught the side of his cheek with a flash of pale blue light. The impact spun him around, and he hit the ground hard on his hands. Pain shot up his arms when the rocks cut his palm.

Mikáryo walked around him and knelt down. The body he worshiped was hidden by her cloth, but her scent and perfume wafted around him, and he couldn't help but remember the softness of her skin. She reached down and hooked her fingers under his chin and pulled him up until he met her eyes. "What do think this is between us?"

Tears ran down Rutejìmo's face. He opened his mouth then closed it when he realized he didn't have an answer. Mikáryo wasn't responding the way he thought she would.

"Do you think you love me?" she whispered.

Rutejìmo gulped and nodded.

Mikáryo gently lowered him back to the ground. She stood up and the rocks underneath her scattered. "This isn't love. There will never be love, or anything else, between us. Jìmo, it's sweet, but our time together ended this morning."

She turned and returned to her horse.

Forcing himself back to his knees, Rutejìmo remembered the comb. Digging into his pocket, he pulled the black one out and held it up with both shaking hands. "K-Káryo?"

Mikáryo stopped and looked over her shoulder. Her eyes widened for a moment before she returned to him. "A bribe? Really? Do you think I'm that shallow that I would choose my companions on some tiny gift?" She pushed the cloth back from her head, exposing her tattooed face to the bright sun.

Rutejìmo realized how pathetic he looked and flushed hotly. He lowered his hands, but she caught his left wrist.

With a sad smile, she plucked the comb from his fingers. Flipping it over, she returned it to his palm. "Safe journeys, Jìmo, and good-bye."

"W-Why?" he gasped.

She crouched down, her knees spread and the black cloth rustling along the ground. "Because, my dear, pathetic, and utterly hopeless idiot, I can never love you."

The whine in his throat turned into a wheeze from the pain in his chest.

"There is nothing," she said, "that will ever change that. I have no room for love in my world. And I can't let you keep this shikāfu any longer."

Mikáryo brought his wrist to her lips. The comb trembled in his grip as she rotated his hand so his palm faced up and planted a single kiss right on his wrist. "And if the only way for you to lose your flame is to snuff it out, then I will do that." Her eyes were hard for a moment, though they shimmered with her emotions.

He gasped, unable to do anything.

"Be safe, Jìmo. Find someplace to be, somewhere you can survive."

She stood up and walked away. Reaching her horse, she vaulted on the back and set off for the passing caravan and scorpions.

Tsubàyo reared his horse. He followed after his companion with only a single cruel smile for Rutejìmo before he disappeared into the darkness of the cliff.

Rutejìmo stared at the dark shadows. "But," he whispered to no one, "I don't have a clan anymore."

---- Chapter 14 ----

Drowning

Many choose suicide when ostracized, though the choice of death varies on the character of the abandoned.

—Waryoni Pokīmu

Rutejìmo slammed the mug down on the table. A splatter of foam splashed out and struck him across the face. It dripped down along the bridge of his nose. Snorting, he wiped it off with his other hand. He tilted the clay mug up to see if more liquid remained inside, but only a few droplets chased each other to the bottom rim.

He slammed it back down and shoved it across the bar. The effort brought out another twinge along his countless injuries. It also left a small splatter of blood on the counter. "Another."

The young woman on the other side looked at him with disgust. "Money?"

Rutejìmo dug into his pocket. The tines of the comb scraped against his hand and he yanked it out. It was pathetic and small, and a waste of twenty pyābi. He tossed it on the counter and returned to dig in his pocket.

The bartender shook her head. The bright yellow feathers in her hair shook with her movement. "Money," she repeated in a firmer tone.

"I'm," he struggled with his words, "getting it." When he found the last of his pyābi, he pulled them out. The heavy coins rested in his palm and he stared at them for a moment, wondering how things had gone so wrong so quickly.

He knew the answer, but he didn't want to admit it. He had ruined everything. He even knew what he was doing when he set out across the city after a black horse. Mistake after mistake kept piling in his memories, things he should have done, things he knew were mistakes. It would have been better if he never met Mikáryo in the first place.

Rutejìmo didn't know what he was going to do anymore. He could continue his job, running contracts and treaties between cities, but as soon as the word got out, he wouldn't be able to work with any clan associated with the Shimusògo. Even the Kidorīsi and Mafimára, the two clans he had spent years running between, would turn him away in fear of insulting the Shimusògo. He might get a single job out of it, but then his brother would have a reason to hunt him down. And Rutejìmo wasn't sure if Desòchu would stop before killing him.

Tears burned his eyes. He could feel them welling up and blurring his vision. He sniffed and used the back of his arm to wipe his face. He lifted the money for the bartender but she had left.

"Is that the last of your money?"

Hearing Mapábyo's voice punched him in the gut. He closed his eyes tightly and let his hand drop to the table. The coins rolled from his fingers, rattling on the wood. He took a deep breath and then winced at the aches from the beating earlier that morning.

"What are you doing here?" Rutejìmo said in a broken whisper. "Desòchu will do the same thing to you."

"Great Shimusogo Desòchu and the others have already left." Mapábyo's curt voice continued to slash him. He knew where she stood, but he didn't dare look up at her. "They went home to tell the others."

Rutejìmo grunted.

The chair to his left scraped on the floor. He felt it more than heard it over the din of the crowded bar. "I spent days looking for you, Rutejìmo. We all did."

"You shouldn't have."

Her hand, black as night, pressed against the table along the corner of his vision. "Why do you think you aren't worth anything?"

Rutejìmo reached out for his money, but Mapábyo slapped her hand down on it.

"Tell me, Great Shimusogo Rutejìmo! We all looked for you! Day and night, through the city and the lands around. We were worried, and you... you..." Her voice cracked. "You were fucking some night-bred horse bitch!"

He jerked at her shout. Dragging his fingernails along the table, he pulled his hand back.

"Well!?"

The din quieted, and Rutejìmo could feel the attention of others on him. His stomach lurched and a wave of dizziness slammed into him. He clutched the table. Slowly, he shook his head before speaking in a calmer voice, "I don't have an answer, Great Shimusogo Mapábyo." The clan name had become a bitter taste in his mouth. "Other than to suggest you turn around and—" he almost said "leave" but the memories of Mikáryo saying the same thing froze the word in his throat. He shook his head again. "Just go away. Go back to your life. I'll be back in a year... maybe."

Her chair scraped on the ground before she shoved his arm. "What's wrong with you!?"

Rutejìmo stood up and slapped the table. With a glare, he bellowed at her, "You know what's wrong with me!? I'm pathetic! I'm the slowest runner in the clan. I'm a sand-damn outcast that no one ever liked! I'm not going to ever get a place of honor in our damned clan because I won't ever amount to anything! I will never be anything! That's my problem!"

The bar grew silent.

Mapábyo half-stood from her chair. She was dressed for running, a white shirt with tight trousers trimmed in orange. Over her shoulder, a mail delivery bag bumped against her travel pack. She stared at him with red-rimmed eyes, and her lips parted with an emotion that Rutejìmo guessed was shock.

Continuing, he gestured toward the east and her home. "Even now, Desòchu is probably telling himself that he should have cut my throat when he had the chance! Just like he's told me so many times that he shouldn't have saved Mikáryo. You know what!? I don't care anymore." He slammed back down in the chair and crossed his arms.

Tears ran down his cheeks, and he closed his eyes tightly. "He should have killed her. Just let her bones bleach in the sun and not ruin my life."

"I-I..." Mapábyo said in a cracked, soft voice. "I liked you."

He said nothing.

A blast of wind ripped past him, sucking the air to his left. Napkins and glasses fell off tables. He snapped his head around to look at her, but she was gone. Only a path of destruction marked her passing from where she ran out of the public house at full speed.

With growing dread, he watched sparks shoot out from two magical globe lights on each side of the door leading to the street. The one on the right flared brightly and then shattered, sending shards of glass in all directions.

A high-pitched whine rose up from the second one. Patrons dove to the ground. Among the smoking shards of the first, the increasing light turned the bar into a hellish world of smoke and brilliance. The hum continued to rise until Rutejìmo's ears rang out in agony.

The lights had reacted to Mapábyo's magic and the feedback of two sources caused the more delicate artifacts to crack. Even a trivial item such as that light cost hundreds, if not thousands, to bring into the city since the effort to make it compatible with the Wamifūko's resonance took a great deal of skill.

An explosion shook the bar sending more glasses and pottery cascading from the shelves. The whining globe sparked and then burst. He flinched before shards of glass speared across the room.

"Mapábyo!" Rutejìmo scrambled to shove the seat back. It fell. He kicked it aside to grab his own pack and hoist it over his shoulder. Taking a deep breath, he sprinted out of the bar after her. His eyes looked for a clear space he could accelerate enough to summon Shimusògo.

He slammed into the metal chest of a Wamifūko warrior and staggered back.

"Great Shimusogo Rutejìmo," said Gichyòbi in a low voice, "I was not expecting to see you."

Rutejìmo gasped and stared at the armored warrior. Gichyòbi had his sword out, and the blade hummed with ripples of power rolling down its length. An azure name flickered down the length of the blade, the name it was given when Gichyòbi first took a life with his weapon.

"Now..." Gichyòbi started and he looked around. The horse-shaped helm seemed to follow Rutejìmo with its eyes. The warrior looked down the street. "You seem to be running rather fast. You weren't thinking about chasing that spirit bird of yours, were you?"

Before Rutejìmo blinked, the warrior stood in front of him, inches away and peering down with piercing green eyes shadowed by the visor. Rutejìmo tried to step back, but Gichyòbi followed with a thud of his boots.

"Because I would hate to kill you."

Rutejìmo shook his head. "N-No, I'm trying to stop someone from making another mistake."

Gichyòbi stepped to the side and gestured down the street. Rutejìmo couldn't pretend not to see Mapábyo's passing, a straight path cut through smoke, debris, and screaming people. City guards were rushing to the damage, many of them already struggling to calm the panic and quiet the screaming.

Magenta sparks still rose from the destroyed artifacts in Mapábyo's wake.

Rutejìmo moaned. "Sands."

"Walk with me." Gichyòbi rested his gauntlet over Rutejìmo's shoulders and forced him down the street. It wasn't a request.

Rutejìmo tensed, but then let the warrior guide him. If Gichyòbi wanted to kill him, he could have done it in an instant.

"You know the penalty of using this type of magic in the city, right?"

With a groan, Rutejìmo nodded. He glanced at a stall that used to have glowing flowers, now they were burnt and wilted. It took centuries to work magic to be harmonious with the city's resonance and every artifact had to be tested against the city before it was allowed inside. No doubt, the flowers that Mapábyo had just destroyed would cost more than he made in a year.

"Don't worry about that," Gichyòbi said quietly, "I'd worry more about your clan mate who ran off. Which one is it? The warriors? The older couple?"

"Mapábyo." Even as he said it, he realized that he had just put Mapábyo at risk. He inhaled sharply, holding his breath.

"Ah," Gichyòbi chuckled. "The young girl."

When Gichyòbi didn't respond with anger, Rutejìmo let his breath out in a rush. "Please don't kill her. It wasn't her fault." Sorrow draped over his thoughts, darkening them. "It was mine."

Gichyòbi boots crunched through a glass vase. "Really? Because she was the one running, not you."

Rutejìmo let out a long sigh. "I guess she was trying to help."

They walked in silence. Gichyòbi didn't say anything, but Rutejìmo could feel the heavy armored arm over his back, firmly guiding him down the center of the destruction that lead to one of the western gates.

Rutejìmo looked around at the damage and felt despair clutching his stomach. There was no way he could afford to repair the destruction, much less save Mapábyo from the Wamifūko's vengeance. There were magenta fires burning from stalls and along the sidewalks. A large crack had sheared off the front of a store, the various runes that protected it hissed and popped among the jewels. A pair of guards stood over the jewelry, but no one else was nearby. The rest were rushing to fight a fire growing along one block and others were gathering up the shards of scorched glass. Even the dirt from the road had been blasted away and he could see it painting storefronts on both sides.

Finally, Rutejìmo had to say something. "I made a mistake."

Gichyòbi remained silent.

"My brother... my clan is dead to me. Actually, I'm dead to them."

The warrior came to a sharp stop and looked at him with a scowl. "What did you do?"

"I spent the last two nights with Great Pabinkue Mikáryo."

At Gichyòbi's piercing gaze and silence, Rutejìmo worried his lip for a moment. "I didn't tell them I was going to, and they were upset."

Gichyòbi pushed toward the gate. "Can't imagine why. They spent two days tearing apart the city looking for you."

"They really did?" Rutejìmo tried to halt himself, but the hard hand forced him forward.

"Yes, they pulled favors from a number of clans to look for you, including Wamifūko. In fact, I seem to recall spending most of my last night looking in the gutters for you myself." Gichyòbi shoved Rutejìmo forward.

Rutejìmo shook his head and clutched his stomach. The urge to throw up rose in his throat, burning the back of his mouth with bile. "I'm sorry, I didn't think—"

Gichyòbi grunted.

"I don't have a word, actually, for what I did." Rutejìmo bowed his head. "I ruined at least one life, if not two."

"The little runner girl?"

He nodded. "Please don't kill her."

"I'm curious, Rutejìmo, why you're worried about her if you were the one banned from your clan? Who is she to you?"

"It isn't her fault."

"Why?"

"Because she's young and upset."

"Upset about what?"

Rutejìmo couldn't answer. "I don't know."

They came up to the final street leading to the gate. A crowd had gathered, but Rutejìmo could see the helms of more Wamifūko guards over their heads. Wavers of magic rose up from the center and Mapábyo's sobbing drifted through the crowds. He could feel the Wamifūko magic around him; it itched along his spine and sent a throbbing ache through his head.

"Maybe you should work on figuring that out. Come on." Gichyòbi strode forward. "Move!" he bellowed and the crowds split before him.

Rutejìmo followed, his cheeks burning with humiliation and shame. People screamed at him, shaking their arms and broken merchandise. Someone threw fruit and it splattered against his chest. He flinched and brushed it off his leg. It dropped onto his feet but he couldn't shake it clear while walking.

At the gate, only feet from being outside of the city, Mapábyo knelt on the ground. Shoulders shaking, she sobbed loudly and held her hands up in a pleading gesture. "I didn't mean it!"

Four warriors, blades drawn, stood around her. Unlike Gichyòbi's open helm, the warriors' closed visors hid any hint of humanity. One of them creaked with movement, but Rutejìmo couldn't identify which one shifted.

Rutejìmo gasped and started forward, but Gichyòbi's gauntlet held him back.

The armored warrior shook his head. "Don't run."

A fifth guard strode to Gichyòbi. Giving Rutejìmo a brief glance, he held something up to the man escorting Rutejìmo. Gichyòbi looked at it for a moment, gave a nod, and then whispered a command. The guard ran off, leaving Gichyòbi to walk past the guards surrounding Mapábyo and Rutejìmo to follow.

"What's your name, girl?"

"S-Shimusogo Mapábyo, Great Wamifūko." Tears ran down Mapábyo's face.

Gichyòbi knelt down, his armor creaking.

Mapábyo looked up, and Rutejìmo's heart almost stopped at the devastation in her face. "I-I didn't mean to. I'm sorry, I was —"

"You just did a lot of damage to my city, girl."

"I know, but I—"

"And, there is a price to pay for that damage."

Mapábyo sobbed. More tears ran down her cheeks, soaking her shirt.

Rutejìmo stumbled forward. "Kill me. It wasn't her fault."

Mapábyo looked up at him, confusion written across her face.

Gichyòbi chuckled. "I'm not going to kill either one of you."

Rutejìmo's heart skipped a beat. "W-What?"

Standing up, Gichyòbi shook his head. "I'm going to ban you from the city." He turned to Rutejìmo. "Both of you."

Mapábyo let out a sobbing gasp.

Rutejìmo clutched his side, staring at the city guard. Dizziness slammed into him and bile rose in his throat, but he didn't know why Gichyòbi would have spared either of them when it was his right to kill them. "W-Why? The damage—"

Gichyòbi patted Mapábyo on the head. "You're lucky that Rutejìmo was willing to speak for you, girl. He doesn't have a lot of favors left with this city after what he just did. And he just used most of his to keep you alive."

Rutejìmo jerked and stared in confusion. Gichyòbi didn't owe Rutejìmo any favors, and he probably never would. He was a warrior of his clan and had no reason to save either of them.

Sniffing, Mapábyo looked up at Rutejìmo, looking just as confused as Rutejìmo felt.

"Stand up, girl." Gichyòbi's voice was powerful and commanding.

She staggered up.

When Gichyòbi gestured for Rutejìmo to join her at the entrance of the city, Rutejìmo obeyed with a scuff of his feet. When he stopped, he stared at the ground.

The crowds inside the walls continued to yell and scream at the two Shimusògo couriers.

Gichyòbi stood in front of them, a scowl etched on his face. "I am Gichyòbi and I speak for Wamifūko. You two are banned from this city on the pain of death until a time that the clan allows you passage once again."

Mapábyo pressed her hand against her mouth. Wamifuko City had been one end of her mail route for a year.

Rutejìmo nodded slowly while the guilt tore through him. Somehow, he managed to ruin her life as quickly as he did his own. In the back of his mind, he already prepared a route to flee for a different part of the desert to start a new life.

"I think two weeks is enough. Though, I expect the both of you," he emphasized the word by tapping their shoulders, "to return to this city and tender a formal apology. I think treating me to dinner would be appropriate."

Mapábyo gasped. "T-Two weeks? That's how long it takes for me to deliver, um, that's my normal mail run. I-I don't understand."

Gichyòbi's frown cracked into a smile. "Imagine that. Then, I will see both of you ready to apologize for this in two weeks. Until then," the smile dropped back into a scowl, "get out of my sand-damned city."

Stunned, Rutejìmo turned and walked away. Next to him, Mapábyo did the same, her feet scuffing on the rocks.

Behind them, the jeers and cries rose up in a wave.

────────── Chapter 15 ──────────

Rutejìmo Walks

A clan's saying, such as "Ryayusúki ride," is more than just words. It is inspiration and encouragement when the clan's skills, loyalty, or reputation are questioned.

—Martin Debosun, *Clans of the Desert*

With a pulsating headache and an aching body, Rutejìmo staggered away from Wamifuko City. He walked alone lost in his sour thoughts, making no effort to run or even jog. He didn't have anywhere to go, and the simple thrill of running no longer appealed to him.

He scuffed across the sands, his bare feet scraping along the rocks and ripples of sand that gathered along the hard-packed road that wound before him. The cuts and scrapes of Desòchu's and Chimípu's beating burned along his skin, the tiny grains of sand adding irritation to burning pain.

Rutejìmo didn't know where he could go. No city or village in the area would take him if he didn't have a clan. He didn't know if anyone would give him shelter. He didn't even deserve to wear the reds and oranges—someone might take the Shimu-sògo embroidered on it to be associating with his former clan.

For the briefest of moments, he considered lying, claiming he was still a Shimusògo. But as soon as the thought drifted across his mind, a cold shiver raced down his spine. He grew up with tales about warriors who tried to claim a clan not of their own; none of them survived, and all of them died horrifically. Rutejìmo tore his thoughts away from that possibility.

A year of loneliness loomed before him, and he shivered at the imaginary shadow crossing his life. He tried to imagine months but couldn't. It was too long, too abstract for him to imagine. He wasn't even sure what would happen by the end of the week.

Wind rushed past him, and he saw a flash of feathers before a cloud of sand peppered against his back. Reflexively, he held his breath until the cloud settled and then let it out between pursed lips.

Mapábyo came around in a wide circle before returning to him. Her movement had torn through the ground, ripping up sand and rocks in a deep furrow. She stepped out of the gouge and stood before him, her body still shimmering with fading magic and feathers. Grains of sand bounced off her shoulder and rolled down the creases of her white top. "Great Shimusogo Rutejìmo, why aren't you running?"

Rutejìmo shrugged and stepped to the side to walk around her.

Mapábyo shifted to block him. "Great Shimusogo Rutejìmo."

"I'm not Great Shimusogo Rutejìmo anymore, remember?"

"But you w-will be." Her voice cracked and she inched closer.

He scoffed and tried to get around her again. "Not for a year, if I make it that far."

Mapábyo ran her hands through her black hair, shaking the strands to dislodge the last of the sand. "What are you going to do until then? Just wander the desert with almost no food or water? How long do you think you'll survive until you die of thirst?"

Not soon enough, he thought. Instead, he said, "Where can I go? Wamifuko City is no longer a choice. Everywhere else is too small to hide in and eventually they'll find out that I'm dead to the clan."

Mapábyo gestured to the road behind her.

With a frown, Rutejìmo peered down the shimmering road. Mirages wavered along the hills and dunes as the road snaked its way to the southwest. "What's there?"

"Monafuma Cliffs. It's a good place."

"Why there?"

She turned and pointed to her mailbag.

Rutejìmo shook his head. "No, no, I can't go there. That's a Shimusògo contract, and I'm not Shimusògo."

"But," Mapábyo said with a bright smile, "it will take us a week to get there and a week to get back. Then we can come back, and you can stay in Wamifuko City or," she hesitated, "whatever you decide to do next."

He didn't know what to say. Anger and frustration warred inside him. He wanted her to go away and leave him alone. She needed to stay away from him. With a growl, he gestured across the sands away from any of the roads. "What I want to do is head that way, until I can't walk anymore."

A frown crossed her face. "If you want that so bad, why a-ren't you?"

Rutejìmo gulped and glanced at the waves of sand. Only death waited for him out there, but it came in many forms: painful thirst, starvation, or exposure. If he managed to survive those, it would be wild animals, bandits, or a score of other horrors that would take his life.

"Great Shimusogo—"

"No," snapped Rutejìmo, "I am not Shimusògo!"

Mapábyo stepped back at his outburst. She cocked her head. "Rutejìmo?" When he gave a disinterested shrug, she cleared her throat. "Then, Rutejìmo, why are you still on the road?"

Rutejìmo turned away to hide the tears gathering in his eyes. He wanted to go out in the sands, but the dread stopped him.

"Please, Rutejìmo?"

"I-I don't have the courage. I don't have the courage to walk out there. I want to. I want to make this all end. But I can't."

"Papa says that death is a hard thing to run to."

He shivered at her soft words. She was right, but he didn't want to admit it. The desire to kill himself had been tempered by the fear of pain and suffering.

"Come with me," she said.

Rutejìmo dragged his feet along some rocks. "Do you know what will happen if the Shimusògo catch you with me? They'll drive you from the clan. I... you can't do that to yourself." The tears began to burn his eyes again. "You aren't even supposed to see or hear me."

Mapábyo's footsteps scraped along the ground. "Yes. I know."

He frowned and looked up. She had moved closer than he expected, and the smell of a light perfume danced in the air between them. Inhaling, he started to back up, but then froze. "Y-Yes?"

She nodded. "Yes, but I see you." She reached out and rested two fingers of her right hand on his chest, right above his heart. "You're right here."

Rutejìmo's heart thumped and he wondered if she could feel it through his ribs.

"Come, Great... Rutejìmo."

He struggled with his words. "W-What if Desòchu finds you?"

Mapábyo cocked her head and her lip curled up. "Then, I'll just say you've been following me. Then you'll have your death, but it will be a lot faster than dying out there." She pointed to the sands he had been contemplating.

Rutejìmo rolled his eyes, but a small blossom of hope rose up. "Just for two weeks?"

"To the city and back. And then you can run away until you want to come back. But you have to run until then." She stepped back and gestured.

"What if Shimusògo leaves me?"

"He won't."

"What if?"

Mapábyo pulled her fingers back, but it still felt like her fingertips burned his skin. "Then we walk. But until then, Shimusògo run."

Rutejìmo's stomach lurched.

A shadow of annoyance flickered across her face, but a smile quickly replaced it. "Fine, Rutejìmo and Mapábyo run."

With a wink, she was gone in a rush of air, a cloud of dust, and a sparkle of translucent feathers.

He stood there and watched the plume behind her. She was running slowly enough that he could catch her, if he wanted.

Slowly, he looked over the unforgiving desert. Death waited for him if he had the courage to keep walking.

He turned his attention back to the runner receding in the distance. He needed a different courage to follow her, one that he wasn't sure he had. But Mapábyo offered a lot less pain. At least until Desòchu caught him.

Clearing his throat, Rutejìmo chased after her, walking at first, then running. He pushed himself until he felt the power of Shimusògo flood his veins and the world became nothing but sand, feathers, and bliss.

————————— Chapter 16 —————————

Banyosiōu

Lying about one's clan has only one consequence: death. Painful, screaming, agonizing death.

—Chizoki Miyóna, *A Traveler's Introduction to Kyōti*

As evening came, Rutejìmo desperately wanted to stop running, but guilt refused to let him slow. Sweat soaked his shirt and pants. His breath came in ragged gasps. He strained to run through the pain of his injuries and maintain enough speed to keep Shimusògo racing ahead of him. Every time he licked his lips, he could taste blood along his split lip.

The reason he couldn't stop ran a few feet in front of him and to the right. Mapábyo ran exactly his pace, unwavering from her position even though she didn't look back at him. She had maintained her distance from him ever since a brief water break at lunch. Her dark skin flashed through the howling wind and the translucent feathers that streamed around her and pulled him into her wake.

Past the shifting sands and howling winds, he saw colorful smoke rising high into the air, advertising an oasis ahead. He took a deep breath and began to slow, preparing to walk the last mile as he normally did.

To his surprise, Mapábyo continued to match his pace, slowing down. The swirling winds began to die down and the golden feathers faded away.

Guilt slashed through him. No one had ever slowed down when he dropped back. Startled, he forced himself to speed up again and maintain her pace.

Mapábyo accelerated with a smile. The guilt rose along with humiliation. He forced his attention to the camp to temper the boil of emotions rising in his throat.

He didn't know the oasis ahead of him, but the plume of colored smoke that rose into the air had marked it long before he could see the few trees and buildings around a spring. He had used similar camps most of his life, though the clans that protected each oasis differed as greatly as the ground underneath his feet or the wind across his face.

Mapábyo circled around to the west side of the camp before angling steeply toward a small wooden structure.

He followed and slowed down when she did. He stumbled when the power seeped away from him, but he managed to keep running under his own abilities.

She came to a halt next to two clan warriors and a less-armored individual, all of them female. Panting softly, she looked at him with a silent question. It was the task of the group elder to introduce the members of an approaching clan.

Rutejìmo almost spoke the familiar words, but they froze in his throat. He couldn't speak for Shimusògo, not with what happened. He shook his head and stepped back, blushing hotly. "G-Go ahead," he said in a whispered croak.

Her eyes widened for a moment. She leaned toward him, as if asking for confirmation.

He nodded sharply and stepped back again.

Mapábyo straightened before turning around. She bowed deeply. "Good evening. I am Mapábyo, and I speak for Shimusògo."

Rutejìmo fought a surge of despair that rose in his throat. The others were looking at him. The eldest in a traveling group usually spoke the formal words of greeting. He obviously wore the Shimusògo colors and carried years over her but his reluctance brought frowns of confusion.

All three of them looked at Rutejìmo briefly before they turned to Mapábyo.

The unarmed one spoke while bowing, "Good evening, I am Tijikóse, and I speak for Naryòshi. Just the two of you?"

Mapábyo's shoulders tightened but she nodded.

"We have three other clans already camped here." She listed the groups, Rutejìmo had heard of all of them. "Do you have issues with any of them?"

"No, Great Naryoshi Tijikóse. The Shimusògo will never war with anyone."

Tijikóse glanced at Rutejìmo again, a frown on her face.

Rutejìmo gulped and looked away. He felt sick to his stomach, and the sweat drying along his skin itched.

Tijikóse said, "Along the southern side, Great Shimusogo Mapábyo. One plot marked with one green and two blue flags."

Mapábyo bowed. "Thank you, Great Naryoshi Tijikóse."

Rutejìmo and the warriors bowed in turn before Rutejìmo followed Mapábyo to walk around the camp.

Mapábyo let out a nervous giggle. "I thought she was going to insist you speak."

He sighed and nodded.

"What would you have said?" She slowed so they walked shoulder to shoulder. "You won't say you speak for Shimusògo, will you?"

"No, I can't. And I won't lie about my clan."

"Are you really going to say you are banyosiōu?"

Banyosiōu, those without clan, was the name for those who never found a clan spirit or those who abandoned their clans later in life. In society, very little stood below the clanless who spent their lives in the refuse of culture: shoveling garbage, caring for the dead, and other unclean duties that no civilized person would ever suffer.

Rutejìmo ground his jaw together. "I have to, don't I? I," he tugged on his shirt, "probably should change my colors."

She gave him a reassuring smile. "I'll speak for you."

"Thank you, Great Shimusogo Mapábyo."

She stretched her body with her hands high above her head. "Of course, that means you'll make dinner because you're going to be last in the camp." With a giggle, she jogged forward.

Rutejìmo stumbled and ran after her. The sand kicked up behind him with every step to catch up. The injuries from his beating slowed him down, but he managed to keep up.

Mapábyo only jumped over the roped out area for their camp a few seconds before he did. She hopped in place and spun around. She dropped her pack and kicked it toward the outer edge of the camp. The mail bag followed but with more care. "You start dinner, and I'll get the water."

Rutejìmo dropped his own pack next to hers. "Isn't that my job?"

"I won't tell anyone." Mapábyo winked at him before picking up the water skins.

He watched her stroll to the center of the oasis where the merchants were already chatting. Tradition dictated that they bring food and tales for everyone to share, though Rutejìmo didn't know how he would face the inevitable questions.

To avoid souring his thoughts, he started dinner. On the road, meals consisted of dried meats and fruits. To heat both, he used an alchemical gel that responded to his breath. It cooked the meat with faint flames and thin streamers of acidic smoke. He made enough for four and spiced it with some of the herbs and seasonings that came from their home valley. When the aromas of sizzling meat drifted around him, he patted out the flames and set the meat aside to cool.

He glanced again toward the center of the oasis. More clans had joined at the dinner by the waters. Sounds of laughter and stories drifted over the sands. He felt sick to his stomach and turned his back to the center. He liked meeting people on his runs, more so when he ran alone. That way, no one could compare him to the other Shimusògo.

Steeling himself, he worked on setting up the rest of the camp including the two tents and bedrolls. Mapábyo hadn't returned by the time he finished, so he pulled his book from his pack and settled down to wait.

"Rutejìmo?"

He looked up from the far side of the tent. When he couldn't see Mapábyo, he set down the book and stood up. He had spent the last half hour reading the same page but the words refused to sink into his head.

Mapábyo stopped in front of him, her bare feet scrunching on the sand. She favored him with a hesitant smile. "I got you something, but I wasn't sure if you really wanted them." In her hands, she carried a small stack of neatly folded clothes. Unlike the normal outfits they wore, the plain fabric had no additional embroidery or colors. Just off-white fabric ready to be dyed into a clan's colors.

Rutejìmo gulped. Banyosiōu wore uncolored cloth to indicate their lack of clan. If Rutejìmo donned the clothes in their plain state, he would be telling the world that he lost his clan.

He closed his eyes tightly for moment, fighting the tears that threaten to come.

"I can return them," whispered Mapábyo.

"No," he opened his eyes and held out his hands. "Thank you, Great Shimusogo Mapábyo. It's time that I acknowledge it."

She handed him the clothes with tears in her eyes. Her fingers trailed along the side of his arm before she pulled back. She opened her mouth to say something, but then closed it with a snap. Turning around, she started to walk away but stopped near a large platter of food Rutejìmo made to share with the others.

"Thank you," she whispered before she picked it up and headed back to the oasis, leaving him alone with his thoughts.

———————— Chapter 17 ————————

The Wrong Words

It only takes a single word to change everything.

—Kyōti proverb

Just as the run reached its apex, they came to a halt. Searing heat bore down on Rutejìmo while he walked the last few rods to an outcropping of rock that Mapábyo had pointed out.

She walked next to him and gestured to the near side. "There's a great spot for a break."

He trudged into the shadow and looked for scorpions or snakes. Seeing none, he sat down heavily and pulled his water skin around to take a swig. The new fabric of his shirt scratched and he rubbed his shoulder. It felt wrong to be wearing white. His mind kept wanting to see orange and red against his brown skin, instead of plain cloth and no embroidery. He kept his tazágu, though, and the dark hilt of his weapon was the only splash of color to his plainness.

Mapábyo joined him, hauling her pack and mail bag from her shoulders before setting them down. She dropped to her knees in front of him and gave him a smile before dragging her bag closer.

Rutejìmo watched as she dug into the pack.

When she pulled her hand out, she had a pair of travel rations in her palm. With a wink, she tossed them over to him.

He caught them. "Do you want—?"

Mapábyo shook her head. "You looked hungry."

His stomach answered and she smirked. With a blush, Rutejìmo ducked his head and worked the oiled paper off the dried fruit of indeterminate origin and a twisted hunk of salted meat.

Still smiling, she dug her fingers into the sand and began to scoop out a hole. After a few seconds, he heard her fingernails scrape against something buried in the ground.

Realizing that she had a supply cache hidden in the sands, Rutejìmo bit down on the jerky and crawled toward her to help. He stopped when she twisted around and started to dig another hole. His eyes took in the sight of her kneeling away from him and the tight lines of her muscular legs that led to her buttocks. He trailed his gaze along the line of her spine up to her shoulders and his heart beat faster.

Suddenly, she wasn't just an eighteen-year-old girl that he grew up with. She was something else: a woman. A woman that he had recently learned how to please, thanks to Mikáryo's instructions. When he imagined doing the same to Mapábyo, his manhood responded with his thoughts.

"Damn you, Mikáryo," he whispered to himself.

"What?"

"Oh, nothing," Rutejìmo said. He glanced back. Thankfully, Mapábyo sat down, and he could turn back to her without embarrassing himself.

She grinned and pulled a small box into her lap. "I had to use some first aid last time."

He watched her move supplies from her pack to the box. He dug into his own pack to add some of his own, but she waved him away. "Don't worry about it. I bought these in town before..." Her face paled, "um, before things got frantic."

Rutejìmo gave a bitter laugh. "You don't have to protect me, Great Shimusogo—"

"Pábyo," interrupted Mapábyo. "Just call me Pábyo out here." She waggled her finger at him while grinning. Then she pulled out some rations and her own water skin.

He froze. Mikáryo had insisted on using the familiar tone herself, and the similarities between the two was too much. "I-I can't."

"Why not?" Mapábyo gave him a curious look while she set out her rations and dug out a few spices.

He tried to come up with some reason. "I-I, um, it isn't appropriate."

Mapábyo took a bite of her dried meat. "Why not?"

He tried to find something, but then decided to be honest. "Mikáryo insisted on me calling her Káryo. She did that for everyone."

Poking him with her finger, she shook her head. "I'm not that horse bitch."

"I know," he sighed, "but it feels wrong. I'm only here because you.... you, um...."

"Convinced you not to run out into the desert and die? But you weren't really interested in that final run, were you?"

Rutejìmo stared at her for a moment.

She raised an eyebrow. "Well?"

He wanted to deny it, but they both knew the truth. With a sigh, he shook his head. "Sands," he muttered.

She giggled. "Eat."

Sullenly, he tore off a hunk of meat and chewed. He thought about how Mikáryo rejected him the second time, tearing out his heart with her curt words. The meat turned to ash in his mouth but he forced himself to swallow.

"Jìmo?" Mapábyo interrupted his thoughts. "What was so good about her anyways?"

Shocked by her question, the food stuck in the back of his throat. He choked.

Mapábyo swore violently and reached for him, but Rutejìmo managed to cough hard enough to clear his air passage. He bowed forward, hacking as he tried not to think about humiliating himself in front of her and failing.

She offered him her water skin and he took it gratefully.

Gulping the water, he managed to swallow the remains of his lunch before handing it back. "Thank you."

She pointed to his cheek. "You have a bit of, um, drool."

Cheeks burning, he wiped his mouth with the back of his hand.

Mapábyo leaned back against the rocks. "So, what was so good about her?"

Rutejìmo looked down at his lap. He didn't want to answer, but he didn't know why. "Nothing."

"Two days is a really long time for nothing."

He peered up at her and, when he saw her hard look, he cringed. "I thought there was something, but...."

"What happened?"

"She ripped my heart out." Rutejìmo let out a gasping breath before he continued. "She said she would never love me, and there was nothing that would ever change it."

"But," Mapábyo said in a soft voice, "you've held a shikāfu for years. Didn't that mean anything to her?"

Rutejìmo snorted. "She knew about it. I guess it was obvious, actually." He sighed. "Everyone in the clan seems to know I held one for her. Then she went and tore out my heart to make sure I knew there would never be a sands-damned chance of ever being with her."

She rested her hand on his knee. "I'm sorry."

Rutejìmo realized he was crying. With an angry swipe, he shook his head. "I should have known better." His fingers gripped the tooth necklace around his neck. He yanked down, snapping the leather. "Damn that bitch!"

Before his eyes could blur with tears, he crawled out from the shadows and stood up. With an inarticulate yell, he threw the tooth away as far as he could.

It sailed in a long arc before landing in the sand with a puff.

Mapábyo's feet scuffed the sand and she inched closer. She rested her hand on his shoulder, but said nothing.

"Damn her," he gasped. "Damn her to the sands. And after I went back to her, begging to just give me a second chance." He sank to his knees. "I should have never tried to give her that comb."

Even as he spoke, he knew that it was the wrong thing to say.

Mapábyo's hand slipped from his shoulder. "Second... chance?" She said. "You went back?"

Rutejìmo closed his eyes and nodded. "After she kicked me out of her tent."

"After Desòchu s-sent," her voice cracked, "you away? You went back to her and begged for her to take you again?"

He prayed silently that Tachìra would strike him dead right then and there. "Sands," he muttered.

Mapábyo stepped away from him. He listened to her feet on the sands. She headed back to the rocks, but then she came back a few seconds later.

He heard a whistling sound and turned toward her.

Her pack slammed into his face. The impact sent stars across his vision and he staggered back.

"What is wrong with you!?" she screamed.

Rutejìmo groaned and held his face, trying to blink through his blurry vision.

"She kicked you out, and you went back!? Are you really that stupid!?" Mapábyo swung her bag around again. "Maybe if someone hits you hard enough, you'll stop being a skull-rotted moron!"

Rutejìmo flinched in anticipation, but she didn't step forward to hit him again. Instead, she spun around again. The strap on the bag stretched out and whistled loudly in the air. He caught a glimpse of her mask of rage each time she turned around. The rotations grew faster until the bag began to glow and became a streak of golden flames.

He stared in shock for a moment before he realized what Mapábyo was doing. She was going to throw it at him.

"Shit!" Stumbling, he turned on his heels and sprinted away. Three steps later, Shimusògo raced past him, and he threw everything he could into putting as much distance between the two of them. His breath came raggedly with his effort to run faster. His injuries slowed him down, and he knew he wouldn't make it.

He had sprinted a quarter mile when the burning pack slammed into him. It impacted between his shoulders, picking him off the ground and throwing him across a scree of gravel and against a short rock that caught his hip. The canvas exploded behind him, peppering him with underwear, eating utensils, and travel supplies.

His landing drove the air out of his lungs, and he slumped to the ground. Gasping for breath, he felt a rumble shake the ground. Smoke and flames blew away from him, but he could do nothing but helplessly open his mouth and try to draw air into his lungs.

A second boom rumbled through the air.

He flung up his hands, trying to protect himself from a second hit.

After long seconds, nothing came.

Flailing, he flipped over to see Mapábyo racing away in a cloud of feathers and dust.

Rutejìmo dropped his head to the ground. His lungs jerked back to life, and he inhaled sharply, choking on sand that tickled the back of his throat. "Sands. Damn the sands and damn the sun and," he lifted his head to scream, "damn every single person in my sand-damned life!"

Pushing himself up on his knees, he continued to scream. He bellowed until his aching lungs emptied and he had to draw in a long, gasping breath. He let out another yell, but it died in his throat after a few seconds.

He considered remaining on the sands until the sun baked away his skin, and his bones were scattered by the wind. A sob ripped from his throat, and he slumped forward, his hands slapping to the ground. He struck something hard underneath. Curious, he dug his fingers into the hot grains until he felt a sharp edge of bone digging into his palm.

Pain pushed away his sorrow. He sat back up and opened his palm. It was the chipped tooth that Mapábyo had around her neck. One end had been snapped off with a rock and she had used an awl to bore a hole in it. A droplet of blood oozed along his palm and he watched it fill the hole she had made in the tooth.

Years ago, Mikáryo had chipped a tooth off a giant snake and given it to him. He had done the same as Mapábyo and had bored a hole in the middle to wear it. He had worn it ever since. Even after ten years, he was still lost.

Rutejìmo stared at Mapábyo's tooth, trying to focus through his discomfort. Mapábyo wasn't searching for meaning like him. As far as he could remember, there was no question of her remaining in the clan or even becoming an adult. Everyone loved her.

He shook his head, that couldn't be it. Sniffing, he rolled the tooth in his hand and smeared the blood across his palm. She was the only other one to consider wearing a tooth around her neck. He still remembered the pain and sorrow on her face when Tejíko and Desòchu asked her to remove it. But there was no reason for her to wear it in the first place.

He groaned with frustration. He didn't always understand things, and this was one situation where he was truly lost. He wished he had someone to talk to: Chimípu or Pidòhu would be best, but even Gemènyo would help him figure out why Mapábyo was so nice to him or why she responded so poorly to his attempt to return to Mikáryo. But they were alone in the desert, and he had no friends to ask.

Not that they would. When the clan had taken Rutejìmo and the others into the middle of the desert, they abandoned them without explaining their reasons. He had seen it other times when they led a fighting couple and let them resolve it in the open.

He lifted his head and focused on his thoughts.

It was the Shimusogo Way to let the desert solve problems. Both of their coming of age rituals involved taking them far from home and then leaving them alone. Gemènyo even said they chained Hyonèku and Kiríshi together when they were struggling with their marriage.

Other memories bubbled up: of Kiríshi insisting he buy something for Mapábyo, the strange way he was evicted from his table and forced to sit next to her, even the little smiles from Gemènyo after Rutejìmo talked to her.

He stared down at the tooth. The rest of the world fell away until he saw nothing but it in his palm. He realized he knew the answer, but his mind refused to let him focus on it. Staring at the tooth, he saw how she had made it just like his. It was because of him she did it. To be like him, to be with him.

Mapábyo had come back when he fell behind. And then encouraged him to keep running even when he wanted to give up. He didn't expect her to show up in the public house. She risked everything, including her own clan, to talk to him. Only a fool would do that, or someone in love.

"Sands," he muttered hoarsely. "Sands damn me to the furthest limits of the desert."

She had a shikāfu for him, and he never noticed it. Everyone else did, even Gichyòbi. That was why the warrior sent them away together without punishment. Like everywhere else in the desert, they were abandoned to figure out their feelings for each other. No, Mapábyo already knew what she wanted. They were out on the sands because Rutejìmo needed to figure it out.

"I'm an idiot. A sand-drowned, blinded idiot who couldn't even—"

With a gasp, he looked up and around. He could no longer see the plume of her passing. If she got too far or was too angry, he would never catch up and apologize. It didn't matter if she never wanted to see him again, he had to tell her he finally figured it out.

Moving desperately, he crawled around and used his fingers to comb the possessions that had burst from her bag. He stripped off his shirt and turned it into a makeshift bag and then stuffed it full. A few straps from her ripped bag sealed it shut. He staggered to his feet, fighting through the agony of his injuries, and ran back to the rocks.

He found his bag out in the shadows. Gathering it up, he looped both packs over his shoulder and took a deep breath. He had to apologize, or at least beg for forgiveness.

He started forward, but came to a stumbling halt. Turning around, he raced to where he had thrown his necklace and frantically searched the sands. It hadn't taken long for the wind to almost cover the tooth. He yanked the leather out of the hole and held both teeth in one palm. They were almost identical, except for the ten years that separated them.

He turned and looked in the direction Mapábyo ran. Biting his lip against the pain, he sprinted after her.

$$\text{---------}\quad \text{Chapter 18}\quad \text{---------}$$

Darkness

Decisions of the heart are rarely announced in public.

—Fakinori Détsu

Rutejìmo raced across the sands, his heart pounding in time with each strike against the hard ground. Feathers and dust poured around him, solidifying the earth under his feet before exploding into a cloud that stretched for at least half a mile behind him. He knew he was in pain and he would suffer, but he had to catch Mapábyo. He had to keep running.

Shimusògo, the tiny spectral bird, was always three steps ahead. Unlike him, it ran effortlessly over the sand and rock. Rutejìmo would never catch it, but that didn't stop him from trying. He knew if he could, then maybe he could finally run fast enough to catch Mapábyo before she ran out of his life forever.

He ran against the setting sun. He could feel it reaching the horizon. When it sank below, all the power would rush out of him, and he would be forced to run with his own strength.

Rutejìmo would also suffer the full brunt of his exhaustion and injuries. Over the day, he had felt blood drying in the wind but there was no pain. The power of Shimusògo kept it away from him while he ran, but that would all stop once the magic ended.

The knowledge that he would be in agony hung over him. Every few seconds of running meant a hundred less feet he would crawl in agony. He strained to keep moving, to avoid stumbling and losing precious seconds.

In the distance, to his right, he spotted a plume of colored smoke that marked a guarded oasis. Turning toward it, he pushed himself to run faster. His feet flew across red-tinted sand, and he fought back the discomfort beginning to push through the euphoria of running.

He didn't make it before the sun dipped below the horizon. Between one step and the next, the power slipped away and he stumbled forward. He planted his feet to come to a sliding halt, his efforts leaving a rod-length furrow in the fine sand.

Rutejìmo crawled out of the gouge. When he reached the top, a wave of dizziness slammed into him. With a groan, he slumped to his knees. Agony throbbed in his joints, adding to the discomfort of the cuts, bruises, and scrapes that peppered his skin. The blow Mapábyo had made across his back still burned painfully. Underneath the injuries, the burn of torn muscles and the ache of fatigue throbbed.

He tried to push himself up, but his strength fled him and he fell forward.

For a long moment, he remained on the ground, breathing through his nose. The grains of sand clung to his nostrils. It would be so easy to remain there until darkness came. But then it would be too late.

Groaning, he forced himself back to his feet. He trudged along a dune, his bare feet digging into the sand. His entire body shook violently with the effort. Once he reached the top, he looked around for his destination.

Rutejìmo spotted it a quarter mile away, a glow in a haze of colored smoke. Without his magic, it was an insurmountable distance and one that he would have long since given up. He sighed and looked around for a closer shelter: a rocky outcropping or a cliff.

Shuddering through the agony that assaulted his senses, he shoved his hand into his pocket. When his fingers caught on the sharp tips of the tooth necklaces, he froze. He forced his fingers along the sharp edges and explored it. He looked back toward the oasis. It was a quarter mile of agony, but there was still a chance.

He groaned and turned to the oasis. He glanced down to the ground. Shaking, he forced himself to take a step. Agonies reported themselves along his senses, sharp pains mixed with deep aches. Wincing, he gripped the teeth tighter and then took another step. When it didn't hurt as much, he took another.

"Please be there. Please, Shimusògo, please let her be there."

Chapter 19

Exhaustion

The banyosiōu are dead to everyone, unseen and unheard.

—*Forgotten Ghosts* (Act 1)

Over an hour later, Rutejìmo staggered into the light of the camp surrounding the oasis. His breath came in ragged gasps, ripping from his throat in a wheeze. Behind him, his footsteps formed a ragged line through the smooth sand, leaving behind a wake of disturbed sand and, he suspected, the occasional splatter of blood.

An armed man strode forward to meet him in the center of a pool of light created by four torches. The dark-skinned man wore a close-fitting shirt that strained over his muscular chest. "I am Tijìko and I speak for Tifukòmi."

From underneath boxes and around a wagon, a pack of six dogs came out. They didn't bark or growl, but Rutejìmo could hear them panting and the scuff of sand underneath their paws. They circled around him, a faint breeze rippling their short, wiry hair and bringing the scent of fur and blood to Rutejìmo. He gulped and waited until they sat down around him.

Rutejìmo took a deep breath, automatically saying the familiar words. "I am Rutejìmo and I speak for..." His clan name froze in his throat. He no longer had the right to use it.

He glanced down at his plain shirt, missing the orange and reds he normally wore. His chest ached. He saw the dark bruises on his skin and felt the scratches underneath the fabric. Everything hurt but, somehow, losing his clan stung the deepest.

"... I speak for no one." He didn't really know the proper greeting for a banyosiōu. He sighed and looked up helplessly.

The warrior's face twisted into a scowl. Around Rutejìmo, the dogs began to growl in a low, rumbling done. "Then go. We don't have a place for your kind."

Rutejìmo glanced over his shoulder at the blackness around him. Without sunlight, he couldn't see a foot in front of him much less enough to find a place to camp. "But it's night, and I can't see."

Wrapping his hand around the hilt of his sword, the guard pulled a few inches of the weapon from his sheath. "Go, before I tear you apart and feed you to the vultures."

The dogs stood up, growling as one.

Rutejìmo clutched himself, careful to avoid going near his weapon. Sweat prickled his skin. He looked out into the darkness and then back to the oasis where an audience stood up to salute a bard who had just finished a story. He cleared his throat. "Could you tell me if Great Shimusogo Mapábyo is here?"

"Go!"

One of the dogs charged at Rutejìmo, teeth bared and snarled.

Rutejìmo let out a yelp and backed away, stumbling toward another dog that nipped at his thigh. The sharp pain of teeth cut across his skin and he backpedaled away from both dogs.

The pack circled in front of him, growling loudly and moving with disturbing synchronization. He cringed when they completely surrounded him.

"Go!" yelled the warrior.

An armed woman joined him with more dogs following her.

The warrior yelled again, "Go until you can't see the light! If I see you again, the pack will tear you apart!"

Rutejìmo continued to work his way back until he no longer stood in the pool of light. A trickle of blood ran down his thigh and he hissed in pain. Bending over, he started to press one hand against it to test the injury when the dogs surged forward.

Crying out, he turned on his heels and staggered into the darkness.

As he ran, he heard the man tell the woman. "And tomorrow, there will be one less fool."

———————— Chapter 20 ————————

Waking Up Alone

Footsteps on a beach are quickly forgotten during a storm.
—The Shadow King's Lament (Act 3)

Rutejìmo crawled out of unconsciousness with a groan. He struggled to place himself, the nightmares still swimming through his head. Gulping, he looked around at the darkness surrounding him and tried to calm his rapidly beating heart. While his hands reached out for one of his lights, he relived Desòchu's and Chimípu's brutal punishment and Mikáryo's rebuke. But instead of a blanket underneath his hand, his fingers brushed against cold sand. A sharp edge of a rock scraped his palm and he yanked it back. He rolled away from it, trying to force his mind away from his nightmares and focus on the world around him.

He cracked open one eye and stared ahead of him. It was morning, a few moments before the sun rose. There was nothing but waves of sand as far as he could see through his bleary vision. He blinked slowly and tried again, his eyes slowly coming into focus. Still, he saw nothing but sand and rock.

Rutejìmo closed his eye and pried both open. He blinked and stared at his surroundings, hoping to see something besides the desert. When he didn't, he rolled back over and stared in the other direction, his mind somehow struggling to take in the miles of barren land.

And then it struck him. He was alone.

Completely alone in the desert.

Images flashed through his mind: of Karawàbi with his throat cut, of the bodies he had stumbled on over the years, and the sight of the massive snake that Mikáryo killed when he was sleeping. There were horrors in the sand that preyed on loners.

His heart began to beat faster and he felt ice drip along his spine. There was no one else with him. He could picture faceless men coming up to cut his throat, or creatures burrowing under the sand only inches away from slaughtering him.

Crying out, he scrambled to his feet and fumbled for his tazágu. Yanking the weapon out, he spun around and waved it in front of him, scanning the horizon for attackers. He didn't spot any, but that didn't stop him from turning around frantically and brandishing his weapon.

After a few rotations, he was sure he was alone. The anticipation of danger continued to itch and he spun around again to make sure.

Groaning, he came to a stop and used one hand to shake the sand free from his black hair. It bounced off his bare chest before cascading to the ground.

His injuries still ached along his body, but the scratches had managed to scab over and a few of the bruises didn't hurt as much as they did before he slept. Sleep, he decided, had done some good, though he berated himself for closing his eyes.

He didn't need to look to know the sun rested right below the horizon. In a few seconds, he would feel it breach the horizon and the familiar rush of excitement would course through him. He felt sick, though, as if he questioned if he still deserved the powers that Tachìra and Shimusògo granted him.

Another part of his mind wondered if he would lose his powers with the new day. Or would it take longer before the sun punished him for his transgression?

Memories of his mistakes slammed into him and he fought the urge to crawl back into the sand and cry. Clamping his mouth tight to avoid whimpering, he knelt down and brushed off the two packs before hoisting them over his shoulder.

He grabbed his water skin and shook it. The light weight and faint sloshing brought a fresh surge of despair. He had precious little left. He could survive for a few hours by running fast enough to lose himself to magic, but he only had enough for a single stop.

Frowning, he tried to picture the map of the area. Like most of the couriers, he knew the areas he ran intimately, not only to avoid dehydration in the sand but also to find alternative routes when storm or bandits threatened his run. But Rutejìmo didn't know Mapábyo's mail run any better than Hyonèku's or Gemènyo's routes. It took six days, that much he knew, which meant there were still four more days of running before he reached the destination.

He turned back the way he had come. He couldn't see Wamifuko City, but he knew how to trace his steps back. He shook his head and turned his back on the city, he couldn't return there for days. Even if he did, there would be no shelter waiting for him.

Turning around, he scanned the horizon until he spotted the southwest road that would eventually take him to Monafuma Cliffs. The cliffs were on a river, but they were four days from here, enough time to die of thirst before reaching water.

His other choices weren't any better. Shimmering waves of sand and rocks surrounded him. To the north, he spotted a dark line that could be cliffs, mountains, or a sand storm. To the southeast, nothing but gravel and rock until the horizon.

As he pondered his choices, he gathered up the ring of travel lights he used to push back the darkness and stuffed each one in his pack. The pale light wouldn't keep larger predators at bay, but he didn't dare spend the night in darkness. He growled to himself, he didn't plan on sleeping either, but exhaustion had taken him when he wasn't expecting it.

Standing up, he looked around in hope of a path before him. There was none, only faith and hope; he didn't enjoy a large share of either.

Rutejìmo took a swig of his water and held it against his tongue before swallowing. Closing his eyes, he faced the sun and whispered prayers to Tachìra; the whispered words felt more precious than ever before. He knew he was begging for his life and a second, or third, chance. Not that Tachìra had any reason to ever give Rutejìmo anything.

He ended with a whispered plea. "Please, don't let me die out here, Tachìra. I beg you."

The sun peeked over the horizon. When the light struck his body, he felt a shiver of power and the rush of heat. The sun felt good again his skin, and for a brief moment, he no longer felt ashamed.

With a tear in his eye, he gave the sun a deep bow before turning to the southwest and the Monafuma Cliffs.

———————— Chapter 21 ————————

Silence

They are the rotting rats scurrying along the shadows of society.
—Chyobizo Nichikōse, *The Lost*

Rutejìmo ran because it was the only thing he could do. His pains had intensified over the hours of running in the sun. The sharp edge of dehydration turned the discomfort of his injuries into piercing agony.

He tried to get water from two separate oases, but the guards at each one rebuked him. After the second attempt, he toyed with the idea of using the Shimusògo name for just one stop, but the words wouldn't come. He wasn't sure if it was pride or honor, but he couldn't muster the courage to the claim the clan, even in his mind.

He focused on the road ahead of him, trying to cling to the faltering euphoria of running. His head ached, and his body screamed in agony with every strike of his foot against the hardened ground, but he couldn't stop running. Every time he considered it, the image of Mapábyo rose up in his mind. The look of hurt, betrayal, and anger kept playing over in his thoughts, reminding him that he had missed the most important thing in his life. She could be halfway to the cliffs by now, and he would be running for no other reason than to speed his death, but his memories drove him forward as much as the spirit bird running before him.

Ahead, a thin wisp of colored smoke rose from the side of the road to mark the presence of a guarded oasis. He hoped they would give him water, but doubted it would end differently than the last three attempts. His guts were already twisted in knots, and the ache burned along his limbs. If the world needed to remind him of his failure, it had been proven beyond a doubt that the desert hated those without a clan.

He needed water. Needed it more than anything else in his life. Any amount would be salvation at this point, even if he had to suck it off the rocks or through sand. The oasis could be his last chance. Though he already knew they would chase him away, he angled toward it in bitter hope.

What felt like a day later, he came to a skidding halt in front of the oasis. Being mid-day, the dirty camping plots around the stone-covered well were empty. A few teenagers swept them clean while some women were repairing a sheltering wall on the outer edge. On the far side, he spotted a wagon filled with wood and a group of a dozen men emptying it into a stack near the central fire pit.

Scattered among the clan were more of the stocky dogs he had seen a few days ago. They were sleeping in the shade or watching the work around them. He recognized the name on the banners that hung off the walls: Tifukòmi.

The clan, human and canine, looked up at him where he stood. Rutejìmo stepped toward the nearest of them, but his arms and legs didn't seem to work. A wave of dizziness slammed into him, and he fell, flailing around before landing heavily on one knee. He pitched forward. The ground rushed up. He groaned from the bolt of agony that shot up from his knees.

Stars burned across his vision. He clawed at the ground until he found purchase, but when he went to lever himself, his strength failed him, and he slumped forward.

Hands grabbed him and pulled him up.

Rutejìmo gasped for breath, each breath a dry wheeze. His lips were cracked, and blood dribbled down the side of his mouth.

Someone offered him a mug, but when his fingers refused to grip it, they held it to his mouth. He gulped down the cool liquid.

"Slowly now, don't choke." An old man knelt on the ground next to him. He held the mug up to Rutejìmo. His green eyes bore into Rutejìmo, and he did not smile.

Rutejìmo struggled to drink and breathe at the same time. What should have been an easy thing took most of his concentration. After a few seconds of drinking, he gasped and pulled back.

The old man set aside the mug. He cleared his throat until Rutejìmo looked at him. "I am Kamanìo and I speak for Tifukòmi."

"I-I am Rutejìmo and I can't speak for anyone."

The hands holding him up tightened and he saw the old man's face twist into a scowl.

Desperate, Rutejìmo pawed at the mug. "Please? All I ask is for some water and I'll go."

Kamanìo's eyes softened and he shook his head. "You just lost your clan, didn't you?"

Rutejìmo gasped. "H-How did you know?"

"You're running alone in the desert, and you speak for no spirit. You don't know the way of the banyosiōu, yet you obviously are dressed as one. Only one who recently died would even consider the desert. It would be suicide. No one will help you out here, not if you have no clan."

"I'm learning that. In fact, your clan helped with that lesson."

"You come from the northeast, that means Tifukomi Tijìko?" At Rutejìmo's nod, Kamanìo sighed. "I can't speak for my son, but he was right. If you were on your feet, I would turn you away just as he did."

Rutejìmo's eyes burned. "I'm sorry. There... aren't a lot of lessons for what to do and I," he inhaled roughly, "wasn't really planning on traveling alone."

Kamanìo's eyes narrowed for a moment. "Who were you meeting?" He held up the mug to Rutejìmo.

Taking the cup, Rutejìmo sipped from it and felt his stomach beginning to unknot.

"I ran with...." The words died in his throat. He couldn't let anyone know that Mapábyo traveled with him willingly, that would risk her own life among the clan. Gasping again, he bowed his head. "I run with no one."

"And your former clan?"

Rutejìmo couldn't name his clan either, in fear that it would reveal Mapábyo. The Shimusògo were well-known along this route. He shook his head.

Kamanìo gestured to the others with his chin. Hands pushed Rutejìmo firmly into a sitting position before the clan members withdrew and returned to their duties in the camp. In a few seconds, only two gray dogs and the old man remained near Rutejìmo.

With a grunt, Kamanìo got off his knees and sat down.

Rutejìmo watched, his stomach beginning to clench in fear.

"She isn't supposed to be running with you, is she?"

Searching the older man's face, Rutejìmo tried to figure out what he was pushing for. The green eyes, one hazy and one bright, watched him sharply.

"No," Rutejìmo said finally, "she isn't." Guilt bore down on him and he bowed his head.

"You put both of your lives at risk by doing this, you know. If someone determines you are chasing after her, they might suspect she knew about it."

Rutejìmo nodded mutely.

"But," the old man said, "you are both young and foolish. Which is probably why she went back for you."

Rutejìmo lifted his gaze, his breath quickening. "She did?"

Kamanìo nodded slowly.

"Sands," groaned Rutejìmo. He tried to push himself to his feet, but the two dogs growled sharply and he froze.

"No, young man, you need to stay here."

"I-I have to go back."

"If you leave then you will surely die."

Rutejìmo whimpered and looked across the shimmering sands. Heat waves rose up from the road, wavering at the edge of his focus. The idea of running in the heat, even with a little water in his belly, sickened him and all he wanted to do was curl up and cry.

Kamanìo patted him on the leg. "It never gets better, you know."

"But I have to apologize to her."

The hand on his leg froze.

"I screwed up so many things, and she... she didn't deserve what I did. What I'm doing to her either."

Pulling back his hand, Kamanìo stood up with a guttural groan. Both of the dogs came up to him, one on each side, and pressed their bodies against his knees. He reached down to rest his hands on the large hounds' heads. "How badly do you want this?"

Rutejìmo looked up, his eyes burning but no tears coming. "More than anything, Great Tifukomi Kamanìo."

Kamanìo held out his hand, and Rutejìmo flinched. Instead of hitting him, Kamanìo held his hand out to help Rutejìmo to his feet.

Trembling, Rutejìmo took it and stood up.

The old man pulled Rutejìmo close enough that Rutejìmo could feel his breath and then turned him around. With a firm hand, he pushed Rutejìmo toward one of the shelters. "First, you need water, food, and sleep."

"I-I—"

"This is how things work, young man. You remain silent and do what you're told. For now, you need to recover because, in four hours, the first of the clans will be arriving for the night, and you cannot be seen."

Rutejìmo nodded. He struggled to understand the sudden change in the old man's attitude.

"While our guests are here and then until about an hour after midnight, you will gather up the refuse around that way," Kamanìo gestured to a hill, "and take it to a dump about a mile to the south to burn. You will not be seen and you will make no noise. You will remain hidden from the mind and senses."

"How—" Rutejìmo stopped when Kamanìo's hand tightened on his shoulder.

"You will remain silent. I will detail a guard to guide you, but she will not touch either the garbage or the body. Those are not her duties."

Rutejìmo inhaled sharply. He knew that banyosiōu were the ones who dealt with the unclean things in life, but he wasn't expecting it to happen to him.

"The corpse was my daughter's first hound. She died two nights ago from age. She is to be burned to ash, separately from the garbage." His voice grew tight.

Rutejìmo nodded and remained silent.

"Do you know the way?"

He shook his head.

"Can you read?"

At Rutejìmo's nod, Kamanìo grunted. "I have a book of rituals to perform and a vase for her ashes. There are rites for her body, follow them exactly if you value your life. There are directions for which spices to use and when. Requirements for how much ash must remain behind. When you come back, I will have a blanket and food by the garbage pile. You will remain behind the garbage until the last of the visiting clans have arrived. I will send for you."

Kamanìo pushed Rutejìmo into the shade of a shelter.

One of the dogs came up with a basket filled with food and two waterskins. Rutejìmo's stomach rumbled at the sight of it.

"Now, remain silent, eat, and sleep. You will be woken."

Rutejìmo sank down on the ground, struggling to wrap his mind around the sudden change in his life. It was hard to concentrate through his pounding headache. "Great..." he paused and looked into Kamanìo's eyes, wondering if he could ask one question.

The old man sighed and looked away. "Why?" he asked into thin air.

Rutejìmo nodded.

"I may be a fool, but Great Shimusogo Mapábyo has been a joy in the last year." Kamanìo held up his hands before he continued, "She has brought smiles and laughter to my clan and those we protect around the oasis. And last night, I saw all the laughter gone from her eyes as she regretted leaving you. I may be cursing her to join your path, but I am driven to see her smile once again."

Kamanìo stepped away. "I am also bound by other obligations not to do this again. Rutejìmo, this is the one and only time you will have solace in this camp without a clan. You have one day exactly—twenty hours—and you are no longer permitted to remain. If you return, I will not see you again and it would be in your best interest that Great Shimusogo Mapábyo speaks for herself with you nothing more than a shadow of the dead barely visible in the corner of my eye."

Rutejìmo watched the old man stride away. He struggled not only with the desire to say something but also the sadness that welled up. It squeezed his lungs and burned his eyes, but he had no more tears left for his own mistakes.

With a heavy heart, he reached for the food and drink. He had a lot of work to do.

Chapter 22

The Ghost

How do you deal with the unseen? Treat them as if they weren't there and
let them see your answer.

—Chyobizo Nichikōse, *The Lost*

Sweat pouring down his back, Rutejìmo swung the pickax
over his head. He swung it and drove it into the ground. A
small chunk of earth flew up, bouncing twice before rolling
away. He grunted and swung the ax up and over again. He
couldn't stop, despite the protest of his muscles and the ache
in his back. As soon as it hit, he yanked it back and swung a-
gain.

He had been working hard since early morning. Even before
the other clans had left for their travels, he spent the time cleaning out the garbage pits and scraping out the cleaning pots behind a dune. When it was safe to be seen again, he hammered,
lugged, and dragged whatever was placed in front of him. He
ate when he could, stealing scraps off plates while scraping
them into the garbage or grabbing a gulp of water from the bottom of a bucket.

No one spoke to him or even looked at him. Instead, they
pointedly set down whatever tool he needed when he walked

nearby. He worked numbly, bound by the generosity they were giving him but also by the realization that he couldn't return to his old life.

He continued to dig while watching the shadows grow shorter. With every swing of the pick ax, he planned his route: back along the road and circle around the oases that threatened him. If the Tijikóse allowed it, he would grab two more water skins, but he wasn't sure if that would be enough. It was a long run back to Wamifuko City and he might never meet up with Mapábyo again.

Along the outer edge of the oasis, he spotted two teenagers carrying his pack. They said nothing to each other or even looked in his direction. Instead, they left the pack for him and continued along their way. One of the clan dogs dragged a large water skin over, dropped it on the pile, and then trotted away.

The stack of supplies pointedly reminded him that he was running out of time. Tearing his attention away from it, he bore down on the pick and continued to dig out the hole. If he had to leave, he would thank them properly with silent labor. He dug faster, feeling the seconds sliding away by the shortening shadows. Blisters broke along his palms but the pain only drove him to move faster.

He finished just as the sun reached its apex. Panting for breath, he wiped the sweat from his brow and peered around for whatever would go into the hole. Seeing nothing, he dragged the pick ax over to a shed that they used to store tools and set it down.

He slipped around the shed and trudged along the outer perimeter of the campground. His breath came in ragged gasps. He felt like a ghost flitting from shadow to shadow, unheard and unseen.

The Tifukòmi were generous: three skins of water, enough food for two days, fresh supplies, bandages, twisted knots of rofōshi roots for pain, and another change of plain clothes. He secured everything into the two packs before swinging the straps over his shoulders. It weighed more than usual, but he had a long run ahead of him.

Rutejìmo resisted the urge to take one last look at the camp. They had given him enough: shelter for the night, water, and lessons on what his new life would be like.

Taking a deep breath, he walked away from the camp. The muscles of his arms and legs ached with every step, but most of the discomfort came from his work around the campsite instead of his injuries. He pushed himself to jog, working out his body until his movements grew smoother and more familiar. He could barely feel the limp that slowed him down before.

He feared going faster, in case Shimusògo had somehow abandoned him in the night. His feet pounded against the ground in steady, slow beats. It didn't take long before the heat began to bear down on him and the slowness plucked at his mind.

Rutejìmo was a runner, and he needed speed. Grunting, he pushed himself to accelerate.

When Shimusògo appeared, he let out a sob. He sank into the familiar chase after the tiny speckled bird racing before him. The world blurred around him and he found comfort in his speed. As long as his spirit came to him, he could survive the year.

He cried out in joy, thankful Shimusògo was still there, and threw himself into running. He needed to find Mapábyo.

D. Moonfire

Chapter 23

Reunion

Rarely do declarations of love come at opportune times.
—*Lament of Talsir* (Act 2, Scene 7)

By the time the sun touched the horizon, Rutejìmo's excitement had faded into a stubborn determination with a hint of despair. He was about to lose his magic to the night, and he still had too many miles to go. He pushed himself to his limits—the point where his body refused to move any faster—and his lungs burned from his effort.

A thousand nightmares ran across his mind, mostly of Mapábyo turning him away once he caught up with her. He didn't know if she would still be angry at him for wasting her time trying to find him, or simply furious that he spent nights with Mikáryo. Doubt seeped through his thoughts, and he had to fight to avoid slowing down in defeat.

He came up to one of the many oases along the road. They were all heavily guarded, though now he could tell there were only four clans that claimed the string of oases along this road.

Coming into a wide arc, he circled around the camp at a respectful distance, far away from the guards. He searched for the familiar red and orange of his clan. After a second lap, he saw neither Mapábyo or Shimusògo's colors.

With a groan, he sprinted away. He wouldn't make it to the next oasis before sunset. Not that anyone would welcome him to the oasis without Mapábyo. If the last few days were any indication, he couldn't travel anywhere in the desert by himself.

It didn't matter if he was stuck in a city or at the cliff for the rest of the year, he couldn't live with himself if he couldn't apologize to Mapábyo for what he did. He tightened his jaw and raced along the road, his body moving in time with the rapid-fire rhythm of magic and speed.

A mile later, he felt a tickling of power rising up behind him. He looked around, but he couldn't see anything through the dust.

The feeling didn't subside. Instead, it grew in the back of his head, a wave of familiar energy. After a few seconds of trying to identify it, he pulled himself to the side of the road and slowed until he barely held on to Shimusògo. As he ran, he repeatedly glanced over his shoulder at the boiling cloud behind him.

Seconds later, Mapábyo came running up behind him, bursting through the dust in a cloud of translucent feathers and power. Her speed dragged his own plume after it, the curls of dust swirling like a flower.

Rutejìmo slammed his foot down to stop. His sole, hardened by the power of Shimusògo, tore through the ground and he came to a halt only a few chains later. The sand kicked up by his passing rolled over him and bounced off his face before cascading down.

When the dust cleared, Mapábyo stood on the opposite side and a few rods down the road. "Jìmo!"

She jumped out of the gouge her own feet made and sprinted down the road. She moved fast enough for the wind to kick up, but the dépa disappeared when she launched herself into him and tackled him with a hug.

He tripped on the ground and let out an inarticulate yelp. One arm windmilled before he landed back in his trench and then rolled.

The smell of Mapábyo's body swirled around him, a light flowery scent coupled with sweat and smoke. She didn't have her travel packs, and she wore a lighter outfit than they usually wore while running. The thin fabric of her shift clung to her body, rippling from the wind swirling around her. To his surprise, the feel of her body against him brought other lessons Mikáryo taught him welling up into his thoughts.

Embarrassed, Rutejìmo struggled to extricate himself, but her arms caught one of his and she pinned him down with her weight.

"I'm sorry, Jìmo!"

He froze and then shook his head. "No, no. This is my—"

Mapábyo lifted her head and pushed the hair from her face. Tears glistened on her cheeks. "Jìmo—"

Rutejìmo realized how close their faces were and his heart thumped. He gulped for air and then shook his head. With an effort, he pushed her up and off his legs. Quickly, he curled his knees underneath him.

She stared at him, eyes wide and shimmering. He could see her toes curling and uncurling, matching the flex of her hands.

"Mapábyo...." He struggled with the words. Taking a deep breath, he said, "Pábyo, I've made mistakes."

"I don't mind—!"

He held up his hand, and her mouth closed with a snap. "Great Shimusogo Mapábyo... please, let me say this?"

She nodded twice with tears rolling down her face.

Rutejìmo clenched his own hands into fists. "I'm not the fastest or the smartest."

She opened her mouth to protest, but then closed it. "Sorry," she whispered.

His cheeks burned, and his heart pounded in his chest. "I'm never going to be either. And, if my life is any indication, I'm not exactly the most observant person on the sands either." He let out a short, bitter snort. "Actually, I know I'm not because it took me so long to figure out that you... actually like me."

Mapábyo sniffed and pressed her hand against her nose. More tears ran down her cheeks, tracing her almost black skin along her throat and collar.

He reached out for her.

She started to inch closer, but he grabbed her hand and held it tight. "Pábyo... Great... Pábyo, I wish I were a better man for you, but I don't think I can be anything more right now. I'm dead to the world, and you are the only...." He didn't know how to finish the sentence. "I don't even know what you are to me."

Mapábyo sniffed and inched closer. "Jìmo?"

A shiver coursed along his body. He wanted to look away but he forced himself to peer into her green eyes. "Y-Yes?"

"You know I've held a shikāfu for you for years, right?" She inhaled, and he watched her breasts rise with the movement. With a shaking hand of her own, she pressed two fingers against his throat. "I've loved you as long as I can remember."

"I-I," he struggled to breathe, "I didn't know."

The corner of her lip lifted into a smile. "I kind of figured that out."

He chuckled and wiped the tears from his eyes. "I'm an idiot, Pábyo. Dense, slow, and—"

She silenced him by raising her fingers to his lips. "Jìmo? Shut up."

Rutejìmo snapped his mouth shut.

She smiled and inched closer. She parted her thighs to straddle him before settling into place. "You are stubborn, brave, and occasionally you need to be beaten over the head—"

"Or with a pack."

She blushed. "—but the clan never saw you the way I saw you."

Her body molded against him. He felt tight and hot and choking, all at the same time. He reached around her and brought his hands to the small of her back, it felt right to pull her close.

He wanted to deny it, but the words wouldn't come.

"I see you," she whispered. She brought her lips to him. "You may think you're dead to the world, but I see you. And I... will never stop seeing you."

She crossed the infinitely short distance to press her cracked lips against his.

And then he lost himself in the fire of her kiss.

Chapter 24

Tijikóse

Even the most forbidden of people will find their place once they stop and listen.

—Roger Mistork, *The Hidden Society of Prisons*

A day later, Rutejìmo followed Mapábyo into the Tijikóse camp. He remained running up until the last minute, but stopped sharply a few chains shy of the camp. They both agreed that she had to approach the camp by herself.

Mapábyo continued to the edge and stopped in a cloud of dust. She didn't look back at him, but he knew he was on her thoughts. Instead, she stood up straighter and walked the last rod into the camp, her bare feet leaving a ragged trail across the sand.

Tijikose Kamanìo walked out of the shadows for her. Like Mapábyo, neither he nor the rest of his clan even looked at Rutejìmo. He stopped in front of Mapábyo, and they spoke for a few short minutes.

Rutejìmo wondered what they were saying, but then realized it didn't matter. It was no longer his place to greet strangers. He would remain silent, as was now his place. He glanced at the camp and saw that they had planted poles in the holes he had dug, creating a new frame to store more firewood. He stepped to the side to get a better look.

Movement near the front drew his attention back. Mapábyo bowed deeply and walked to the side, moving around the camp in a wide circle instead of passing between the campsites. He watched her profile, her nearly black skin contrasted against the pale sands.

He followed a chain behind her, circling the camp in a much larger circuit until he saw where she stopped. The plot was the furthest one from the fires and, he noticed, the closest to the dune hiding the garbage that he had tended before. Knowing his place, he continued around the ridge of sand until he came up to the familiar place to hide until dark.

He didn't have to wait long. A few minutes later, one of the dogs dragged the shovel around the dune and set it down. The hound panted for a moment and ran off, leaving it behind.

Rutejìmo picked it up and began cleaning. To his surprise, he felt content with what the Tijikóse expected of him. The shovel settled into his palm, against healing blisters. Without hesitating, he got to work.

Hours later, when the sun had long dipped below the horizon, he staggered around the dune and looked across the camp. Most of the campsites were occupied by various clans, just like before. Most had a number of tents, but a few had wagons. One even had a snail-like vehicle that smoked from its tentacles. Small fires had been set among the tents and wagons with a larger bonfire in the common area of the oasis. The crowds gathered around the larger fire, sharing dinner, laughter, and conversation while they forgot the world for a moment.

Mapábyo, on the other hand, sat next to an empty fire pit. She had her tent set up, and there was a spot for a second one.

He came up along the sands, his bare feet scrunching with every step.

She jumped at his sound and scrambled to her feet. "Jìmo —"

Rutejìmo held up his hand to silence her. Coming up, he came close enough to feel her breath against his skin. He grinned and leaned toward her, enjoying the sight of her tilting her head up to meet his kiss. He kissed her.

A Tijikóse guard walked near.

He pulled away from her to step toward the shadows, watching the guard warily.

Mapábyo whimpered softly and sat down. "I don't like this."

Without a word, he unrolled his tent between hers and the dune. It would remain hidden from the central area of the camp, something he thought would be appropriate. He worked quickly to pitch the tent, and started making food to donate to the central fire.

She shifted to watch him. In the light of the flames, her eyes glistened with tears.

Rutejìmo tried to smile encouragingly when he could, but he remained silent.

When she left to take the food to the others, he slipped into his tent and sat down heavily. He wanted to cry or scream. The urge to bolt out of the tent and bellow for everyone to pay attention to him rose up, but he fought it. He yanked the small book of poetry from his pack and distracted himself by reading.

Twenty minutes later, Mapábyo pushed aside the flap of his tent. "You forgot to eat," she whispered.

He looked up, unsure if he could find any words. The lessons before held, and he nodded silently.

She knelt and carried in two heaping plates of food of all varieties, each clan contributing their specialties. He recognized the small yellow peppers from a horse clan who shared bodies with their mounts and the spiced pepper that many clans bought from the south. With a smile, she held up her finger and left. He saw that the gathering had started to break apart, but then the tent flap blocked his sight of the others.

He listened to her footsteps fade before he took a deep breath. His heart felt heavy and his throat tight. He waited for her to return, knowing that she would but still fearing that she had abandoned him.

The long minutes stretched out with only his imagination keeping him company.

When he heard her walking back, he almost sobbed with relief.

Mapábyo crawled back into his tent with a carafe of fermented milk and a large mug. "I could only get one. You don't mind sharing, do you?"

He shook his head and smiled.

They ate in silence and passed the mug back and forth. They said nothing, but Rutejìmo felt a pressure between them, a tension that felt like a thread about to snap. He felt clumsy and nervous, lost and excited at the same time. In the moments between bites, he couldn't help but watch her.

Eight years younger than him, Mapábyo wasn't anything like Mikáryo. She was almost as nervous as he was. She fumbled with her plate and glanced at him through her hair. Her slender body somehow looked vulnerable in the tent, but it was the closeness to her that quickened his heart. She was beautiful, and he wondered how he missed her growing up.

She was nothing like Mikáryo, who moved like a feral mare brimming with confidence. He couldn't help comparing the two women, he saw both when he looked at Mapábyo. He didn't know if it because Mikáryo was his first or if it was his ten year shikāfu, but he struggled with both the differences and similarities of the two, starkly different, women.

He couldn't forget Mapábyo's kiss when they first reunited. He tried to bring it back, the tenderness and intensity quickly fading with his memories.

"J-Jìmo?"

Rutejìmo looked up.

"Tomorrow, could we camp out there? Where you can talk?"

He nodded, a smile stretching his lips.

"Jìmo?"

Rutejìmo shivered at the sound of her voice. It reminded him of the sound Mikáryo made when she drew him back to the tent.

Mapábyo set the mug aside and crawled over to him. Her breath washed across his face, and he drank in the sweetness tinged with soured milk. She smelled like the sweetest amyochíso fruit in that moment. She inhaled sharply and leaned into him until they were an inch apart. "I still see you."

And then she kissed him again.

Chapter 25

Mikáryo

Love blossoms in quiet words and gentle touches.

—Tateshyuso Shifáni

Two days later, at the end of their run, Rutejìmo and Mapábyo stopped at the same time. Their feet dug through the sand and dunes, tearing two large gouges through the ground and leaving a cloud of sand to scatter across a valley.

Mapábyo, giggling, pushed her hair from her face. "You didn't stop running this time."

He blushed and gave her a sheepish smile. "I can't when I'm running with you. I start to slow down, then I realize that you wouldn't want me to, and both my heart and feet start going faster."

"Good."

Rutejìmo followed her up a short hill. At the top, a rock plateau stretched out in a wide circle almost a rod across. In the center, a clan had erected a waist-high circle of stone to shield against the desert winds. The clan's name was engraved on the rock, but Rutejìmo didn't recognize it.

"Jìmo?"

He stopped at the top of the wall. He looked over his shoulder to where Mapábyo stood a few feet away with her hands held behind her back. She twisted back and forth, with a smile.

His heart beat even faster.

"You set up the tents, I'll make dinner."

He nodded, unsure of what to say. "I'd like that."

In the brief silence, Rutejìmo finished crawling over the wall and held his hands out for her.

She took them and pulled herself up.

His muscles and injuries screamed in agony, but he fought to keep his discomfort from his face. When she reached the top, he relaxed and straightened.

Mapábyo stepped closer and reached around him. Catching his wrists, she pulled him into her and placed his palms on her hips.

Rutejìmo tried to pull away, but she held him there. "Jìmo?" She whispered, "You want to continue your story?"

Rutejìmo smiled. He had been telling Mapábyo about his rite of passage. For the first time, he didn't hold anything back, including the most humiliating moment in his life, when he peed his pants as Mikáryo first pressed her tazágu against his throat.

He nodded, and she released him.

Time passed quickly as he told his story. He was relieved that she didn't laugh during his whispered telling of the darkest points when he almost failed at being a decent man. Instead, she just asked a few questions and listened.

He finished in the middle of dinner. The cold food rested on his plate, and he stared at it, drained from his storytelling. In his mind, he kept seeing that last moment when he begged everyone to not kill Mikáryo and Tsubàyo.

Mapábyo padded around the small fire and sat down next to him. "You loved her, didn't you?"

Rutejìmo sighed. He wanted to forget that moment when Mikáryo's life was in his hands. His own life would be better if all he could remember was when she told him to leave. But then he would be lying. He sighed and set down his plate. "I don't want to get hit again."

"Silly, I'm not going to hit you," she said with a grin, "unless you answer dishonestly."

He chuckled.

"Please?"

When he looked over, he could see her pleading. Her dark skin accented the ridge of her nose and the green of her eyes. In his mind, he could see Mikáryo sitting next to her, brown skin covered in black tattoos compared to Mapábyo's darker coloration. They were night and day in his world and he didn't know which one he wanted more.

He took a deep breath. "I loved her." He felt sick to his stomach saying the words. "She was the only woman in my life, even as a fantasy."

"What about Chimípu?"

Rutejìmo gave her a playful bump with his shoulder. "Of course, there was Chimípu and Faríhyo and Kiríshi and everyone else. They were women," he sighed, "but Mikáryo was... the first I ever thought of as something other than a parent or sister."

Mapábyo inched closer. "No one else? I would have thought you and Chimípu would have done it," she paused for a heartbeat, "at least once. Isn't that her duty? To teach you about fucking?"

"I couldn't." He sighed. "We tried, but it just..." He closed his eyes tightly. "Every time we get close, all I see is the people Chimípu killed. Not just her fighting for me against Tsubàyo or Mikáryo, but in the years since, she's killed so many people to protect me."

She leaned against him, saying nothing.

"I despise the violence of the desert. I hate that people try to kill me just to stop some treaty from being registered. When I take a message to deliver, I'm afraid someone is going to kill me. I cringe every time I come up to a corpse along the road. I'm weak, though, and thankful someone is always there to protect me. Chimípu, Desòchu, that guard in the city, a dozen others. I've fumbled through life being... being...."

Mapábyo reached up and kissed him. "You're you."

Rutejìmo smiled and kissed her back. It still felt strange that she was even kissing him, but he found that the tiny little touches were addictive.

"And there is nothing," another kiss, "wrong with that."

"I just feel like I'm doing things wrong, but I can't stop. Desòchu said I got lost on the path and I wasn't worthy of Shimusògo." He rested his hand where his necklace would be. "Everyone knew that I had a shikāfu for Mikáryo, but it was harmless. Until, that is, we met up again and then...."

Mapábyo rested her head on his shoulder. She hooked one arm around his waist and pulled him close. Her body was warm and smelled sweet.

Rutejìmo let out his breath and shrugged. "I knew I was making a mistake, but I kept doing it. Ten years of being told I wasn't good enough, that no one would love me, that I was different, and I couldn't stop myself. I needed to see her and then," he realized he was crying and wiped his tears, "I ruined everything by staying."

"You didn't ruin anything."

"You hit me with your pack."

"I was surprised and probably responded harsher than you deserved."

He grinned. "No, I was stupid."

She looked up at him. Her frown caused him to cringe. "You should stop doing that."

"What?"

"Insulting yourself. I don't like it when you do that."

Rutejìmo looked away.

She reached up and pulled his chin back. "Stop being pathetic."

He snorted. "Yes, Great Shimusogo Mapábyo."

"That's what Mikáryo tells you?"

"No, she just says I'm pathetic. Never to stop. Most of the time, I think she's trying to tell me that I need to be," he chuckled dryly, "less pathetic, but I can't always figure out what I'm doing wrong. At least with the Tijikóse, they would set down the shovel next to what they wanted me to dig. Or put my dinner near the fire. Guiding me without helping."

"Or when papa or Gemènyo drop their rolls where they want to help you to set up the tent."

Rutejìmo jerked. "They do?"

"Yeah, whenever you were gasping as you came in, I saw them moving their rolls or pretending to accidentally unroll it."

He closed his eyes and groaned. "I'm betting they've been doing that for years, and I never noticed."

"Yes," she said and leaned into him. She kissed his lips before pulling back. "Now, eat," she commanded.

Rutejìmo picked up his cold food and ate. He felt raw and vulnerable, exposing his past to someone he didn't notice a week ago. He expected to feel fear and terror, but instead it felt almost comforting knowing that she wouldn't laugh at him.

"What was she like?"

He had to swallow the food in his throat. "Mikáryo?"

Mapábyo nodded.

"She's insulting, to say the least, and rough. She never uses formal names out here in the desert, and she thinks everyone is beneath her."

"Even in the tent?"

For a moment, he almost couldn't answer. But then he saw the seriousness in Mapábyo's eyes and then he nodded. "Yes, but also generous. She encouraged me to learn, all the while telling me I was pathetic. Fortunately, that time I listened and got... better, I guess."

Mapábyo turned slightly and leaned the crook of her neck against Rutejìmo's arm. "My first was Desòchu."

Rutejìmo had guessed his brother was the one to teach Mapábyo, but avoided thinking about it. When Mapábyo didn't say anything more, he struggled with the idea of his brother teaching her the ways of adults, but then pushed it aside. He nodded, not trusting his words.

"He was very demanding: do this, do that, never do that. One way, his way."

Rutejìmo chuckled. "Mikáryo never said never. I asked about..." He blushed at the memory and had to clear his throat, "something and she showed me why it could work."

"What?"

His body grew hot at the memories. He leaned forward and whispered it into her ear.

A heartbeat later, Mapábyo's cheeks turned dark. "Doesn't that... I mean... how..."

He had to shift to relieve a sudden hardness between his legs. "It wasn't too bad after the second time. I kind of liked it."

Mapábyo gulped and looked away, her cheeks dark and the muscles of her legs holding her thighs together. Her breath was low and deep, almost panting.

Rutejìmo, worried that he had gone too far, looked the other way and stared out into the desert. It was black with few stars hanging above him and barely visible over the dim light of the campfire.

"Rutejìmo?"

He shivered at her whispered voice. "Yes?"

"What...." She cleared her throat and looked down. "What are you going to do? When we get back?"

Rutejìmo tore his thoughts away from lust and darkness and focused on his future. He had spent most of the day thinking about his options. "Maybe stay in Wamifuko City? I'm sure with a city that big, someone will need a courier. I still have Shimusògo and I might be able to pick up odds jobs, just not as one of the clan. I think I know how to listen now, when someone offers without saying anything."

"I wish you could go home."

He hated that her voice almost had tears in it. "I can. In a year."

"No running off into the desert?"

"No," he chuckled, "I want to keep you happy."

"You do want that." She kissed him. "Wamifuko City is at the end of my route."

"I know the city, at least."

"Maybe we can get an inn between my routes? You, me, and nothing else?"

"I'd like that." And, he meant it. "As long as you will have me."

Mapábyo smiled and stood up. She took the few steps over to Rutejìmo and took his plate before scraping the remains of both into the fire.

He watched, admiring her movements to avoid troubling himself with the fear of his future. Life as a banyosiōu was harder than he would have ever guessed. If he couldn't figure it out, he would be in trouble. Fortunately, if she would still take him, he could move somewhere else with her protection.

She stood next to him, "Next time, you only need to set up one tent."

Rutejìmo's skin tightened and a flush rose inside him. "Then where will I sleep?"

"The same place you'll be tonight." She held out her hand.

Chapter 26

Return to Wamifuko City

Ostracization is a subtle dance of willing ignorance and looking the other way.

—Tamin Gamanin, *Freedom From Vo*

With a groan, Rutejìmo slumped against the rough stone. Sweat dripped down his back and neck, soaking into his colorless clothes and prickling along his skin. The cold night air washed over him and muted the stench coming from Wamifuko City.

He wiped the sweat from his brow and leaned to the side to watch Mapábyo approach the city gates. They had been running since early morning, trying to get to the city before dark, but they were still a league away when the sun dipped below the horizon. Despite running so long, Mapábyo only had a few beads of sweat on her dark skin.

Rutejìmo clamped down on a brief surge of jealousy. Mapábyo had done so much for him in the last two weeks. Without her, he would have died in the desert or would be forced to remain in Monafuma Cliffs, a border town uncomfortably close to the pale-skinned foreigners.

"There you are, Great Shimusogo Mapábyo!" boomed Gichyòbi from behind Rutejìmo.

Rutejìmo jumped. He spun around to see the warrior striding toward him, inches away from the stone wall and on a collision course with Rutejìmo. Without thinking, Rutejìmo stumbled back toward Mapábyo.

Just as Rutejìmo drew even with Mapábyo, Gichyòbi took a step to the side and bowed to Mapábyo. "I'm glad to see you have returned safely to the city. The desert can be dangerous for a single courier."

Mapábyo bowed even deeper. "Thank you, Great Wamifuko Gichyòbi."

"Come, you must be exhausted from running all day."

Mapábyo gasped. "H-How did you know that? What... I just got here."

"The stones tell me many secrets. I would be honored if you stayed at my home for the night. The inns will be packed because of the sun festival today." Gichyòbi held out his arm and turned her into the city. That brought them both face to face with Rutejìmo.

Rutejìmo tried to step to the side, but guards were blocking his way. He flinched to avoid touching them. Spinning around, he looked for some way to avoid the guards, but the only way free was further into the city. It took him a heartbeat to realize that Gichyòbi was doing the same as the Tifukòmi did, leading without acknowledging his presence. Understanding, Rutejìmo walked backwards and to the side to let others pass so he could follow.

As soon as they did, Rutejìmo followed in their wake. He kept his head bowed and focused on the backs of their heels. He knew the route to Gichyòbi's home, a house made from stone near the center of town. It was the quieter part of the city, in an area the Wamifūko set aside for their own privacy.

"It was a shame you couldn't make it yesterday, Great Shimusogo Mapábyo. My boys and girl were hoping to meet you, but their grandmother insisted on taking them for the night. It will just be you, me, and c tonight."

"Kidóri?"

"My wife. She is looking forward to trying out a new recipe. I hope you don't mind." Gichyòbi snorted. "It smells great, but I'd rather have a strong lager or a piece of my new bread recipe, if you know what I mean."

"Um," Mapábyo said in a confused tone, "I don't."

Rutejìmo grinned. Gichyòbi had a massive cellar filled with wooden casks of beer from every part of the desert. He also baked as a hobby, collecting recipes from the various travelers who passed through the gates.

They walked for a few minutes and talked about the sun festival and the weather.

"Um," Mapábyo said in a pause during the conversation, "Great Wamifuko Gichyòbi?"

"Yes, Great Shimusogo Mapábyo?"

"Can Wamifuko warriors have children?"

Gichyòbi laughed. "Just because I'm not capable of siring them doesn't make them less my children. A father is made by action!" He slammed his fist into his metal chest plate.

Rutejìmo and Mapábyo both jumped.

"And love, of course," finished Gichyòbi.

"The Shimusogo warriors don't have children. They are dedicated to the clan as a whole. At least," she coughed, "that is what I'm told."

"And that works for Shimusògo. Me? I like having a little one screaming my name as I enter the house. And a horde of brigands is nothing compared to a night when every child in the house is pouring out their stomachs and blowing out their backsides. It's a challenge that I willingly face; it reminds me of my willingness to die for my clan."

"Oh," Mapábyo said in a soft voice.

"Ever think about children?"

Rutejìmo tensed and stumbled.

Mapábyo started to look back, but then stared straight forward. Rutejìmo could see her cheeks coloring darkly with her thoughts.

Gichyòbi broke the silence to talk about the history of a bathhouse they were passing.

Mapábyo seemed to jump at the segue, and they spoke about places they'd seen while they made their way to the heart of the city.

Twenty minutes later, they came to Gichyòbi's home. Two guards stood outside, both at attention.

Rutejìmo frowned. He had never seen anyone guarding Gichyòbi's home before. When Gichyòbi held open the door, though, he passed inside and stepped to the side.

The door closed with a click, and then suddenly Gichyòbi grabbed Rutejìmo into a powerful hug. "Good to see you made it, boy."

Rutejìmo tensed for a moment, then leaned into Gichyòbi. It wasn't comfortable with the warrior wearing metal, but somehow the warmth was a balm against the last few weeks of being unseen.

Gichyòbi squeezed tight before releasing him. "I see you learned a bit about silence."

Unsure if he should talk, Rutejìmo nodded.

"Don't worry about being heard here. The two outside will make sure no one interrupts us. And, I had the little ones spend the night away because they won't understand..." Gichyòbi looked over Rutejìmo and sighed. "They are all too young to know the difference between those who are dead and those who have to pretend to be dead."

"I'm sorry for this," said Rutejìmo.

Mapábyo stepped up. "Excuse me, why are you...?"

Gichyòbi gestured to Rutejìmo. "Talking to him? Because I choose to, and there are things that need to be said." He pulled off his helm, revealing a gray-haired man with a child-like, rounded face and an easy smile. "And, being one of the elders gives me privileges that most can't afford." He winked. "At least in private."

He turned to Rutejìmo. "Boy, I can only do this once. I cannot give you shelter or protection, nor can it be known that I see you." Gichyòbi's eyes glistened before he cleared his throat. "This is the way things are, as you probably figured out."

Rutejìmo nodded and clenched against the brief hope of staying that had been crushed. He nodded again as soon as he regained his composure. "Thank you, Great Wamifuko Gichyòbi."

"Call me Gichyòbi, boy."

It was a subtle reminder that they couldn't be friends, otherwise Rutejìmo would be told to use the friendly version of his name, Chyòbi. To hide his discomfort, Rutejìmo grinned.

"I've brought some lagers up from the basement, loves." Gichyòbi's wife, Kidóri, entered the room with four large glasses filled with beer. Her large breasts rested on top of the glasses and she held her elbows along her wide hips. Turning a brilliant smile on Rutejìmo and Mapábyo, she gestured with her chin to the table before setting down the glasses on a low table in the center of the living room. It was the largest room in the house—and where most of the chaos focused when Gichyòbi's children were present.

Surrounding the table were cushions over every square foot of the room, except for ragged paths leading to the sleeping area and another to the kitchen. In the far back, beyond the kitchen, was the bathing area. He had only used it once but he still remembered using the indoor toilet that cleaned itself with a magical rune.

"Ah," boomed Gichyòbi, "the most beautiful woman in the desert, my wife. I fear every day that Tachìra will turn his back on Mifúno to woo her instead."

Kidóri rolled her eyes, but she smiled. "Oh, shush. Are you going to introduce me to the young lady?"

"This is Mapábyo, a courier of the Shimusògo. She delivers mail between here and Monafuma Cliffs."

Kidóri bowed again and then looked at her husband. "Are you going to wear your armor for dinner?"

Gichyòbi rolled his own eyes. "Fine, will you—"

"Go," commanded Kidóri.

Making a show of grumbling, Gichyòbi stomped toward the sleeping areas.

"Boy," Kidóri said, "there is some food in the kitchen. Cut up the cheese and meats and bring it here."

Normally, to call someone other than by their name was an insult. But, somehow, having her speak to him muted any indignity. He bowed and headed back.

Rutejìmo realized that he had not talked much since entering the city. He knew he could, at least in the protection of Gichyòbi's home, but an invisible pressure held back his tongue. Just because he could, didn't mean he had to.

In the kitchen area, he could smell some of Gichyòbi's bread in the oven. A prickle of heat and energy rippled along his senses from the magic used for cooking. He pawed through the cabinets until he found an appropriate platter and started to prepare the food.

As he did, he listened to Kidóri and Mapábyo asking each other about the happenings in the city and Mapábyo's route. They talked about Mapábyo's route to the Cliffs and back, mostly focusing on the various clans traveling back and forth. Rutejìmo felt a strange sense of ease. Even though he wasn't part of the conversation, he could imagine that he was a normal person just like everyone else.

"I heard what your brother did," said Gichyòbi in a low voice.

Rutejìmo jumped and peeked at the man approaching. The warrior had switched into a thick, gray robe. It strained against his muscles and his broad chest. Even though Rutejìmo knew that Gichyòbi wouldn't attack, it helped when the older man wasn't armed with a massive spear.

Gichyòbi patted Rutejìmo's shoulder. "I'm sorry, Jìmo."

Rutejìmo hesitated, the knife hovering over the slices of meat. "I deserved it. I wasn't the best of bro… clan."

"A year is a long time, even for that. Usually a month or two is sufficient."

The knife quivered in Rutejìmo's hand. He forced himself to set the blade down.

"Here, let me get my bread out." Gichyòbi patted Rutejìmo on the shoulder.

Rutejìmo stepped aside.

Gichyòbi opened up the metal box and peered inside. Waves of heat rose around him and rippled the air. He grabbed a towel and pulled out a tray with four loafs of bread. The smells flooded the kitchen and Rutejìmo's stomach rumbled in response.

Gichyòbi set it down. "So, do you have plans?"

"I… I was hoping to stay here in the city."

"Jìmo, I can't help you here."

"I know, but I'm safer here than any other place. At least I know the streets." He hesitated and then sighed. "I hope."

"You'll have company. There are groups of banyosiōu in the city. I can't point them out, but you'll find them soon enough. There are always jobs for those who still have the gifts of the spirits, but without the clans to guide them."

A small measure of hope filled Rutejìmo. "Thank you."

"It's a hard life, but you'll survive." Gichyòbi glanced at Rutejìmo and smiled. "That's one of your best traits."

Rutejìmo stared at him in shock. "What? How would you know?"

Gichyòbi turned and dragged the tray to the opposite side of the cooking area and set it aside. With a grunt, he pulled another loaf from a box and began to slice off thick wedges with a serrated knife.

Rutejìmo stood for a moment and watched Gichyòbi. When the warrior didn't say anything else, Rutejìmo returned to preparing the rest of the food. When he finished, he peered into a pot bubbling over a heating rune. Inside was a thick cream stew bubbling with meats and vegetables.

"It's Kidóri's new recipe. She traded for it with one of the Tsubyòmi a few months ago, but we never had a chance to try it." Gichyòbi reached over and stuck his finger into the stew to scoop out a hunk of meat. He licked his finger before returning to his bread. "The little ones aren't big on things they don't understand."

Rutejìmo chuckled. "I know the feeling."

Gichyòbi nodded in approval. He gathered up the food and added it to the platter Rutejìmo had been filling. "Come, Kidóri is probably inflicting Mapábyo with her paintings. She just finished one yesterday."

Rutejìmo followed after Gichyòbi. In the living area, Kidóri and Mapábyo were sitting on the cushions next to the central table. Kidóri had her book of watercolor paintings. She had done them over the years from various points inside and out of the city.

Mapábyo pointed out one. "That's the gate we came in, isn't it?"

Gichyòbi peered over. "No, that gate is on the east side of the town. You came through its twin."

"Oh," Mapábyo said. "How can you tell?"

Kidóri gestured to a dark spot on the painting. "This is where Gichyòbi had his head slammed into the stone by a horse. I even painted the blood," her finger trailed down, "that stained the cracks."

Mapábyo looked up at Gichyòbi curiously. "Really?"

Gichyòbi turned and showed off a scar on the back of his head.

When Mapábyo gasped in surprise, Gichyòbi slumped down. "You'll love this story. It was early evening..."

Rutejìmo listened to the familiar tale with a smile on his lips. It was comforting to hear it, both remembering the first time he heard it and also the way Gichyòbi's and Kidóri's children listened with wide eyes even after hearing it countless times. It reminded Rutejìmo of better times, when he listened to a stranger's tale while being treated as if he was a long-lost cousin.

Gichyòbi's story ended with flair, and Kidóri followed up with one of her own. Before she married Gichyòbi, she had been a city farmer in charge of the rooftop gardens. Her tales were almost as fantastic as Gichyòbi's, and violent and bloody in their own way.

Rutejìmo had heard them all before, but he sat and listened. When Kidóri finished hers, Gichyòbi convinced Mapábyo to tell the story of her rites of passage.

When Mapábyo finished her own, Rutejìmo knew that he could speak up, but discomfort silenced him.

Mapábyo glanced at Rutejìmo with a question, but Rutejìmo shook his head. He was still dead to the clan, and it didn't bother him that he wasn't asked to join in. Their company gave him comfort, despite knowing that the next day he would no doubt be digging in trash for food or even begging.

Gichyòbi started up another story, distracting everyone. They swapped stories well into the night. As midnight approached, there were empty plates and glasses on the tables. The story ended and only the soft sounds of the city intruded in the silence that followed.

Kidóri leaned against Gichyòbi's arm, one leg on his, and snored softly. A thin line of drool soaked his robe. Rutejìmo wasn't sure, but he thought she had passed out somewhere during one of Mapábyo's quieter tales.

Gichyòbi held his wife closely and swirled a half-finished glass of stout with his other hand.

Rutejìmo looked over to his love. Mapábyo sat on the edge of the table, staring down. He wasn't sure what to do, so he picked up plates and started to carry them to the kitchen.

"Gichyòbi?" Mapábyo's voice stopped Rutejìmo at the door.

"Yes?" Gichyòbi's words were slurred with exhaustion and drink.

"Why did you let us go?"

Rutejìmo tensed at her question. The plates in his hands rattled, and he had to calm himself down before turning back around.

Gichyòbi looked over at her, his eyes rimmed with red. "You mean instead of killing you?"

Mapábyo shivered and nodded.

"I'm supposed to, you know." Gichyòbi snorted. "You did almost three hundred thousand pyābi in damage that day. It took us days to figure out the extent of damages and deal with the screaming. A lot of promises were made to keep everyone happy."

Mapábyo blushed and bowed her head. Her dark skin looked black in the light filling the living area. "S-Sorry."

"Normally," Gichyòbi pried his arm from underneath his wife with a grunt, "if we didn't kill you for the blood price, we would have ransomed you off to the Shimusògo to pay for the damage. Your clan would have paid for you, but other clans just tell us to kill off the offend—"

She sat up straight and a horrified look crossed her face. "You didn't tell the clan, did you!?"

"No," said Gichyòbi, "the Wamifūko paid for the damage."

Rutejìmo spoke before he could stop himself. "Why?"

The warrior looked at Rutejìmo. "You, of course."

The plates slipped from Rutejìmo's fingers. He gasped and knelt down to catch them and banged his knee in the process. One of the plates clattered on the floor before thumping against the table. "S-Sorry."

Kidóri looked up. "What? Oh, you don't..." A sad look crossed her face. Then, she slumped back against Gichyòbi. "I forgot."

Cheeks burning, Rutejìmo gathered up the plates and set them near the stove. He returned to the table.

"Sit, boy," Gichyòbi commanded.

Rutejìmo obeyed. As he did, Kidóri sat up and Mapábyo shifted closer to Rutejìmo.

Gichyòbi pushed himself up and leaned toward Rutejìmo. "Do you know why I saved her for you?"

Rutejìmo shook his head. "No, Great—"

"Do you know what warriors do?"

"Of course, they defend their clan."

Gichyòbi nodded. "It's more than that, but close enough. When I know there is a Wamifūko in trouble, there is something," he thumped his chest, "inside me that rises up and commands me to do something. It's a compulsion so strong that I would sooner rip off my own balls than disobey."

"But," Mapábyo whispered, "why did Desòchu—?"

"Kick Jìmo out?" Kidóri picked her book of paintings off the floor from beneath the table. "Because it takes a lot to overcome the compulsion of the clan spirit, but it can be done in anger, rage, and..." She looked at Gichyòbi, "love."

Gichyòbi smiled back and pulled her into a hug. They started to kiss, then Kidóri cleared her throat and gestured to Mapábyo and Rutejìmo. With a faint color in his own cheeks, Gichyòbi turned his attention back and Mapábyo giggled.

"So," he said, "what do you think I'd feel if I saw you in danger, Mapábyo?"

Mapábyo shrugged.

Gichyòbi nodded. "Exactly. I don't need to save you. I will because you are Shimusògo and useful to our city. You are also a pretty girl—"

Kidóri glared at her husband.

"—and it is in the city's interest to save those who need it, but it is a choice I made, not a compulsion that commands me."

Mapábyo looked down. "Oh."

Glaring, Kidóri thumped her husband with her fist. "He's also not one of Chobìre's shits."

Rutejìmo smirked at the insult. Chobìre was the spirit of the moon and night. He was also the enemy of everything the day clans stood for.

"Oh yeah, that too." Gichyòbi rolled his eyes. "But I said that already."

"Really?" said Kidóri, "when?"

"Yeah, I said it's in the city's—"

"You would do it because it is the right thing." Kidóri thumped her husband.

"Yes, dear."

Rutejìmo grinned.

Mapábyo straightened. "What about Rutejìmo?"

Gichyòbi looked at Rutejìmo. His hand rested on his wife's hip and he stared for a long moment. "I'm strongly suggested to save him."

Rutejìmo felt a shiver of something coursing along his skin. "A suggestion?"

"It isn't a compulsion, it isn't Wamifūko, but something else. I respond as if you are clan, but I know you aren't. I've seen other warriors do the same. You," he pointed to Rutejìmo, "will never be a warrior, but there is more than one clan looking out for you. Maybe every clan that walks the sands?"

"Plenty of warriors have tried to kill me, Chyòbi."

Gichyòbi pointed a finger at him. "Don't test me, boy."

Kidóri pulled Gichyòbi's hand down. "Have you ever noticed that whenever you flee for the city, there is usually half a dozen clans involved in the fight? The last time you were running from those archers, there were at least a dozen warriors on both sides killing each other. Does that seem a bit unusual for a single courier carrying a treaty?"

The world spun around Rutejìmo. He stared at Gichyòbi in shock, unsure of what to say.

"What does that mean?" asked Mapábyo.

Both Gichyòbi and Kidóri looked at each other.

"We aren't exactly sure...," Kidóri said. She looked down. "But..."

They were both lying. Rutejìmo knew it, but he could also tell they were worried about him. He slumped back in the cushions.

Mapábyo shook her head. "No, you have to know. I can tell —"

"Mapábyo," Rutejìmo interrupted.

"Jìmo! If they know then—"

Rutejìmo remembered something Pidòhu once told him. "Then it will make it harder for me to find my place."

The older couple looked at him with surprise.

Rutejìmo blushed. "Pidòhu once said that knowing your path makes it more difficult to accept. That is why the rites of passage are a surprise, and they keep the young ones in the dark. It makes it easier to find a path when you aren't looking."

Kidóri smiled and gave a barely perceptible nod.

The world still spun around him. Rutejìmo let out his breath, wincing at the gasp. "I guess, if this is what I'm supposed to do, then I'll accept what will happen. Things seem to happen for a reason. Without Desòchu… I would have never figured out that I loved Mapábyo as much as she loved me."

When he looked at her, he froze. She was staring at him with her mouth open and eyes shimmering with tears. He gave a hesitant smile. "I really do, you know; with all my heart, Pábyo."

He heard Gichyòbi and Kidóri stand up. He knew, somehow, that he had to be gone when either woke in the morning. But until then, they had given silent consent for the two lovers to remain in the living room.

And Rutejìmo intended to prove to Mapábyo that he loved her.

—————— Chapter 27 ——————

Two Months Later

The underbelly of society is far larger and more organized than anyone could imagine.

—Milifor Krum, *Hidden Dangers of Kormar*

Rutejìmo ran along the outer circuit of Wamifuko City, following hidden paths that circled the city and kept him away from those who still walked with their heads held high. One more delivery and he would be done for the day.

Since he started, people called his delivery route The Dépa Trail. There were three couriers who ran along the trail with magic, and two of them followed dépa spirits. The only difference came from the source of their power: Rutejìmo followed a spirit of the day, and the other gained power when the moon rose above the horizon.

They also worked for the same woman, a dour-faced hag who managed to know everyone in the dark parts of society. A banyosiōu just like him, she had been abandoned by the Wamifūko when she used her powers to carve out a little dominion of her own. Now, she was unseen like the others and a surprising ally.

Rutejìmo wasn't living richly, but he had a comfortable spot to sleep in her house and enough money to buy little presents for Mapábyo. The rest of his money went into saving for the time between Mapábyo's mail routes.

With a smile, he jumped across a chasm and landed on the far side. His bare feet dug into the ridges of the rock, and he took a sharp turn to head down from the hills and into the plains where the various clans camped when they didn't want to enter the city. It was along the eastern side of the city, so the clans present would be ones who gained power from Tachìra. The moon clans always entered from the north or south.

Down along the sun-baked plains, he raced between two herds of sheep. The clan colors, white and red on one side and blue on the other, were as sharply contrasting as the two clans screaming at each other. Knives and swords flashed in the air with their threats.

The noise quieted for only a moment when he ran past, until they realized he wore gray and white—the colors of the banyosiōu.

His destination came up on the right, a large tent flanked by two armed guards. The clan warriors watched him with narrowed eyes when he came to a halt just outside the rope that identified their temporary territories. He turned and looked over at the rest of the warring clans, his skin crawling with the sight of so many brandished blades.

Turning back to the tents, he bowed, but said nothing.

Rutejìmo didn't speak much anymore. The lessons he learned in the desert still held true in the city. He was unseen even when he stood in the sun. Those who still had a clan would look away from him, but it didn't stop them from using his services. It just took him a while to learn the cues of being unseen but useful.

A herder swore at a small flock of sheep and guided them past Rutejìmo. His eyes never drifted toward Rutejìmo and Ru-

tejìmo did the same. Not even his sheep seemed to look at Rutejìmo.

Something thudded between his feet. Glancing down, he
saw a small purse. He toed it and guessed it was full from the
heavy weight. Without looking up, he pulled out a thin tube
from his shirt and held it at his side.

A herd of sheep came walking by, their bodies bumping a-
gainst him.

He counted to three and let it go, dropping it into the animals that crowded him. He didn't feel it hit the ground.

It took a moment for the herd to pass him. As soon as he
could, he picked up the coin purse and shoved it into his pocket.

Rutejìmo didn't know what was in the tube, and he didn't
care. He stepped back twice and turned around. The two clans
were still screaming at each other, seconds away from a fight,
but no one paid any attention to him. He was invisible, a ghost
among the others.

He lifted his head up to the sun and smiled. The heat baked
down on his face. It felt good, not only from the rush of power
still coursing through his veins, but because noon meant that
Mapábyo would be meeting him at Higoryo Inn in less than an
hour.

With a grin, he sprinted away from the fight and between
the two warring factions. The dust he kicked up blew across
both groups. In a few short hours, they could be dead, still
fighting, or licking their wounds, but he wouldn't care because
he would be in Mapábyo's arms.

Rutejìmo ran in record time, circling the city in less than
thirty minutes. He passed a number of couriers going the opposite direction. Most of them didn't use magic to travel, but
there was the occasional rush of a clan, or former clan, member racing by on foot or mount. In the moments when the
moon rose above the horizon it was more crowded, but the cur-

rent steady traffic gave Rutejìmo comfort. He had found his place in the city.

By the time he reached the western gates, he was almost jumping along the road. He slowed down smoothly and watched Shimusògo disappear between one step and another. Continuing forward, he reduced his speed until he reached his destination, a trail leading up to some rocks. He jogged up a small path that led to a flat plateau that gave him a clear view of the incoming traffic and, he hoped, the familiar sight of a plume of sand rolling with golden feathers.

He reached the top of the ridge and slowed down to a crawl. There was already someone sitting at the top. It was a clan warrior in bright yellow and green holding a spear. The warrior glanced at him but as soon as his green eyes focused on Rutejìmo, they slid away.

Rutejìmo stepped to the edge, to the side, and then sat down.

Neither spoke across the two worlds that divided them, but Rutejìmo's muscles grew tense in anticipation of an attack. He would have moved, but the ridge was the best place to see Mapábyo approach.

The warrior did the same. Rutejìmo had never noticed it when he was just a courier, but the subtle tightening of the arms and the way the warrior shifted his weapon in reach told him enough.

Heart pounded faster, Rutejìmo focused on the roads leading into the city. He wasn't sure if it was the warrior next to him or the hope of seeing Mapábyo coming home. She had finished two mail runs before leaving for the third. Each time, she remained in the inn instead of running back to the home valley and her parents.

He smiled and rested his hands on his thighs. A year of being without a clan didn't seem so devastating when he was in her arms, just as two weeks felt like forever when she left for her delivery route. Sooner or later, she would have to go back, but for the next week, she was his.

The horizon in the distance began to waver. A blur formed along the road leading to the cliffs, and his heart beat faster. Panting, he strained to watch it expand into a cloud of dust tipped by a dark figure racing toward the city.

Even though he wanted to, Rutejìmo waited until he saw the boiling cloud of translucent feathers before he jumped to his feet. Jogging a short distance away from the warrior, he threw himself into a run, blasted his way across the trail, down to the road, and then accelerated to his limit.

Minutes later, they were close enough to see each other smile. Mapábyo yelled wordlessly, jumping and holding out her hand. She didn't slow down.

Rutejìmo caught her hand, the world slowing down with a rush. When he gripped her sweat-slicked fingers, nothing else mattered.

They began to spin around. The pulse of the world accelerated with them. A liquid sensation poured out of his body and his speed blended with hers. He slowed her down while she pulled him faster. It was the final power Shimusògo gave both of them, the ability to share the momentum of their run. The warriors used it to make hairpin turns or, rarely, launch themselves a hundred feet straight up. For a few precious seconds, Rutejìmo's heart and feet ran faster than he could ever run alone.

The world accelerated, and so did they. Spinning rapidly like a top, they kicked off each other and shot out in opposite directions.

Rutejìmo, moving faster than he could on his own, rocketed across the sands before slowly circling to come back at her. A large plume of sand and rocks followed him, sucked in by the wake of his passing.

They came to each other again. This time, they caught each other with both hands and leaned forward to kiss. The transference of their speed sparked along their lips and then they were rocketing apart.

The two ran together for almost an hour in a meandering line across the sands and over the crowded roads. Their two trails met in kisses and clouds of dust. Rutejìmo ignored the curses they left behind. His entire world had collapsed into a single woman.

It scared him how much he looked forward to her return, but it also felt right. Mapábyo, though eight years his junior, was a good listener, and he enjoyed listening when she needed to talk. She was wonderful, not just slipping between the blankets but also simply running next to her.

They came together to kiss again.

Mapábyo grabbed his hand. She didn't spin him, but simply directed him back down the road toward the city.

They rushed along the side of the road, past the merchants coming up to the lines and the masses of herds slowly making their way across the desert. As they approached the gate, they slowed.

Rutejìmo stopped to the side of her. He watched her slip into line and her eyes slid away from him. The moment she had to pretend not to see him was the worst, the moment when he wondered if she would ever come back to him. He sighed and paced next to her, neither part of the line or blocking it.

It took them almost ten minutes to get to the gate. To his surprise, he recognized the horse-helmed warrior that stood at the entrance.

"Good afternoon, Great Shimusogo Mapábyo," boomed Gichyòbi, "you are in good spirits."

Mapábyo smiled and bowed low.

They shared the greetings, and Gichyòbi reminded her of the rules. The entire time, his eyes never glanced toward Rutejìmo though Rutejìmo knew the warrior could place him within an inch, if it came down to a fight.

When Gichyòbi finished his speech, he cocked his head. "May I ask where you plan on spending the night, Great Shimusogo Mapábyo?"

"Higoryo Inn, Great Wamifuko Gichyòbi, as last time."

"And the time before, if I recall."

She blushed and nodded. Rutejìmo's heart skipped a beat at the smile on her lips. He wanted to reach over and kiss her. It took all his willpower to remain standing to the side, unseen but not forgotten.

"Yes, Great Wamifuko Gichyòbi. May this humble courier treat you and your family to a meal?" Every time Mapábyo returned to the city, she shared a private meal with Gichyòbi and his family. Rutejìmo listened from the side, but he wasn't allowed to join in. He earned his right to eat by cleaning after the others left the room.

Gichyòbi cleared his throat. "Maybe not tonight."

"Tomorrow?" Mapábyo smiled at him, her teeth visible between the lips Rutejìmo wanted for himself.

The armored warrior held up his hands. "We'll see. Things are about to get complicated. Do you mind if I join you? I have some business at the inn."

Mapábyo tensed but then nodded. "Of course, Great Wamifuko Gichyòbi." She bowed and took a few steps into the city before waiting for the warrior to join them.

Rutejìmo followed after the two. He kept his head bowed but watched the streets around them. It surprised him, even after two months, how pervasive the dead were: beggars sitting on the corners, men and women picking up garbage, and even someone digging a dead animal out of a gutter. They were unseen by Mapábyo and Gichyòbi, but Rutejìmo saw them with a sinking heart.

As he walked, he loosened the coin purse he just earned and pulled out a few pyābi. He dropped them into open hands while he walked. The beggars mutely bowed their head in thanks. When he first came to the city, he had to beg for a few days before he found employment and a few kind banyosiōu had dropped coins in his hands and gave him a chance to survive.

The Higoryo Inn was a large stone building just off the fountain square. One of the earliest inns in the rebuilt city, it commanded a steady share of the business of the traveling clans. Rutejìmo liked it because they let him buy a room, through an intermediary, at the end of a long hallway where they wouldn't be disturbed.

He had already been to the room and dropped off his pack. Though he slept in a cramped apartment while Mapábyo was gone, he paid for more comfortable quarters for privacy and her comfort when she was there. It took most of the money he saved up, but money had no meaning without her.

Rutejìmo was interested in something else at the moment, but it was something that required a soft bed to properly show his appreciation for her returning. In many ways, he learned more than he realized from Mikáryo's lessons.

When Mapábyo and Gichyòbi reached the front entrance, Rutejìmo stepped to the side and started around to the back. He would enter from the kitchen and meet her in the room. But as he came around the corner, he skidded to a halt when he saw two Wamifuko guards in the gap between buildings. The heavily armored figures had their back to him, but their wide shoulders blocked the alley completely.

Rutejìmo worried his lip and turned away, only to notice a pair of guards standing a rod away and partially blocking the road. A prickle of fear ran down his spine. Rutejìmo glanced around, spotting more guards marching across the road before standing in the middle.

In a matter of seconds, they had cut off his escape routes. He would have attracted attention to himself if he tried to leave.

He looked around for some way to avoid touching anyone, but he was trapped. His stomach clenched and a sour taste tickled the back of his throat. Clenching his lip, he rested his hand on his tazágu and slipped into the inn after Mapábyo.

Only to run into Mapábyo's back. He recoiled and slipped to the side, backing along the wall. He tried to orient himself. When he caught sight of red and orange, he froze. His eyes widened with fear and his heart slammed against his ribs.

The Shimusògo were there. He looked into the faces of Chimípu and Desòchu. Both warriors stood on either side of Rutejìmo's grandmother and head of the clan, Tejíko. Behind the three, Hyonèku and Kiríshi. There wasn't a single smile in the room and Rutejìmo felt the air pressing down on him, squeezing out his lungs. He looked desperately around until he settled on his grandmother's face.

The only relief, though minor, was that no one looked at him. They all knew he was in the room, but not a single eye even flickered toward him. The feeling of isolation grew, and he choked at the sensation of being unseen.

"Do you know why we're here, girl?" growled Tejíko. She sat on a padded chair with a glass in her right hand. Her long hair, as white as a cloud, hung over her shoulder and danced against the floor. The heavy ring she wore swung lightly against her thigh, the twisting of the ring betraying Tejíko's anger.

Mapábyo trembled as she stared at the people in front of her. She gulped loudly and clenched her hands into fists before she answered. "B-Because I haven't come home in a while."

Tejíko set down her glass. "Were you planning on ever coming home?"

"Yes! Um, yes, Great Shimusogo Tejíko."

"When?"

The simple question hung in the air. Rutejìmo closed his eyes and fought the urge to speak up. He didn't know what would happen, but he was already dead to the people in front of him. It didn't matter if he had grown up with them, or was related to two of them, he was unseen.

Mapábyo took a deep breath and her pack slid to the ground. "Soon."

A tic jumped in Desòchu's neck.

"The only answer," said Tejíko, "you will give is tomorrow morning."

Mapábyo's head started to turn toward Rutejìmo, but Tejíko snapped out.

"Girl!"

Mapábyo and Rutejìmo jumped. Mapábyo bowed deeply, her body shaking with her fear. "I'll leave tomorrow morning, Great Shimusogo Tejíko."

Tejíko nodded.

Mapábyo's shoulders slumped limply. A shake trembled through her and Rutejìmo saw the glitter of tears. He wanted to hold her, to touch her, but his feet remained rooted in place by the presence of his clan and the fear of losing his love.

Groaning, Tejíko levered herself out of the chair and stood up. Her bare feet were gray and wrinkled, but covered in the same dust and sand as the rest of the runners. Unsteadily, she stepped over to Mapábyo and stood in front of her.

Rutejìmo could see the intense green of his grandmother's eyes. She was feared by everyone in the clan for her firm hand, and also her cruel punishment. While he was growing up, he was frequently the target of her beatings. He had no doubt she would do it again, if she was allowed to see him.

"Girl," Tejíko said, "Rutejìmo is dead."

Rutejìmo jerked at the simple words. He felt like collapsing to the ground.

Mapábyo shook her head. "No, Great—"

"Girl!" interrupted the older woman. "If you don't understand that, you will follow his path."

The muscles in Mapábyo's neck tightened.

Tejíko slapped her. The crack shot through the room.

As Mapábyo ground her fists into her side, Tejíko leaned forward. "No, I mean for the rest of your life. You," she jammed her finger into Mapábyo's chest, "will be dead to this clan, and there is nothing you, your papa, mama, or anyone else, living or dead, will be able to do about it. Do you understand?"

From behind Tejíko, both Hyonèku and Kiríshi paled. Tears glittered in Kiríshi's eyes.

Rutejìmo struggled with his thoughts. He could picture throwing himself to defend Mapábyo, but Desòchu and Chimípu would stop him before he had a chance. Even the thin veneer of being dead wouldn't stop the two warriors from killing him. He forced himself to concentrate on making fists and suffered through his helplessness.

"Simultaneously," Tejíko said suddenly as she lowered her hand and took Mapábyo's hands in her own, "I also know that if I follow through, I'll lose not only you but my... something else important to me."

Surprised, Rutejìmo stared at his grandmother. The change in her words sounded almost deliberate, but shielded like someone dealing with the unseen.

"Great Shimusogo Tejíko?" Mapábyo looked up, her brow furrowed in confusion.

"Yes, my dear?"

"I-I," Mapábyo sobbed as she struggled with her words, "love him."

Hyonèku closed his eyes tightly and reached out for Kiríshi's hand.

Kiríshi's lower lip quivered as the tears welled up in her eyes.

Tejíko reached up and used her thumb to wipe at Mapábyo's tears. "I know, and it is healthy to grieve."

"But he isn't—!" Mapábyo stopped herself, the word hanging in the air.

With another sob, she bowed her head. "Yes, Great Shimusogo Tejíko."

Rutejìmo realized he was struggling with his own emotions. He was a stranger to his own clan, terribly alone in the crowded room. He glanced to the others. Chimípu and Desòchu both were standing rock-still, but Rutejìmo could see Chimípu's eyes glistening with her own emotions. His brother, on the other hand, frowned as he stood there with one hand on his knife.

Tejíko pulled Mapábyo closer, and the younger woman fell into her arms, sobbing.

"I'm sorry, I just love him! I don't want to ever lose him!"

Rutejìmo listened as Tejíko comforted his love, saying soft words that he couldn't hear.

Minutes passed as Mapábyo sobbed. Rutejìmo wanted to join her, to let the tears fall, but he couldn't. He couldn't make a noise; it wasn't his place anymore. He turned away to leave, but Gichyòbi had blocked the exit to the room. The powerful warrior stared forward, pointedly not looking at Rutejìmo.

With a sigh, Rutejìmo stepped away and leaned in the shadows, watching as his thoughts and stomach turned sour. If Mapábyo returned home, he would remain alone. Despair loomed over him as he tried to imagine life without her presence, even once every few weeks. He didn't know if he could do it.

He knew he would. Gichyòbi's words came back. Rutejìmo didn't give up.

Tejíko kissed Mapábyo's head. "There, there. Things will be better when you get home."

Mapábyo sniffed and wiped her face. She nodded, but Rutejìmo could see that all the energy had fled her. She sniffed again. "Yes, Great Shimusogo Tejíko."

Tejíko smiled and slipped to the side as Hyonèku stepped up. "Why don't you take your parents to your room? We'll have dinner with Great Wamifuko Gichyòbi and his family. They no doubt want to hear about your journey."

Mapábyo nodded, but briefly shot a glare at Gichyòbi who just snorted. "Yes, Great Shimusogo Tejíko."

Rutejìmo's heart broke as he watched Mapábyo shuffle toward the back rooms, her head hanging low and her feet scraping on the ground. She leaned into her father and he saw tears sparkling in her eyes.

"Oh, Pábyo?" Tejíko said suddenly, her voice almost cheerful.

Mapábyo jerked and turned. "Yes, Great Shimusogo Tejíko."

The rest of the room tensed also. Rutejìmo noticed his brother's lip pulled back in a snarl just as Chimípu began to smile.

"Take Rutejìmo's cave as your own. If there is some solace in his death, you'll find it there."

Mapábyo stared at Tejíko with a confused look.

Rutejìmo frowned himself, trying to understand the sudden shift in tone and subject.

"I heard that the best place to grieve for your shikāfu is in their former homes. Legend says if you reach out, you can almost touch them." Tejíko smiled and held up her hands helplessly. "I'd always want to think my two husbands, may Shimusògo run with them forever, were haunting my cave," her voice grew tense again, "instead of running around some sand-damn city where we couldn't protect him even if we wanted to."

It took a long moment for Rutejìmo to realize what she was saying. He inhaled sharply and stood up straight, a smile starting to stretch across his face.

Mapábyo, on the other hand, looked confused as she turned to her mother and father and back to Tejíko. Then, like a flower unfolding, realization blossomed, and she let out another sob, this time a happy one.

"Of course," Tejíko said in a hard voice, "if the dead feel the need to speak up or be seen, I'll make sure their bones bleach in the sands. So, if you happen to hear your shikāfu, make sure you are somewhere quiet and private or we'll think you're destined for death yourself, do you understand?"

Mapábyo let out a cry and flung herself over to Tejíko, holding her tightly. "Thank you! Thank you, Great Shimusogo Tejíko!"

Gichyòbi grunted and left the inn, a grin on his face.

Rutejìmo smiled and sank to the ground. He clapped his hands over his mouth to muffle his own sobs of joy. He was going home.

Chapter 28

Second Thoughts

*Closeness makes a punishment worse. It is one thing for a stranger to cut
you down, another for your own brother.*

—Tomas Saldar, *Dalak and the Giants*

Rutejìmo trudged up to the cliffs that marked the valley entrance. A hum of insects greeted him. As he walked, he scratched his palm and worked at the countless splinters embedded in his skin. Other abrasions called for his attention, but he forced himself to focus on the splinters.

Two days of hauling the remains of the eating area had taken their toll. It would have been easier if the pieces of scrap had been large, but when the clan's oven collapsed from age, it rolled over one of the valley's mechanical dogs. The alchemical device that powered it exploded. Thankfully, the injuries from the explosion were minor, but the devastation took days to clean. It would have taken only a few hours if anyone else had helped, but no one offered to relieve him of days of backbreaking work.

He turned and looked back over the sands. Opōgyo, the last of the mechanical dogs of the valley, followed after him. Made of iron and almost as old as Rutejìmo, it moved with slow, shuddering steps. When the right foot landed, the knee joint spewed out a cloud of steam. Tiny wisps rose around the plate on its back, framing the square opening that led to the sensitive alchemical core that powered it.

Opōgyo wasn't intelligent or fast. It went in whatever direction someone turned its head, followed obvious trails, and then stopped when anything stood in front of it. Twenty-five years of abuse had left it scarred and dented, but still useful.

He smiled for the briefest of moments, remembering when Mapábyo was a little girl and bouncing on top of it, trying to get it to move faster.

The smile faded quickly, and Rutejìmo trudged after the mechanical dog. He had been back at the valley for just under a month. Even though there were only eight months in a year, it felt like an eternity. Knowing there were five months left until he was no longer dead stretched out each day until he thought he would snap.

When he first arrived, he hoped life would settle into the comfortable flow he had in Wamifuko City. Instead, he wasn't given a chance to rest or relax. He woke up to tasks waiting for him and went to bed exhausted. He spent his days cleaning, repairing, and hauling. Chores he hated as a teenager were heaped on him. What he thought was an annoyance became a burden when he worked from sunrise to sunset and then well into the night. His directions came from silent cues: a shovel against the door, tools by the gate, or the occasional picture pinned to the blanket covering the cave entrance.

He couldn't speak or touch people, not without risking anger from Desòchu or Tejíko. Every unwitting grunt brought a glare from someone. Every labored breath forced the people he grew up with to turn their backs. The only time he dared whisper was in the bedroom of Mapábyo's cave, until someone made note of strange sounds coming from her cave a few days later.

It was one thing to be ignored by strangers in Wamifuko City, but to be afraid of his own clan tore at his heart. Rutejìmo turned and stared out across the dark desert. He had hoped returning home would be easier, but it wasn't. He was just alone, more so since he intimately knew the people ignoring him.

He considered returning to the city, not the first time he contemplated it in the last few days. While it would mean turning his back on his clan forever, it wouldn't hurt as much as seeing family look away whenever he came near.

Opōgyo lumbered past and the ground shook. A burst of steam stung Rutejìmo's leg.

He stepped aside to avoid being burned further.

Something dropped from the mechanical's chest and rolled across the way to bounce off the far wall.

Shaking his head, he pushed himself off the road and padded across the way to pick up the gear that Opōgyo dropped. He took one last look at the desert and then headed back in to guide Opōgyo up to Pidòhu's forge where the dog could recharge for the morning.

As soon as Opōgyo thumped against Pidòhu's door, Rutejìmo turned his back and jogged away. Even though his friend had bonded with another clan spirit, Rutejìmo couldn't ask for shelter or even acknowledgment from him.

He ran along the back end of the valley, though it was the last direction he wanted to go. The clan shrine stood along the further point from the entrance. Light glowed from the windows and doorway. He could hear chanting from all the adults who had gathered inside. He could hear them singing a dirge for those who died that year.

Bitterly, he wondered if they would include him among the others who died. He ran faster along a dark trail, using his memory to tell him where it dipped and rose and turned. It was a familiar route now, after six weeks, and he couldn't wait to return home to wait for Mapábyo.

He came up to the highest point in the valley just in time to see the moon clear the horizon. The bright orb appeared to loom over him, and he came to a stumbling stop.

Somewhere out in the desert, Mikáryo would be letting out a soft coo of pleasure with her powers awaking. He had seen it only a few times, but it still brought a smile to his lips when he thought of her. He remembered how she rejected him and his smile faded. He shook his head. Mikáryo had the right idea, at least. Stay in the desert and far away from all of the clans. He longed to be where she was, out where being a banyosiōu didn't matter.

He turned away from the moon and back to the edge of the valley. Peering down, he regarded the small shrine below him. Inside, Mapábyo would be singing with the others, the only one not pretending that Rutejìmo wasn't haunting the place.

He snorted. It would have been better if he had fled to the desert and let his bones bleach in the sun. Even his promise to Mapábyo felt foolish after struggling for so long to prove himself.

He stopped in mid-step. He couldn't stay in the valley any longer. It wasn't home for him, and he felt more separated from the people living around him than ever before. He couldn't take many more months of the silence, turned backs, and constant chores. He needed to speak again, to find even that small happiness he had when he ran jobs outside of Wamifuko City.

Leaving would hurt Mapábyo. She was his only reason for remaining in the valley. He shook his head. If he asked her, he knew she would either try to convince him to stay or go with him. He couldn't allow either. In the back of his mind, he started to plan: where to get supplies, the hidden caches that he had stumbled upon over the years, and even where to find the water skins to survive the trip back to Wamifuko City.

Down below, a shadow crept out of the darkness. Rutejìmo watched it for a moment, lost in his fantasy, but then his attention focused on it. One of the teenage girls was crawling up the back of the shrine. He chuckled dryly.

Years ago, he had been in the same place. The vent that let smoke escape was also the perfect place to listen to the conversations and debates that went on among the clan. He dug into his pocket and pulled out his stones, the way of measuring the weight of his decisions in the clan. The ten stones were useless now, and he could not help but remind himself there would be eleven, if he hadn't ruined everything.

With a sigh, he opened his fingers and let the stones slip through. They bounced off his thigh before disappearing into the darkness below him. He listened to the cracking noise and the fading of his worth. Without his stones, he could no longer vote, not that he could as one of the walking dead.

Rutejìmo let out a long shuddering breath and stood up. If he was going to run, he needed to run while the moon hung in the sky. He wouldn't be able to summon Shimusògo, but at least he could be a few miles away before anyone woke.

He jogged along the trail that ran along the ridge of the valley. To one side, the sheer cliff stretched a number of chains to the rocks below. Decades ago, the clan had paid for the cliffs to be cut smooth to protect the valley from invasion. If he fell, there would be nothing he could do but hit the ground.

As the trail led away from the ridge, he followed it. He came up on a switchback and saw a second boy crawling on top of the shrine. The two children nodded to each other and peered down into the vent. They stared at the forbidden world of adulthood with their asses in the air.

Rutejìmo halted next to them. His childhood centered around the shrine's vent. He had tried to steal his great-grandfather's ashes to prove he was worthy of being a warrior. Hyonèku caught him and sent him back to Tejíko to be beaten. Later, he had sat next to the vent while he listened to the elders vote to send him on his rite of passage.

They were voting for the teenage girl now, to send her on a rite of passage. Like everything else, it would no doubt involve taking her deep into the desert and abandoning her. It was the Shimusogo Way.

He had to do something. Starting up again, he jogged along the trail and took the fork that would lead him to the shrine. Soon, he was creeping along the back of the building to the barrel that would let him climb to the top.

Rutejìmo didn't know what he would do, but something drew him. He twisted the barrel slightly to avoid any movement from alerting the others. He climbed up the side and onto the roof; he had done that many times since he became an adult of the clan.

When he finally got to the top and stood behind the two teenagers, he realized he didn't know what he wanted either. He could ruin it for them, by pushing one in or startling them, but it wouldn't stop anything. It was the way of the clan, both the sneaking and spying, but also growing.

Holding his breath, he inched forward until he knelt between the two teenagers. Neither noticed him as they stared intently down into the vent.

The builders of the shrine placed the vent right above the stone statue of Shimusògo. Along the back wall stood hundreds of vases with the ashes of the dead. For those who never returned home, the vases had mementos to cherish their spirits.

Tejíko sat before Shimusògo with two bowls in front of her. The red bowl on the right meant disagreement, the black one on the left indicated agreement. When decisions were made, everyone would throw their stones into the appropriate bowl. Tejíko had a large pile of stones in front of her; she was the oldest in the clan and its leader.

She was right in the middle of speaking when he settled into place. "... and we have an agreement. The girl goes tomorrow."

The teenage girl on Rutejìmo's right let out a happy gasp. He saw her turn toward him with a smile, but it wasn't Rutejìmo she expected to see. She inhaled sharply and froze.

It took all of Rutejìmo's willpower to not smile.

On the other side, the boy turned himself and spotted Rutejìmo. He let out a loud whimper and crawled away sharply, his feet skittering on the stone tiles. One cracked loudly underneath his weight, and he let out a cry.

Rutejìmo started to reach for him, but the teenage girl beat him to it. She jumped over him and slid down the side, grabbing the boy before he slipped off the roof. For the briefest of moments, the boy's legs dangled in front of the shrine entrance before he crawled back to the top.

Fear naked on their faces, both children rushed to the far side and climbed down.

Rutejìmo smiled and waited until he heard them running away. Then, he sat down and rolled on his back so he wouldn't look down the vent hole. The familiar smells of the shrine, incense and smoke, rose around him, and he inhaled the memories. It was home, the shrine and the valley. A place of tears and torture. He already missed it.

"And we have one more decision for the night," announced Tejíko, her voice cracking with age and exhaustion. "The Wamifūko have asked us to dedicate a new runner for negotiations between the Monafùma and Kidorīsi. This is a trade agreement between the cliffs and valley, but as we know, the Kidorīsi are..."

"... difficult," muttered Hyonèku.

"Difficult?" Gemènyo said, "You mean a constant thorn in our asses? They can't make a decision to save their lives. I say —"

Kiríshi's interrupted Gemènyo. "They are very rich and they know they are difficult. The treaty between Kidorīsi and Mafimára has supported us for a great number of years and the Monafùma have a chance of giving us another steady income. I say it's a good deal."

Murmurs of agreement drifted from the hole.

Rutejìmo noticed that no one mentioned his role in the treaty run. It was his job to go back and forth between the two. Even his memory was dead to them. He closed his eyes and slumped back. He wouldn't miss that.

"Who would run it?" asked Hyonèku.

"You," Tejíko said, "or Gemènyo. You are the only ones who dealt with the Kidorīsi before, and they like working with known people."

"Great Shimusogo Tejíko?" Mapábyo spoke up. "I've worked with the Monafùma, and I know the area and the people."

Rutejìmo clenched his eyes tight. She was talking about leaving him.

"Mapábyo, this is a very long job. It's very hard and it takes willpower to stand up to their constant indecision and not lose your temper. You will spend many months on the road, with no time to come home."

"But I'm the best choice, aren't I? I don't mind the resonance of the cities, I have allies among the Wamifūko and Monafùma. Not to mention the clans along the route like me. If anyone should do this route, it would be me."

Silence filled the shrine.

Tejíko broke it with a sad sigh. "You would be our only choice, but realize, Mapábyo, you'll be alone. There are places that your... memories can't go, and this is one of them. There can only be Shimusògo present at the treaties. You'll have Desòchu to introduce you, but it will only be you two. Only," she repeated, "you two."

Mapábyo sighed. "N-No," Rutejìmo's heart broke when he heard the tears, "matter who... what I cling to, I serve the clan."

No one said anything for a long moment. Then, Tejíko grunted. "A vote?"

Everyone threw their stones into the bowls, the clay ringing out from the impacts. He didn't dare look inside, and his heart thumped with the anticipation.

Tejíko grunted. "We send Great Shimusogo Mapábyo in two days' time."

Two days and she would be gone. Rutejìmo pushed himself up into a sitting position and then crawled to his feet. In three, he would leave for Wamifuko City and beyond. He would run until he found some place to hide and not ruin the lives of the family who no longer saw him.

---------- Chapter 29 ----------

His Memorial

—Nilamar Por

Rutejìmo leaned against the entrance to the bedroom and stared at the bed. It used to be his, but now it was Mapábyo's, and he just happened to sleep in it. He took a deep breath and picked up the fading scent of her perfume. The twisted sheets and blankets remained from the night before, when they shared one private goodbye.

He didn't have the courage to tell her he had to leave. Instead, he kept his plans to himself and tried not to think about the guilt tearing at him from the inside until after she left. His efforts left him sick and dizzy. He couldn't eat past the sourness in his stomach that stuck with him ever since he decided to lie to her.

Rutejìmo knew it was wrong. He should have told her, but he couldn't stop her from serving the clan. They needed her and he was willing to step away so she no longer had to make a choice.

Every time she hugged him, he expected her to call him on his behavior. Every time they kissed, he was terrified she would pull back with realization. She didn't. He guessed Mapábyo was too engrossed with her plans to notice his behavior. Or, at least he hoped that was the reason.

A wave of nausea rose up. Groaning, he pressed his face to the cool rock and panted for breath until the agony passed.

As soon as he could move again, he staggered across the room and gathered up his tazágu. The fighting spike scraped against the ground, the sound echoing off the stone walls. He buckled it into place and backed out of the room.

"I'm sorry," whispered Rutejìmo.

It was close to midnight, and no one would see him leaving. His supplies were already gathered and packed into a large bag. It was more than he normally ran with, but he only needed enough for Wamifuko City. Once there, he could return to running errands for the city and settle back into the world that already accepted him.

He tried to tell himself that Mapábyo would forget him, but he knew it was a lie. His stomach twisted violently as he considered what she would do: probably cry herself sick and come after him. She would tear the city apart in hopes of finding him.

Rutejìmo shook his head and took a deep breath. He hoisted the pack over his shoulder and padded for the entrance of the cave. To his surprise, he shook from the effort.

"Hurry up, Dòhu!" Chimípu's voice drifted from the opposite side of the blanket covering the entrance. "I don't want to get caught."

Rutejìmo gasped and yanked his hand back from the blanket.

He heard the scuff of Chimípu's feet right before she pushed the blanket aside and stepped inside. She wore a red dress with orange trim. The flowing skirt moved with the faint breeze, except where her knife pinned the fabric at her thigh. She looked across the room. Her eyes didn't focus on him when she scanned over him.

Pidòhu stepped in past her carrying a large tray of food. The frail man had his short black hair cropped close to his skull. He wore little, a loincloth and nothing else. His brown skin was paler than anyone else in the valley because he spent most of his days in the shadow of Tateshyúso, his clan spirit.

Chimípu released the blanket, and it swung back to cover the entrance. When Rutejìmo returned to the valley, they had replaced it with a thick one with Mapábyo's name on it and moved his old one to the bed. She smiled and peered into the cave. She gestured to a candle near Rutejìmo. "Looks like Mapábyo forgot to put out the light."

"Good for me. That way you don't have to glow and show off."

She chuckled and stepped forward, waves of heat rising off her body before the flames burst around her skin. It painted the walls with golden light and the smell of hot desert wind rippled through the air.

"You didn't have to do that."

Chimípu smirked and continued into the room. "Just scaring away the ghosts."

Rutejìmo continued to back away, watching both of the intruders warily.

The pair spread out, drifting through his cave like intruders.

He squeezed down on the strap of his bag until his fingers ached. He couldn't get around Chimípu to run away.

"Like you believe in those tales," said Pidòhu. He set the tray of food on the table in the main room. Clay pots covered hot food on one end of the tray. The other held piles of sliced meat, cheese, and breads. Three bowls of soup rested in the middle. Next to them, six bottles of iced fermented milk dripped from condensation.

"I don't know, people talk of seeing Rutejìmo at night."

Pidòhu set the clay pots on a shelf near the eating area. There would be food in them, but Pidòhu made no effort to check them or even remove the lids. Instead, Pidòhu grabbed some towels and brought them to the table.

Rutejìmo watched in confusion.

Chimípu dragged one of the chairs. It scraped along the stone. As she approached, Rutejìmo saw her eyes flick down to his travel packs.

He waited for the response, clenching his bag until his hand throbbed.

To her credit, only a single muscle in her cheek jumped with her thoughts. With a sigh, she continued to drag the chair clear around the room until she was centered on the entrance of the cave. A flicker of heat rose around her while she sat down heavily. She pointedly looked at Pidòhu, and said, "I miss him, you know."

Rutejìmo froze at the quiet words.

"Jìmo?" asked Pidòhu.

"Yes. The sun doesn't seem as bright since the day he died." She sniffed and brought her knees up to her chest.

The pack slipped off Rutejìmo's shoulder. It caught on his elbow before sliding down his arm to land heavily on the ground. He stared in shock at her, not only stunned that she would ever speak about him but that they had come specifically for him.

"Yeah." Pidòhu dragged a chair around to the side. "He whimpered too much and usually made a lot of stupid mistakes..."

Rutejìmo glared at Pidòhu.

"... but, in the end, he always did the right thing. Even if he kept crying all the time."

To Rutejìmo's surprise, Pidòhu left the chair and dragged a third one around the table until the three were equidistant from each other. Reaching over, he stacked some cheese and meat on bread before sitting down in the third chair. He left the food behind in front of the empty spot.

Chimípu reached over and grabbed some meat with her fingers. "He was a good man. Though, he had that shikāfu for that horse bitch."

"Great Pabinkue Mikáryo is quite... attractive to a teenage boy. And she had a fondness for walking around in rather revealing outfits." Pidòhu coughed. "I can see the appeal."

"All those tattoos on her body?" Chimípu pulled a face. "That isn't the Shimusogo Way."

Pidòhu shrugged. "I don't know about that. I saw that Mapábyo got a new tattoo somewhere on her last job. Maybe Shimusògo's way is changing?"

Rutejìmo smiled at the memory of Mapábyo showing it to him. It was a small dépa on the curve of her breast, a hidden place when she was dressed. Then, with a start, he looked up sharply at Pidòhu.

"And how," Chimípu muttered with a full mouth, "did you see that?"

"I'm Tateshyúso, the shadows of the valley are all under her wings."

"No, you're a pervert." Chimípu waved her finger and swallowed. "A dirty pervert that likes to look at young women. She was Rutejìmo's, you know. You have no chance when she holds such a bright shikāfu for him."

"The fool didn't know how lucky he was."

Rutejìmo sighed. He didn't know what he had. Guilt slashed through his heart and he slumped against the table. Slowly, he slid down the wall and sat heavily on the ground.

"So, Dòhu," Chimípu asked, "what's the chair for?"

"A place for the dead. I figured he deserved a seat if I'm going to read in his memory."

Tears of guilt burned in Rutejìmo's eyes, he looked up.

Pidòhu made a big deal of pulling a book from the platter. It was a book of poetry, but one that Rutejìmo had not seen before. It was one of their shared interests, ever since Rutejìmo tried to save one of Pidòhu's books from Tsubàyo. In the years that followed, Pidòhu had written and Rutejìmo had listened.

Settling back in the chair, Pidòhu kicked up his feet and held up the book. "Do you mind?"

Chimípu shook her head. "That's why we're here, isn't it?"

Pidòhu held up the book in a toast. "To our little brother, Rutejìmo. May his memory live forever." He opened to the first page. "Oh wait, that's what I wrote in the dedication."

With a chuckle, he flipped the page and began to read the first poem.

As Pidòhu's voice filled the cave, Rutejìmo pushed himself up. He glanced at the entrance of his cave, but he would need to pass the flaming warrior to reach it. Slowly, his eyes slid over to the empty chair. It was obviously an invitation for him to sit, though neither looked at it or him.

Trembling with fear and nervousness, Rutejìmo circled around the room. At the chair, he looked at both of them for confirmation. Pidòhu continued to read, his attention focused on the book. Across from him, Chimípu leaned back with her eyes closed and a smile on her face.

Rutejìmo sank down in the chair. When Chimípu didn't strike him or respond, he leaned forward and grabbed a stack of meat and cheese.

Pidòhu finished the poem and sat there, staring at the page.

"That was nice," Chimípu said after a moment, "when did you write it?"

"About a year ago. I was thinking of Rutejìmo at the time, actually. He held the shikāfu for Mikáryo so tightly he didn't notice Mapábyo trying to impress him. Remember when she kept climbing the rocks whenever he was nearby?"

Chimípu laughed. "Or the times she kept trying to sneak into the shrine, but only when he was sulking on top?"

Frowning, Rutejìmo tried to remember what they had seen. He remembered catching Mapábyo more than a few times trying to sneak into the shrine, but it never occurred to him that she timed it on purpose.

Pidòhu joined in the laughter.

"Poor Jìmo, but he could never take a hint, could he?"

Not feeling anger, Rutejìmo glared at both of them. He listened to them and began to second-guess leaving Mapábyo and the valley. He knew she loved him and it tore him in half to know she would be devastated by his disappearance.

"So, where did he go wrong?"

Rutejìmo tensed at Pidòhu's question.

Chimípu leaned forward and snatched two of the bottles of milk. Sitting back down, she shook her head. "He never went wrong. He really was doing the right thing."

Pidòhu grasped a bowl of soup, pushing one of the bottles of milk toward Rutejìmo as he did. He grabbed another and rested it on the tip of his knee. "Then where did we go wrong?" Setting the bottle down, he picked up the bowl again and slurped from it.

She sighed and shook her head. "I don't know. Every night, I ask myself that same question. We should have shown we loved him, I should have stood up to Desòchu more often when the blowhard started ranting about the Shimusogo Way."

"Great Shimusogo Desòchu was doing what he thought was right."

"Yes, but Rutejìmo is my little brother now."

Pidòhu held up his bowl. "Mine too, you know. I love him with all my heart."

Chimípu nodded and held up her bottle. "To Jìmo, may he live forever."

Grabbing his bottle, Pidòhu held up his own. "To Jìmo."

They held their bottles up for a long moment before Rute-jìmo realized they were waiting for him. Fumbling, he grabbed his bottle and lifted it. He said nothing, but when the other two drank deeply, he brought his bottle to his lips.

With a tear in his eye, he realized they were suffering as much as he was. And, there was no way he could ever leave them. They all had to play their parts out for the year.

He drank in a silent toast to himself.

Chapter 30

Shifted Opinions

You change in an instant. You grow over time.

—Proverb

She was back a month later, but only for a week. In that time, Rutejìmo's despair had eroded under Chimípu's and Pidòhu's tactful companionship. But as much as he appreciated his friends' company, he missed Mapábyo more than he thought possible. He couldn't even consider leaving her anymore and struggled with the guilt of making the decision in the first place.

The night after she returned, she was invited to her parent's cave for dinner. Rutejìmo joined her, since his invitation was tactfully given. He remained silent as the dead and tried to stay out of all of their way to simply enjoy their presence.

"I see you," whispered Mapábyo, her voice too low to be heard by the others in the main room of Hyonèku's and Kiríshi's cave. Her shirt, a ruffled orange with the laces parted enough for him to see the tail of the tattoo on her breast.

Mapábyo came out of the eating area with a platter of food.

Stepping to the side, Rutejìmo pressed his back against the stone opening. A thrill coursed through his veins. He slipped further into the kitchen so she could finish bringing dessert out to the others.

Mapábyo set down the tray, and her left hand automatically went to her belly.

Rutejìmo's heart beat faster in his chest, and he smiled broadly. Mapábyo's monthly cycle was two months late, and already the signs of pregnancy were beginning to show, though only for those who knew to look. He was excited and terrified at the same time. Rutejìmo was about to be a father. The child would be born around the same time he would be allowed to rejoin the clan. Neither he nor Mapábyo knew how the news would be taken, so they decided to keep it quiet as long as possible.

Kiríshi reached over to start serving dessert. She bumped against Mapábyo's elbow.

Mapábyo jerked and pulled her hand away from her belly and grabbed a fork. She smiled sheepishly.

The central area had been cleared out for a large table. There were five chairs set out, but six plates on the table. Gemènyo and Faríhyo sat at one end; Hyonèku and his wife sat at the other. In the center was Mapábyo's spot across from an empty spot for Rutejìmo, though no one ever admitted verbally to his position.

The clan gave him a short respite by giving him no new tasks for a few days, but he continued to perform the duties that he already had. Looking around, he spotted a bucket with the remains of dinner. He picked it up and headed outside to the garbage heap.

He jogged to the entrance of the valley while enjoying the cool air. There, a small pile of refuse and inedible food gathered for the night; he would deal with it in the morning.

He stopped to set down the bucket next to the pile. A breeze kicked up around him, sending sand cascading over his feet. He kicked it off and turned back to the valley, his home.

The two banners to Shimusògo fluttered in the wind, the heavy cloth rippling in the dark. The names glowed brightly from magical thread that took almost two years to adapt to the resonance of the valley before it could be brought home. From a distance, it looked like the words were burning.

Above the sixty-foot banners was the lookout perch. At night, the netting protecting the sheer drop was invisible, but he could see the short metal rods sticking out of the cliff holding it in place.

At the edge of the lookout stood Kiramíro, the eldest of the clan warriors. Next to her was the newest, the teenage girl who Rutejìmo chased off the shrine a few months ago. They were too far away for Rutejìmo to hear, but he could see Kiramíro miming cutting someone's throat.

He shuddered at the casual violence and headed back into the valley. His bare feet echoed loudly in the quiet. He followed the flickering lights and headed up the trail leading back to Hyonèku's cave.

Desòchu slammed him against the wall, his rough hands punching Rutejìmo right below the ribs. He brought his knee up to slam it into Rutejìmo's groin.

Rutejìmo tried to scream out, but the impact against the stone drove the air out of his lungs. The pain ripping through his nerves caused lights to explode across his vision. He gripped Desòchu's wrists, but the tense muscles were too strong for him to push Desòchu away.

"I will kill you, corpse." Desòchu's alcoholic breath washed against Rutejìmo's face. His hands ground into Rutejìmo's chest, the magic rippling off his body in waves of heat and light.

Struggling to breathe, Rutejìmo shook his head.

"You are dead to me, but you continue to be an irritation." Desòchu's hands slid up to Rutejìmo's neck. "You are a poison, a rot. You are sickness and no one else sees it."

Rutejìmo tried to push him away, but couldn't stop his brother.

Desòchu gripped Rutejìmo's neck, squeezing tightly. "You were supposed to take the easy way out, the way you always do. Or sit there and sob like a worm. But you keep coming back, no matter—"

Gemènyo cleared his throat. A breeze washed over Rutejìmo, kicking up a few grains of sand to pepper his legs.

Desòchu released Rutejìmo and stepped back. His eyes slid away from Rutejìmo to focus on Gemènyo and Kiríshi. A low growl rumbled in his chest.

The two adults were standing next to each other, their clothes fluttering with wind and Kiríshi's settling into place.

"What are you doing here?" snapped Desòchu.

"Oh, just enjoying a little stroll with my wife. You know what —"

Desòchu's face purpled. "Kiríshi isn't your wife!"

Gemènyo turned to Kiríshi with mock surprise on his face. "You aren't!?"

"No, I'm not." Kiríshi rolled her eyes and smirked. Under her words, there was a hardness that Rutejìmo had never heard before.

"Want to be?"

"With your pipe?" Kiríshi made a disgusted look. "I'd rather sleep in the garbage. I still don't know how Ríhyo can stand you."

Gemènyo stepped back, his hand on his chest and a dramatic look of horror on his face. "Oh, Great Shimusogo Kiríshi, you wound me!"

"No," she said, "your wife is going to wound you if you make that offer again."

Desòchu snarled. "Stop it! Stop joking!"

Kiríshi turned on Desòchu and gave him an innocent smile. "Stop what, Great Shimusogo Desòchu?"

"Stop protecting him!"

"Gemènyo? He doesn't—" Kiríshi said tensely, the muscles in her neck tightening.

"You know who!" Desòchu's bellow echoed against the stone walls. The echoes reflected down the valley, breaking the silence.

Kiríshi stood up straight, her face turning hard for a moment. "I'm doing what's right."

Desòchu stepped up to her, his body igniting with flames. "No, you aren't. He's dead! Dead to you, dead to me, dead to everyone!"

She didn't flinch. Instead, she stepped up to him until the flames licked her skin and her hair began to curl. "That doesn't mean we forget him."

"That isn't the Shimusogo Way!"

"Yes," Kiríshi snapped, "it is."

She pulled her hands back and slammed them against Desòchu's chest. The impact shot through the air, but Desòchu didn't move. She pulled back and did it again, this time pushing him back an inch. "This is our way because we say it is."

Hyonèku, Faríhyo and Mapábyo raced up. The currents of air spiraled around everyone's feet, kicking up dust devils.

Desòchu shook his head and stepped back. "No, it isn't. He is corrupting us, even… from death!" He pointed at Mapábyo, his finger shaking. "You've seen what she's doing because of him. She wore that tooth around her neck, just like him. She's marked her body like that horse bitch. Everything he touched is corrupted!"

"Maybe," said Hyonèku, "that is just our way now?"

"How can you say that? It's your daughter!"

Hyonèku stepped forward, his bare feet crunching on the piled sand. "Yes, she," he said the word sharply, "is my daughter and the most precious thing in my world. That tooth is now her stone, as you requested. The tattoo? Well," he shrugged, "I don't like it, but it means something to her."

Kiríshi joined her husband, sliding her hand around his waist. "Tejíko didn't seem to mind it when she found out."

"It isn't the Shimusogo Way!"

"Maybe the way is changing?" asked Kiríshi. "Nothing stays the same."

Chimípu's footsteps filled in the space. She didn't run or even jog, but walked down the path.

The others stepped aside.

She came to a stop in front of Desòchu.

Desòchu glared at the other warrior and his flames flared higher. "And you are the worst of them. You and Pidòhu started all of this."

Chimípu's eyes glittered in the flames. "Started what, Great Shimusogo Desòchu?"

"He's dead."

"Yes, he is. And there isn't a day that passes that I don't think about it."

"Of course not, nothing changed for you. You treat him as if he's alive and still part of this clan. He isn't anymore."

"He's been dead to you for many years now, Desòchu. That didn't just start because of a mistake."

Desòchu's teeth ground together before he spoke. "He's a fool."

"He's our clan."

"He is weak."

"And we still love him. He may be dead, but there will always be a place here for him. He tried to be your brother for so many years but you stopped being his a long time ago."

"And you took my place, just like that?"

"Yes," Chimípu said with a smile and a cock of her head. "It may not be the smartest thing to do, but I believe in him. Ever since that day when he stood up and asked for an end to the violence. When he came back and bared his throat to me. When he told me to leave him to chase after Pidòhu, knowing that he risked his own life to remain in the dark. This," she finally moved with a single step forward, "is the man your brother became. He wasn't given our gifts, and he will never be the fastest or strongest. He isn't even the smartest or most observant. But when you pay attention, he has done something remarkable: he never gave up, and he never stopped trying. We have never struggled as much as him, but he has never, ever given up."

Desòchu's flames flickered before he frowned. He started to say something but Chimípu continued.

"Even in death, he works hard and without question. He stands up, because it is the only thing he can do. He runs forward because it is what we do. We run. We run even when we hurt and bleed. We run through the tears and agony and sorrow. Desòchu, this is the Shimusogo Way. This is what we've become. It isn't corruption or wrong, it is just the way it is. He is dead, but we won't stop loving him."

Desòchu glared at the others. "Do the rest of you feel that way?"

Kiríshi, Faríhyo, Mapábyo, and Gemènyo nodded.

Hyonèku cleared his throat. "Actually, I'm kind of pissed at him."

Rutejìmo jerked, for a brief moment he had forgotten he was there, and looked at Hyonèku.

A frown furrowed across Chimípu's brow. She turned to look at him.

Hyonèku shrugged. "I kind of wish he wasn't dead."

"Why?" snarled Desòchu.

A smile crossed Hyonèku's face. "Because I'd probably kill him for getting my daughter pregnant."

Rutejìmo blanched and a shiver of icy liquid ran down his spine. Both he and Mapábyo were afraid of her father's response to her being pregnant. Rutejìmo spent his days imagining all the horrors that Hyonèku could do when Rutejìmo couldn't call out for help.

Mapábyo blushed hotly and ducked her head. She stepped back and slid her hand away from her belly.

Kiríshi rolled her eyes and smacked Hyonèku. The blow staggered him backwards. When he stepped back, she beat him with her palm until he backpedaled out of reach.

"Well," Hyonèku said while defending himself from her, "it's true." He backed away from his wife and up toward his cave. "Sand-cursed ghost giving my girl a child. He deserves to be dead right now." He was almost flippant, but the tone didn't stop Rutejìmo's sudden struggle to breathe.

"I think enough has been said," said Tejíko. She came out of the darkness, her bare feet scuffing on the ground. She wore a ground-length sleeping gown with her bare feet barely visible underneath the white fabric. Her voice was low and cracked with age, yet brimming with power.

Everyone jumped at her words and presence. Hyonèku froze in mid-step and turned around, his cheeks red.

"Your yelling is waking up the valley. Some of us are old and like to sleep through the night."

Everyone, including Rutejìmo, bowed.

"Yes, Great Shimusogo Tejíko." Rutejìmo did not join into the chorus of responses.

The elder stood up straight. With a groan, she held her palm against her back. "Now, go back to your homes. Finish your dinner, but let the dead sleep tonight. We don't need to bring up their memories when we should be celebrating."

Desòchu turned away, taking a step toward Rutejìmo. He stared over Rutejìmo's shoulder and whispered loudly. "If you make a single noise, I will make sure your corpse bleaches in the sun."

It was a grievous offense, to acknowledge his presence. Rutejìmo looked around at the uncomfortable faces and then to his brother's furious expression. He nodded, because it was the only thing he could do.

Wind blew away from Rutejìmo, the streak of Desòchu's flames disappearing through the entrance of the valley and, no doubt, out into the sands. The others returned to their homes.

For a moment, he thought he was alone.

"Even in death, you continue to walk your own path, don't you, boy?" Tejíko stood looking up at the sky. There were tears in her eyes, and she looked far older than her years.

Then she walked back to her home, leaving Rutejìmo in darkness.

Chapter 31

An Unexpected Role

The clans of the desert not of sun and moon speak so little that most forget they exist.

—Paromachīmu

Rutejìmo sat on the edge of a burnt-down funeral pyre keeping his back to the pile of ash and stone. The dying heat rolled against his back as it quickly cooled in the last remains of night. It was early morning, and Tachìra had not risen above the horizon. He felt the anticipation of morning light in his body, a quickening of his pulse that made the heat licking his skin even more intense.

His attention was on an old woman who never spoke to him. He didn't know her name or even her clan, only that she was waiting for him when he arrived to prepare the bodies of the six merchants who died in a caravan attack. She wasn't a banyosiōu, she just dressed like one. Despite the lack of colors between them, something told Rutejìmo that she was more than dead. She felt like she still had a foot in the world of the living; it was a gut feeling rather than something he could easily identify. There was a sense of power in her, a warrior's power, more pure than any other warrior he had ever met. It al-

251

most felt like she followed Tachìra directly. There were no signs of her clan on her clothes, so Rutejìmo was left with a sense of awe.

She stripped naked in front of him. She moved efficiently with no attempt at attraction or even concern for his opinion. The only sounds she made were the soft grunts of age and the whisper of pale fabric scraping off her body. Her hair, an unruly mane of white, stuck out in all directions except for a single braid over the left side of her face.

Rutejìmo watched curiously. He knew she was about to show him something, but she wouldn't speak to him or see him. He wasn't sure how he knew, just that after so many months body language and gestures were enough to tell him when his attention was required.

The old woman finished stripping and stood up. Turning her head to the brightening horizon, she raised her hands above her head and mouthed a wordless prayer. There was no noise beyond her gasping breath and the shifting rocks underneath her feet, but he could see the words passing soundlessly over her lips. It was a prayer to Tachìra. He caught sight of the words "life" and "living" more than a few times.

A tingle ran along his skin. The words were important, and she was teaching him. He focused on her mouth, trying to memorize as much of the unfamiliar prayer as he could. It was hard, reading in silence—though he could puzzle out where it was similar to the rituals he had been taught.

Almost an hour later, she was shaking with the effort to keep her arms raised. Sweat prickled her dark skin, following the lines of wrinkles and pooling in the dust and ash that clung to her.

Tachìra breached the horizon, and Rutejìmo felt the rush of power coursing through his veins.

She responded at the same time he did. Without a word, she lowered her hands and walked toward the rising sun, her bare feet leaving shallow imprints in the gravel.

He turned to watch her walk around the shimmering ash and then head in a straight line across the desert, walking with a confidence that he could only admire. She had nothing, no water, no food. If it were him, it would have been a death sentence.

Rutejìmo stood up to call for her, but was distracted by the sound of paper flapping in the wind. Turning around, he stared at the clothes she had abandoned. Curious, he padded over to them and picked up the plain fabric. A small paper book thudded to the ground, shaken loose from one pocket.

He picked it up. The pages were rough and stained, and the edges were ripped. On the front of the book, in the lower right, was the title: "Ash."

When he stared at the plain cover, the world spun around him and it hurt to breathe. It was used and torn and burnt. Streaks of dirt and dried blood marked the edges. There were smears of ash-covered fingers on the pages from where she had opened it frequently. He held his breath and flipped it open. Inside there were dense, hand-written words that covered every inch of the page.

A faint breeze rippled across the pages and fluttered the edges.

He flipped through the pages, seeing the rites for the dead that he learned from guesswork and instinct. He found prayers for the spirits, not only Tachìra and Chobìre; and other clans, some with names he knew and others that were unknown. There were special rituals for children who died, for plague, for war. Special words for specific clans were written on the rough pages in ash, blood, and ink. Not all of the handwriting was by the same person or even from the same time. It was poetry, much like Pidòhu's, though terrifying in what it represented.

Nestled among the words and actions was something else, a record of those who had died. A history of the desert and its dead.

He paged through the book, glancing over the names of the dead. The lines were ragged and different, written at the point of death with little more than a clan, a date, and the cause.

When he reached the end, he came on two rituals. They were the last of the pages but also the oldest, faded and worn as the cover. He scanned over it, stopped halfway through to start again, this time reading in detail.

The first was familiar: it involved stripping naked and walking toward the sun. He glanced up at the old woman's silhouette slowly growing smaller in the distance. He turned back and kept reading, going through the words. By the time he reached the end, he understood its purpose: to bring the living dead back to life. A way of bringing a banyosiōu back to the living.

He smiled at the sudden tears and sank to his knees. The ritual was what he would need when he finally could return.

Through bleary eyes, he read the second. It was simple, a process for shedding the cloak of the living and willing to become one of the dead once again. It was needed for those who took care of the dead and dying, for the living could not touch death. The ritual ended with a single word, kojinōmi. He had never seen the word before, but kōji meant death and dying.

He stared at the two rituals: one to live and one to die. They were two parts of a whole for those who willingly stepped between the two worlds. A breeze ruffled the pages, casting grains of sand and rocks across the pages. He brushed them aside and continued to read. He could easily picture himself in the old woman's place and continuing the words in the book.

Tears splashed down on the page, rolling across the stained page and adding the faintest of marks. He chuckled and let the sobs come. No noise came out, he had to remain silent, but he could feel it tearing at his dry throat. With the tears came a sensation of coming home, an epiphany that he had finally found his path.

He could become a kojinōmi, a tender of the dead.

The thought and decision settled across his mind, sinking in with the rush of power not unlike when he chased Shimusògo. It filled his body from the inside, spreading out from his bones until it tingled along his skin.

Quick as it filled him, the euphoria faded. He clung to the fading rush but it slipped from his mind and left behind only a vague memory of touching some power far greater than himself. His breath came in fast, short pants.

He looked up to call out to the old woman.

She was only a dark spot on the horizon where her footsteps left a trail directly toward Tachìra. He already knew what she would do; she would live when the sun sank below the horizon. At least until she needed to die once again.

Rutejìmo reached out for her clothes, intending to put them in a safe place, when his hands scraped against only rock. Startled, he looked down. They were gone. Confused, he looked around him, not finding any sign of the white fabric the old woman had stripped off. If it wasn't for his memories, there was no sign the plain white fabric had ever existed.

He knew it could be a trick of his eye, like the others looking away from him when he approached, but it was something else. He closed his fingers through the sand and let the grains slip through the gaps. She didn't need them anymore, not where she was going.

Rutejìmo smiled and stood up. He would follow soon enough, once he could return to the living himself. He pressed the book to his chest. First, he had to learn the path.

Chapter 32

Forbidden Words

Silence is the hallmark of banyosiōu. They do not speak nor are they spoken to. To do otherwise breaks the illusion and demands an immediate response.

—Roman Tomsin, *Observations of the Desert*

It was a beautiful day in the desert, and Rutejìmo wanted to sing. Everything was finally right: the breeze that licked his skin, the wavers of heat from the sun bearing down, even Opōgyo's thudding footsteps complemented the beat in Rutejìmo's heart. He made his way back home with a smile.

Mapábyo had come home late the previous night to a celebration. Her efforts with the other clans had earned the Shimusògo a decade-long agreement at almost twice the original contract price. It was also her last run before giving birth. Her bulging belly was already hampering her ability to race across the sands though it was still two months before the child would be born.

There was only two months left before Rutejìmo could rejoin the clan.

While missing her had taken its toll on Rutejìmo's hopes, Chimípu and Pidòhu were always there just when he thought he couldn't handle it anymore: they read poetry and told stories, brought warm food when he couldn't cook, and talked about how they missed him. For his birthday, which passed in silence, they brought fermented drinks and just sat near him. None of them said anything and neither of them made note when Rutejìmo couldn't stop crying.

Tearing himself away from his memories, he spun around and gave a little dance. Life had reached a peak and everything felt right. His despair over being a banyosiōu had faded. He cleaned and hauled and did the chores no one else wanted. Even the more horrific of duties, cremating the dead, had become a task of honor and something he cherished instead of dreaded. He spent his nights reading from the *Book of Ash* and learned how to be a kojinōmi. Sadly, he also added at least three more entries into the list of the dead near the back.

In his spiritual death, he had somehow found a place. And his role wasn't just among the Shimusògo. As if the other clans somehow knew that the old woman had given him the book, requests had begun to show up for him to tend to the surrounding valleys. Even traveling groups somehow knew about his decision. He had cremated a Ryayusúki warrior only a week ago, and a couple who died at night a few weeks before that.

No one besides Mapábyo talked to him, but the requests were just as clear as a shovel by the cave entrance. Instead of tools, he would find a small token of white or gold—the colors of death—and a strip of paper with the name of the dead. The book told him how to respond, both in approaching the other clan and the rituals that needed to be performed. It was poetic but concise, a beginner's guide to tending the dead.

It took him a day to bring up becoming a kojinōmi to Mapábyo. In their whispered conversations in their bed, she agreed. He thought about telling Tejíko when he could speak again, but then realized no words were needed. He would just do it, silent as the dead. The rest would understand and help just as they had since he returned.

A rumble drew his attention.

Rutejìmo looked up curiously.

A glowing shot burst from the lookout and streaked across the sky. He turned to watch it sail toward a flock of birds, but the burning bola sank too fast, and it slammed into the ground a quarter-mile away. It was almost a year ago when he had tried firing rocks off the cliff, and he smiled at the memory.

Light flashed in the corner of his eye. Rutejìmo frowned and turned toward it, already knowing it was Desòchu running around the valley. From the distance, Rutejìmo could see nothing but flashes of light ahead of a rapidly increasing plume of dust that rippled out in waves and rose into the air. There were very few who could summon enough of Shimusògo to burn so brightly, and Chimípu was a hundred miles away escorting some couriers.

Desòchu circled around and then came toward Rutejìmo. The translucent image of Shimusògo grew with every heartbeat, and Rutejìmo felt the rolling power despite the distance.

Bracing himself, Rutejìmo took a deep breath and waited for his brother to pass. Desòchu would cover the distance in just a few seconds, and there was nowhere Rutejìmo could hide.

The air sucked him toward Desòchu, and then held still as the warrior passed in a blur. Even though there was at least a chain between them, the air reversed and slammed into Rutejìmo. Sand and rock peppered his face from the passing wind.

Rutejìmo considered throwing something at him, but Desòchu was running too fast for either man to see the other clearly. By the time he managed to get a rock in his hand, Desòchu would be on the opposite side of the valley. Despite Rutejìmo's inability to do anything, Desòchu continued to rush past him as the warrior raced around the valley.

Choosing not to respond, Rutejìmo turned and watched his brother sprint toward the far end of the valley. When he saw Gemènyo and Faríhyo only a few feet away, he turned to them.

"I see Desòchu is struggling with his inner demons," said Gemènyo while turning to watch Desòchu rocketing around the valley cliffs. "He's been running for over an hour now, hasn't he?"

It had been almost two hours, but Rutejìmo didn't say anything. He could still feel the passing wind from every lap Desòchu made.

Faríhyo murmured in agreement.

Gemènyo exhaled around his pipe, leaving a cloud of smoke. His bare feet crunched on the gravel. Both of them parted around Opōgyo and Rutejìmo, neither of them looking at the banyosiōu between them.

On the far side, Faríhyo said, "Mènyo, look."

Rutejìmo turned to where she pointed. In the distance, Hyonèku and Kiríshi were chasing each other much like Rutejìmo chased Mapábyo in Wamifuko City. The winding paths and cloud of dust looked like a storm as they came together and parted with blasts of air. With each impact, all movement stopped for the briefest moments before they rocketed apart. The explosion of sand burst into the air as a monument of their touch.

There were other puffs of dust and sand surrounding the valley; other couples spent a few hours enjoying each other's company. Even the young were out, running after Desòchu in a pack that would never catch him.

"Just like a pair of kids who just fell in love," grumbled Gemènyo. "Giving my wife ideas."

"Their daughter is happy and very pregnant. A birth is always a time of celebration, more so when the father is dead."

"I don't see how they can be that happy, Mapábyo is sitting all alone in her cave." Gemènyo inhaled on his pipe before letting smoke rush out from the corner of his mouth. The scent rolled over Rutejìmo who fought the urge to cough. "Poor girl, all alone with everyone out here running like fools. It's going to be hours before anyone returns to the valley."

Faríhyo made another agreeing noise and came back to Gemènyo. She slipped her arm around his waist. Together, they walked away. "At least we get some time alone," she said to no one.

Another rumble of a fired bola passed them.

She looked over her shoulder, "Though, I wish those boys wouldn't do that while watching Nigímo. She's only two years old and still teetering."

Following her gaze, Rutejìmo turned to see another shot rocketing from the lookout. It was a fast shot that exploded into two pieces before sailing to the ground a mile short of the birds.

Rutejìmo shook his head and smiled. Better than his own attempts to hit the birds.

"Don't worry, Ríhyo, they'll be responsible. They know better."

Faríhyo stopped to pull Gemènyo's pipe from his mouth and kissed him. "Run with me." She grinned, twisted the pipe out of his grip, and then exploded into movement.

Gemènyo chuckled and exhaled from his nose. It looked like a bull exhaling on a cold morning. "Yes, love." And then he disappeared with a rush of sand and translucent feathers.

Rutejìmo jogged to catch up to Opōgyo who continued to move with a steady, shuddering walk. He noticed sand in one of the inlet vents and brushed it out, stinging his fingers against the heated metal. It was the last mechanical dog, and Rutejìmo had two months left before he could live again; he didn't relish spending those two months hauling heavy weights on his own.

Another shot burst from the lookout, this one high and flat. It left ripples along the sky as it sailed above Rutejìmo. Rutejìmo turned to watch it and was impressed when it almost hit one of the birds.

Gemènyo's and Faríhyo's suggestion was a good one. A little time with Mapábyo would brighten his day. He rarely got a chance to enjoy her with the sun up. He tapped Opōgyo, though the dog couldn't move any faster.

To distract himself, he focused on the lookout where another vortex indicated a shot about to be fired. He smiled, silently betting himself a pyābi that it would hit.

And then he saw movement. It was faint and barely visible from his position, too short to be an adult. He squinted, peering along the upper edge of the lookout. It was Nigímo, Gemènyo and Faríhyo's daughter. Growing up in the valley, she was precocious and fearless. If Rutejìmo could see her, she had to be standing on the edge of the lookout and waving to her parents.

Rutejìmo lifted his gaze to a vortex rising behind her. Translucent feathers swirled in the column of dust, and he could see the wind spiraling around them.

Ice water ran through his veins. Nigímo had moved too close to the edge. He remembered how hard an adult could be pushed by the wind when someone threw a bola. Unable to call out, he threw himself into running. Two steps later, Shimusògo appeared before him and streaked past. He accelerated rapidly after it, kicking up a plume with his racing.

The bola shot from the lookout in a blast of air. Sand and dust exploded around her, and Nigímo stumbled forward. Her right foot caught the edge. For a moment, she looked like she would remain standing, then she fell over the edge.

She plummeted.

Rutejìmo's heart skipped a beat.

When she landed in the safety net a few feet below, he let out his breath in a gasp. He didn't know if the people on the lookout noticed, but Rutejìmo knew the gaps were large enough that a toddler wouldn't remain caught for long. And there was nothing but a sixty foot fall below.

He wouldn't make it back; he wasn't fast enough. Skidding to a halt, he stared up at her and tried to think of something. He couldn't say anything—no one would listen to him. Desòchu's threat loomed in his head, warring with the sight of Nigímo thrashing in the net; it was quickly crushed by his need to serve.

Silence no longer mattered.

Spinning around, he looked back. Gemènyo and Faríhyo were dancing around only a few chains away. He dug his feet into the sand and sprinted toward them, putting everything he could into reaching them.

Seconds later, he slammed to a halt. "Gemènyo!" His throat tore from yelling after almost a year of whispering, he inhaled and screamed at the top of his lungs. "Faríhyo!"

The couple stumbled to a halt, their bare feet digging into rocks. They jumped out of the cloud that billowed around them and stared at Rutejìmo with dumbfounded looks on their face. Neither would have expected him to break the silence.

Rutejìmo gestured frantically at the cliffs. "Nigímo!" He couldn't think of anything to say.

As one, Gemènyo and Faríhyo lifted their gazes to the cliff. Two translucent dépas raced past them and around each side of Rutejìmo. Before he could blink, Gemènyo and Faríhyo both disappeared as they sprinted toward the clan valley. The wind caught Rutejìmo on both sides, and he was thrown back as Nigímo's parents raced for the cliffs.

He hit the ground hard and saw stars flowing before him. Surging to his feet, he started after them helplessly. Despite his desire to chase after them, helplessness prevented him from running. He would never catch up with them. Even if he did, there was nothing he could do to save Nigímo.

Rutejìmo stumbled to a stop and looked around for Hyonèku and Kiríshi. He could get their attention at least, and both of them were capable of catching up. As he turned, he spotted Desòchu coming out from around the far end of the valley. Rutejìmo's brother was only a speck of light, rapidly growing larger despite his route along a wide loop.

He knew Desòchu could save the toddler if the warrior knew of the danger. Rutejìmo dug his feet into the sand and started to run toward Desòchu.

He only made it a few steps before he realized he could never catch up to his brother; the warrior was running too fast to see Rutejìmo. Even if his brother did glimpse his way, Desòchu would look away: Rutejìmo was dead.

Rutejìmo came to a halt, silently cursing. The only way to force Desòchu to look at him was to be a threat, or at least draw enough attention that Desòchu would be forced to respond. Spinning around, he peered along the ground for something to throw.

A few rods away, he spotted the edge of a large rock sticking out of the sand. The dark ridge hinted that it was much larger than he could see. He exhaled hard and raced over to it. Kneeling hard on the ground, he ripped his shirt off and fashioned it into a crude sling.

He knotted his shirt, dropped it, and dug into the sand. His heart pounded as he fought the urge to look for Desòchu. Every second would count until his brother got close enough. His hand slipped and a sharp pain slashed across his palm. He pulled it up to see a deep cut across his hand. Blood started to well up, flowing around the sand clinging to his skin.

He fought back a whimper by biting his lower lip. He forced his hand into the sand and pried the rock out. It was a heavy hunk of sandstone, far heavier than he normally threw.

Rutejìmo was just staggering to his feet when Desòchu blasted past him. He fell back. "No," he cried out. Hitting the ground, he scrambled to his feet. "Desòchu! Desòchu!"

By the time he could turn around, Desòchu was nothing but a plume of sand and glowing feathers.

Rutejìmo took a step toward him, but despair prevented him from taking another step. He would never catch up to his brother.

With a sigh, he stepped back and dropped the rock into the sling. He didn't know what to do, but he needed to do something. As he moved, he traced his brother's route across the sand with his eyes. The wide loop that Desòchu ran along was more oblong than a perfect circle. Desòchu would be coming back toward the valley in less than a minute but the nearest point to Rutejìmo was over a half mile away.

Rutejìmo looked down at the rock in his shirt. He had never hit anything so far away. If he missed, then Desòchu would be too late to help.

For a moment, Rutejìmo considered racing to the cliff himself, but he would never make it. The others were far faster and more capable of saving Nigímo. The only thing he could do was get Desòchu's attention.

He grabbed the knot with both hands and swung it around to throw it. He came around in a wide loop. When he saw Opōgyo walking toward the cliff, steam belching out of his joints, a new idea came to him. Biting down, he continued to spin in a rapid circle, but his attention focused on Opōgyo as the target instead of his brother.

With every revolution, he remembered how the last mechanical dog had exploded when it collapsed. The roar had blasted through the entire valley, and the rumble shook the sands for miles in all direction. If he could cause Opōgyo to explode, there was no way that Desòchu could miss it.

A small part of him worried that he would be too close to the dog when it exploded, but he pushed the fear aside. Pain wouldn't mean anything if he failed. As soon as the rock became a glowing ring of flame and light, he released it.

The rock shot across the short distance to Opōgyo. It punched into the side of the mechanical dog. Opōgyo staggered a step before tilting over with his metal skin ruptured by the explosion of rock and dust. Twisted curls of metal smoke traced the air before Opōgyo slammed into the ground.

Rutejìmo braced himself for the explosion, but only steam poured out of the gaping wound in Opōgyo's side. The dog shuddered and one leg shook.

"Damn the sands!" Rutejìmo screamed. He raced over and dropped to his knees to peer at the damage.

Inside the gaping hole, he found the metallic vase—a fire core—that fueled the device's movements. Rutejìmo's shot had dented the metal, and a thin flame jetted out from a tiny hole, but it wasn't nearly enough damage. He tried to reach in, but the intense heat pushed him back.

Despair rocked him, and he looked for another rock to smash the core. Only small rocks and sand covered the ground around him. He fought back a whimper. The heat pouring out of Opōgyo seared his skin.

Knowing Desòchu would be out of range soon, Rutejìmo steeled himself and braved the heat to look inside. He traced the foreign mechanical lines that spread out from the core. He vaguely remembered them from when Pidòhu had worked on them. His eyes caught sight of one of the vents that drew air into the dog. Thin streamers of steam from Opōgyo's joints were being sucked into a narrow line. The suction was labored, like a dying creature.

Rutejìmo stuffed his shirt into the intake vents of the core. Wind whistled around the fabric until he forced as much as he could into the narrow slot and silenced it. The whistle ended with a thump and a pressure gauge near the dog's ear began to rapidly rise.

He glanced up to see where his brother was.

Desòchu was coming back again. He was nothing more than a brilliant light with a plume of sand rolling behind him.

Rutejìmo gasped. Inspecting the gauge, he saw it would take too long for the needle to reach the yellow area, much less the red. Panicking, he reached into Opōgyo's side. He remembered when Pidòhu had fixed the core into place with wire. If he couldn't find a rock to destroy the vase, he would destroy it by firing it into the ground.

Heat seared his fingers, and pain shot up his arms. He felt around blindly for the wires until he found the first one. The thin metal cut at his hand, and the smell of cooking skin filled the air around him.

Gasping at the pain and peering through tears, Rutejìmo twisted the wires until he could pull it out. The vase shuddered and the jet of flame caught his skin for a moment, blackening it almost instantly.

The second wire hurt even more. By the time he got it free, he could barely feel his fingertips. His hands were charred up to the wrists. Blood and oil sizzled along the metal, adding to the steam that poured around him.

He had to feel around for the third wire. The angle was impossible until he stood up and leaned over the gaping hole. His hands brushed along the searing metal and his skin felt like it was on fire. He swore loudly, trying to keep his attention focused through tear-blurred vision and fingers he could barely feel. His throat seized up from the effort. When he found the wire, he ripped it out of the smoking body with a sob.

Rutejìmo clamped his shaking hands around the core and yanked it out. A fourth wire, one he missed, resisted for a heartbeat, but he slammed his foot against Opōgyo's chest and pulled with all his might. Something tore in his back, but then he was staggering back along the sand.

Without looking for his brother, Rutejìmo began to spin around as fast as he could. The vase was heavy in his hands, but his fingers were clutched around it. He could feel his skin searing into the metal, like raw meat on a grill. Knowing it would rip off later only pushed him to spin faster.

Shimusògo appeared around his feet and raced in a circle.

He chased the spectral bird and a wind sucked up around his legs before shooting up in a column of dust. Feathers flashed across his vision, blinding him to everything but agony and heat.

Between rotations, he saw his brother racing toward the nearest point. He could feel the core beginning to rattle and crack; even though Opōgyo had been in the valley for decades, the core was not made by one of the Shimusògo and it was responding violently to the proximity of his gathering magic. Flames shot out of the rent in the side, peeling back the flesh of his arm before being sucked up into the vortex of his power.

For the briefest moment, he felt the euphoria of magic fill him. It was a sensation of anticipation, like a held breath before jumping. And then, the power inside him demanded release. He peeled his fingers away from the burning core—patches of his fingertips remained, fused to the metal—and threw it with all his might.

The core burst into light and brilliant sparks as Rutejìmo's power interacted with its magic. Creating a high-pitched whistle that drowned out his ability to hear, it shot forward too fast for Rutejìmo to see, so he focused on the line of burning flames it left behind.

Behind the core, sand sucked up in a spear to follow it, riding the wake of power from the crackling shot.

He was going to miss.

The shot reached the line of Desòchu's run a second too early. Just as it passed, he started to drop to his knees in frustration.

The heart of Opōgyo exploded.

Running too fast to stop, Desòchu dove into the shock wave. As his magic struck the magic of the exploding core, a second explosion blasted out in all directions. Sand tore at Rutejìmo's face, throwing him back and digging into his skin and arms. He vainly tried to shield his face with his hands, the concussive wave pounding sand into his burned palms, stripping away more skin until blood poured down his arms. He screamed in agony.

Rutejìmo staggered to his feet. Swaying, he tried desperately to regain his senses.

Desòchu's fist caught him in the stomach, the force of the blow folding Rutejìmo in half.

Rutejìmo flew back, hitting the ground.

"Do you want to die that badly?" snapped Desòchu. There were cuts over his face and a long scratch down his nose that bled. He stalked over to Rutejìmo, his hands glowing with brilliant flames and a growl in his chest.

Rutejìmo staggered to his knees. He shot back. "If it saves Nigímo, then kill me now!"

Desòchu took another two steps before he stopped. He inhaled sharply. "W-What?"

Blood dripped from Rutejìmo's lips. He pointed angrily at the cliff, and more blood splattered on the sand.

Desòchu's head snapped up. The pupils of his eyes seemed to grow for a moment, and then he inhaled sharply.

On the cliff, Faríhyo was dangling over the edge, reaching for her daughter.

Gemènyo held her up while kneeling near the edge. The smoke from his pipe swirled around them, tracing out their frantic movements.

"Sands!" Desòchu threw back his head, exploded into an i-nferno of golden flames, and screamed. It wasn't the sound of a human that came out of his mouth, but the screech of a bird that echoed in Rutejìmo's head.

The sound crashed into Rutejìmo. It echoed beyond his ears and something deep in his heart responded. He had to obey it, had to do something. It was the cry of Shimusògo himself.

Rutejìmo felt the cry force his attention toward Desòchu. A need to do something rose up inside him, a command that came directly from the clan spirit. He stared into Desòchu's flaming form despite the pain of looking into the brightness. Tears burned in his eyes from the effort.

Desòchu shot forward and the world twisted violently aro-und Rutejìmo. He was ripped off the ground from the blast of air and flipped over before he could brace himself.

Translucent wings spread out before Desòchu as he raced back to cliff. A boiling cloud of dust followed, obscuring every-thing around Rutejìmo. Streamers of sand rolled along the gro-und.

Power rose around him. Looking up, he saw the clan re-sponding to Desòchu's cry. Every adult of the clan converged on the valley, each one leaving a trail of golden flames. The chil-dren who were playing were knocked aside by adults all sprint-ing toward the entrance.

Staggering to his knees, Rutejìmo tried to join but couldn't. His legs shook, and his arms couldn't take his weight. Blood dripped from his ears, and he couldn't hear through the rin-ging. He watched the rest of the clan racing back to the cliffs through blurry vision.

He focused through the haze and dust toward the cliffs. Fa-ríhyo hung over the edge of the cliff, struggling to reach her daughter. Her hands flailed around as Nigímo dangled from the wires, her feet kicking out helplessly above the drop.

Desòchu reached the cliffs. He was moving too fast to stop, and Rutejìmo didn't know how he could turn fast enough to reach the top. Not even Chimípu could stop quickly when running so fast.

The answer came as someone rushed from the entrance of the valley. Even from a distance, Rutejìmo could see the bulge of Mapábyo's belly and the translucent feathers circling around her. He let out a strangled cry and limped toward the valley. She shouldn't answer Desòchu's call, though Rutejìmo could feel the overriding desire to do so rising in himself. It was Shimusògo's voice that called all of them, his pregnant lover included.

Desòchu's dépa accelerated straight for Mapábyo. The spirit bird she chased did the same. The two impacted in a flash of light and then there was only one spirit of Shimusògo shooting straight up in a streak of light.

Rutejìmo's cry caught in his throat, and only a wail came out. He knew what would happen if they struck; he also knew he was too far away to stop it, and too spent to take her place.

Mapábyo threw herself into a slide, her outfit fluttering behind her in a streamer of sand.

Desòchu leaped, covering two chains in an instant. The warrior landed on her, and a burst of energy exploded around them; their forward momentum grew fluid and transferred directly into Desòchu.

Rock and dust exploded in all directions.

Desòchu rocketed straight up and his body became a spear of gold. He punched through the net and both he and Nigímo disappeared in a flare of his magic. The line of flames sailed up and over the cliffs and into the valley.

Less than a rod away, Faríhyo was torn from the safety netting and thrown up into the air. She reached the apex of her short flight and then she came down, her arms and legs windmilling. Even from his vantage point, Rutejìmo knew she wasn't going to reach the cliff edge or the net. He cried out, holding out his hand as if he could stop her. If he had the power, he would have stopped time to save her.

Gemènyo jumped out on the net and grabbed her. He spun his wife around violently and then threw her back on the cliffs. The momentum drove Gemènyo further away from the cliffs and then into a curve toward the ground. His pipe smoke marked the plummet to the hard rock below.

Rutejìmo couldn't tear his eyes away. The body of his friend hit the ground in a cloud of dust. He forced himself to his feet with a sob and ran for the cliffs.

Instead of hearing the boom that rolled over him, Rutejìmo felt it vibrate in his bones. Though he was dizzy and could barely run straight, he had to return.

By the time he reached the cliffs, the rest of the clan were already there. One knot circled around Mapábyo who wailed in agony. It took him painful seconds to peer past the gathered clans to his love.

She was in a deep crater, the result of taking Desòchu's speed and launching him straight up. It saved Nigímo, but she was in pain from the effort. The ground packed hard from centuries of the passage of a multitude of runners had cracked around her.

And then Rutejìmo saw blood pooling underneath her. Most of it was pouring out from between her legs. He stumbled to a halt and stared, not wanting to believe what he saw. Mapábyo reached out for him but then dropped her hand before she slumped back.

Something cracked inside him, and he dropped to his knees. The words wouldn't come, he couldn't make a noise and he felt as if someone had ripped out his heart.

Noises came back, with Tejíko the loudest. "Don't move her. Pidòhu!" A heartbeat later, Rutejìmo's grandmother yelled. "Get the healer from Ryayusúki! Now!"

Pidòhu disappeared in a rush of wind and the massive wings of Tateshyúso, his spirit, shot out across the sands.

Rutejìmo stared without blinking. He couldn't move, he couldn't cry out. It was as if his mind had emptied out in an instant. He wanted to cry, but no tears fell. His emotions had been lost in the gaping chasm his heart had once filled.

He wanted to run to Mapábyo, but couldn't. Not with everyone circling around her. He was dead, he couldn't be seen and in that moment, he knew it was one thing he wasn't allowed to do.

Bearing down on the growing dread, he looked up at the other group. Faríhyo knelt next to her husband, screaming at the sky. Tears ran down her bloodied cheeks. Nigímo cried near her, cradled by Kiríshi while the others stood silently around him. Half of them stared with tears in their eyes while the others were looking away. The choked cries filtered through the crowd.

Desòchu stood in front of Gemènyo, his face twisted in a mask of rage and regret. His hands were bloody and waves of heat rolled off his body.

Gemènyo gasped for breath. He shook violently. Blood poured out from the side of his mouth and his legs were twisted unnaturally. Bright white of bones stuck out from his sides and legs. The ground beneath him was stained with blood and marred by the indentation of his impact.

The wind pushed Rutejìmo to move. He couldn't go to his love, but he could go to Gemènyo. Fighting against the agony that tore through his mind and body, he staggered to his feet. Shuffling, he stepped forward. It was one of the most painful steps of his life. As soon as his bare feet struck the cracked ground, he took another step.

The crowds parted around him, though no one looked to see him coming.

He came to a halt before Faríhyo and Gemènyo. His movement caused blood to run down his own neck and shoulders, reminding him of the injuries he continued to ignore. His ears still rang, yet he could hear the wails through the noise.

Faríhyo held Gemènyo tightly and screamed shrilly. There were no words, only tears and cries.

It was obvious no one could save Gemènyo with mere bandages or splints.

Gemènyo's eyes focused on Rutejìmo. It was the first time he had looked at Rutejìmo for almost a year. A slow smile cracked his lips. "J-J... Jìmo."

Around him, the din grew instantly silent.

Faríhyo clutched him and wailed shrilly, her cry was the only sound in the silence. It scraped at both Rutejìmo's ears and heart.

Gemènyo stared at Rutejìmo and worked his mouth for a second. "I see you."

"No!" screamed Faríhyo. "You can't see him! You can't! I won't let you!"

"Funny," Gemènyo's breath caught and a large gout of blood burst out of his mouth. It splattered against his stained shirt and ran down his neck. "Because I should have told you I've never stopped seeing him."

"No! No!" her scream was shrill, echoing against the walls. She clutched him tightly, squeezing with all her might. "You can't see him!"

And then Great Shimusogo Gemènyo was gone.

Chapter 33

Cremation

No one suffers more than a mother who buries her own daughter.
—*Queen of the River* (Act 1)

Rutejìmo slumped on a boulder near the funeral pyre and stared into the flames. The smell of incense and spices washed over him in a choking cloud that burned his eyes and seared the back of his throat. He coughed softly and then closed his eyes until the breeze blew the smoke away before opening them again.

When his vision came into focus, the first thing he saw was Gemènyo's corpse smoldering in the center of the pyre. The flames obscured the shadow of his friend's body.

Rutejìmo glanced down at the *Book of Ash* in his lap. He had already written in the death, but he couldn't close it. Instead, the charcoal stick he used to write with hovered over the line. He wanted to write something more than just a clan, name, and death. "Fell off a cliff" didn't even hint at the memories of a man who helped Rutejìmo grow up and survive. Gemènyo was a teacher and a friend, he needed more.

Sniffing, Rutejìmo lowered the stick, but then lifted it off the page. All the names in the book were just lists. There was no life, no story. He stared at the page, desperate but afraid to break the silent tradition before him.

A breeze washed over him, bringing stinging smoke to blind him.

He wiped his eyes, wincing at the dryness of tears that had long since faded. The empty hole in his heart remained. The memories kept replaying the sickening fall and Gemènyo's final words. Faríhyo's scream echoed through his head, the high-pitched shrillness of someone losing their love.

The breeze stopped abruptly.

Rutejìmo looked up to check the flames, but they were still roaring before him. He sighed and glanced down. When he saw that he marked the page with the stick, he froze. He stared at the tiny curve, not even a letter, but it was the beginning of a word. The magnitude of his action caused his heart to beat faster.

The world spun around him. He stared at the tip of the charcoal stick. It ground against the page, leaving little crumbs of darkness. He knew if he wiped it off, it would only smear.

It took only the faintest of efforts to continue the letter, drawing it out. When he finished, he started another, and then another. Supposing that his actions would offend the spirits, he continued to write slowly, trying to come up with words to express what tore at his heart.

"He was my mentor and my friend," he wrote. Rutejìmo remembered how Gemènyo tried to teach Rutejìmo the ways of the clan without actually speaking. It was the Shimusogo Way, actually the desert way, to demonstrate without speaking.

He finished the line, and Tachìra didn't strike him down. The sun spirit would have been sleeping at night. He looked up to see that the moon, Chobìre, was also below the horizon, which meant his death could come when one of the great spirits rose. Mifúno, the desert mother, did not seem to desire penance.

Rutejìmo realized he didn't care anymore. While the flames buffeted him with heat and the breeze tickled his skin, he continued to write. Grains of sand bounced off his face, hands, and legs, but none of them stuck to the page he was writing.

There was no way to document everything grand about Gemènyo. No man could ever reduce the richness of anyone's life down to a single page or even a book. Rutejìmo had to skip over the little things to focus on what was important. He didn't have Pidòhu's flair for poetry, so it came out as a short list.

Somehow, it was enough. When he reached the bottom of the page, the words stopped. He looked over the items he wrote and felt a sense of not only pride but also relief. It was a eulogy for his friend, poorly written and probably doomed to anger the spirits, but at least Gemènyo's life would be remembered by the next kojinōmi.

When he couldn't write anymore, he didn't resist. Setting the writing stick between the first page and the cover, he held the book open and lifted his gaze to the fire.

The wind shifted, and the stinging cloud came back to him.

He closed his eyes and waited for it to pass.

It did, but only for a second. Moments later, it came back harder. It brought heat and ashes coursing around him.

Rutejìmo turned but the wind followed him. He blinked at the tears and turned his back to the flames, feeling guilty for his action.

With the light behind him, he could see the path that led back to the Shimusogo Valley. There were lights burning at the entrance, an hour's walk away.

He remembered seeing Mapábyo in a puddle of her own blood and a sob rose in his throat. He had no tears left to shed, despite knowing how close he was to losing his love. He closed his eyes tightly and turned away in renewed anguish, welcoming the burning of the fire.

A blast of wind slammed into him. He staggered back, choking from the heat. He held out his hand for balance and felt it streaming around his fingers, pushing him away from the flames. He snapped open his eyes and looked around. When he felt a tickle along his feet, he glanced down.

The sand was pouring over his feet, racing back along the path in streamers that looked like snakes. The grains scoured the top of his feet, leaving tiny scratches.

He looked back in the direction of the sand. It followed the path leading to the valley. A sick feeling rose in his stomach, and he shook his head.

The wind blew harder, cutting at his skin and yanking at his clothes.

He shook his head more violently. "No, no, I can't lose her. Please, don't take my—"

The funeral pyre flared up into brilliance and heat clawed at his back. The scent of incense and spices grew stronger and thicker. It choked him. The inferno pushed him further away, down the path toward the valley.

Rutejìmo sobbed and cried out. "No!"

The wind stopped abruptly.

He staggered back toward the fire before he caught himself. His foot tapped against a funeral vase that was for Gemènyo's ashes. He looked down at the clay pot with feathers shaped into the side. Someone had decorated it with glass and beads. Gemènyo's pipe rested on the top.

Despair rose inside him as Rutejìmo stared at it. The smoke from the funeral pyre seemed to gather in the bowl of the pipe before spilling out, tracing a smoky line in the same direction as the wind.

He took a deep breath and looked back. It didn't matter if his lover died, he had to go back. With eyes burning, he left the funeral pyre and headed down the trail, praying to the spirits that they would keep the fires burning until he returned.

The entire way back to the valley was filled with nightmares. He imagined Mapábyo's corpse waiting for him at the entrance. He imagined holding her frail form to his chest. Did he have the strength to carry her back? Could he still be a kojinōmi for his lover?

His thoughts made him sick, but he forced himself to keep walking. When he faltered, he imagined there was a wind pushing him forward, and he stumbled forward.

Before he realized it, he arrived at the entrance to the valley. No one stood there, not even someone guarding the opening. He glanced up at the lookout but couldn't even see a light.

He dreaded entering the valley. It was dark and still, an oppressive coldness bore down on him.

Only one cave had light spearing out of the uncovered opening. He looked at his home and realized he was about to see Mapábyo's corpse. Somehow, his body found moisture for tears and they dribbled down his cheeks. He made his way up the darkened path. He had to force himself to take every step; he felt every rock and ridge along the familiar path to his home.

When he saw white and gold at the entrance of his home, he stumbled to a stop. The tears came faster and he gasped for breath. Spurred by curiosity and dread, he stumbled forward, rushing the last rod to reach the entrance. The trinkets for the dead were resting on top of a small vase no larger than his fist. It was too small for Mapábyo, too small for any adult. It had no decorations because the person who died had no accomplishments in their life.

It took only a heart-ripping moment for him to realize who had died. With a long shuddering exhalation, he sank to his knees: he had lost his unborn child. His knees crunched against the ground. He shook violently and stared at the undecorated vase. He sobbed as quietly as he could, clutching the ground with one hand and his heart with the other. It didn't take long until his lungs ached. Tears poured down his face, splashing against the rocks.

He struggled not to make a noise. He knew he couldn't attract anyone's attention without reprisal, but it took all of his effort to keep cries from escaping his throat. He clamped his hand over his mouth and bowed down, sobbing until each breath ripped out of his lungs and tore at his throat. He dug his fingers into his jaw and his chest, trying to use pain to stop the tears but nothing would stop.

Ever since they realized Mapábyo was pregnant, they had been dreaming of their child's life: wondering what gender they would become, would they be a warrior or a runner or even a sage of Tateshyúso? A thousand questions and whispered fantasies were ripped out of him, torn out of his heart in an instant. He bowed over his child's funeral vase and let the tears splash against the pottery.

Bare feet stepped out of his cave. He tried to stand away but couldn't. He closed his eyes tightly and let the tears flow. The only thing he could do was clamp down on his throat to prevent the wails from escaping.

A warm hand rested against his shoulder.

Rutejìmo froze for a moment and then looked into Chimípu's shimmering eyes. She was crying herself, her body glowing faintly with the power of Shimusògo. She must have somehow answered Desòchu's call and ran hundreds of miles to return home. The flames were hot against his skin but not burning. She knelt next to him, not saying anything, grief and sorrow painted on her face.

In her arms, she had a bundle of white cloth stained with blood.

Rutejìmo looked at it and then up to her, his lips moving but no sounds coming out. He wanted to thank her for being there even though it did nothing to help tears aching hole in his heart.

With a pained look, she nodded and held it out to him.

He took the bundle, marveling at the lightness of the body swaddled inside but also the heaviness in his heart. Clutching it tight to his chest, he staggered to his feet. He wanted to unwrap it to see his child but didn't. This wasn't a place to display the dead.

Chimípu stood up with him, picking up the vase as she did. She handed it to him.

Rutejìmo took it silently from her trembling fingers, giving her a sorrow-filled smile.

"I'm—" she started to whisper.

Rutejìmo shook his head.

She closed her mouth and started to cry again. Reaching out for him, she tried to give him a hug.

Inwardly, he cringed. She couldn't be seen interacting with him. If Desòchu saw it, there would be only more pain in their lives. He turned sharply away from her. She was living and he was dead.

Chimípu stepped back into the cave. She smiled at him, a wavering smile that was completely different from anything he had seen her express before: it was filled with grief but also pride.

He knew his place. Heading back down the path toward the entrance, he held his child to his chest—a delicate treasure, fragile as spun glass. His bare feet scuffed on the rocks, the only noise in his silent walk.

Rutejìmo stepped past the entrance before he realized someone waited for him. Thinking it was Desòchu, he tensed and turned his body away to shield the child from his brother.

"Jìmo," said Hyonèku in a low, scratchy voice.

Rutejìmo stopped. He looked down, unwilling to look at Mapábyo's father's face.

Hyonèku stepped forward.

Rutejìmo cringed, waiting for the blow.

Hyonèku pulled him into a hug.

Surprised, Rutejìmo could only twist to keep the bundle away but then he was caught in the shaking arms of his lover's father. It was the first time Hyonèku had touched Rutejìmo since Rutejìmo had become a banyosiōu. It was terrifying and comforting at the same time.

"I don't care what Desòchu said," whispered Hyonèku. "No father should ever suffer in silence."

A sob rose in Rutejìmo's throat. He fought to keep it down, but the effort shook his body and he felt it forcing its way up.

"I lost my best friend and my grandson tonight, I won't lose you."

Knowing that it was a son in his arms somehow made the pain sharper. The gender didn't matter, but the knowledge made it more real.

Hyonèku sobbed and clutched Rutejìmo tighter. "You were always the best man for my Pábyo. No matter what I said before, I was never prouder of you."

Rutejìmo strained to keep silent. He shook from the effort to clamp down on his throat and look away.

"I see you, Great Shimusogo Rutejìmo. I always saw you."

The whispered words broke the dam. Rutejìmo let out a loud cry and buried his face in the older man's neck. He grabbed Hyonèku with his other hand, dropping the vase as he did, and held him tight. The sorrow burst out of him, he stopped caring about silence or being a banyosiōu. He just let go and allowed all the grief and pain to pour out.

Chapter 34

Unshed Tears

Death strips the armor off our minds and bares our souls.
—Queen of the River (Act 3)

Hours later, the flames had finally burned away, and the two pyres had become nothing more than circles of smoldering ash. The heat cut at Rutejìmo's feet and knees as he walked to the center of the largest one. He stopped in the center and knelt to scoop out the blackened ash with his bare hand. Mouthing words to a prayer, he held it over Gemènyo's vase and let the ashes slip through his fingers. Small embers caught on his calloused hand before dimming in the relatively cool night air. He ignored the brief sparks of pain and worked in silence. He had to focus on his task to avoid the gnawing grief that clawed a hole out of his heart.

Despite remaining silent, he choked when the prayers came up to Gemènyo's name. The memories were too raw and painful to even think the words, much less say them. He forced himself to shape each word, praying with all his might that the desert would guide his friend's spirit to Shimusògo.

By the time the vase was full, the ashes were cold underneath his body, and the smoke no longer stung his eyes. He held his hand over the top and staggered to his feet, turning around once to orient himself. He staggered to the boulder he used as a seat.

He mouthed one final prayer while pouring wax over the lid and inscribing Gemènyo's full name along the opening.

When he finished, Rutejìmo held up the vase and stared at it. It was night around him, but after a year of performing rituals, he found that he could see well in the darkness. He stared at the vase and tried to come up with some words to say to his friend. No one would hear them, and he knew that Gemènyo deserved more than just a name on a vase.

A cool breeze washed over him, the flames flickering. He leaned into it and took a deep breath to let the incense-laden air fill his lungs.

Memories drifted through his head, and he let them flash across his mind. They were formless, the idea of an event more than specific details, but he didn't care. Scenes from Gemènyo's life flashed and were gone, fading slowly until there was nothing but darkness in Rutejìmo's head.

It felt like he had run out of things to say, though not a word had passed his lips. He set down the vase next to the boulders. He started to reach for the second one, his son's, but his body froze. From the despair in his heart, he felt a welling of sorrow rising up in his throat. He considered the plain vase for a long moment.

Rutejìmo berated himself. He had to keep going. He had a duty. He had a purpose. He was a kojinōmi, or at least learning to become one.

It took all of his effort to grab the vase. His fingers slipped off, and he had to try two more times before he could wrap his fingers around the icy cold opening and pick it up. Glancing at the second funeral pyre, he knew it was cold enough for him to gather ashes, but he couldn't force himself to walk closer. Closing his eyes, he clutched the empty vase to his chest and cradled it like a child.

There were more memories: he and Mapábyo coming up with names, their whispered dreams of what the child would become, and even the playful sex while she grew rounder with every passing night. None of them brought a smile to Rutejìmo's lips anymore. He wondered if he would ever smile again.

Footsteps crunched on the rock behind him. Rutejìmo slowly opened his eyes. He looked at the final pyre but didn't see anything. He focused his hearing on the approaching person.

"Rutejìmo." It was Desòchu. He spoke in a low, cracked voice.

Rutejìmo tensed and gripped the vase tighter. He wondered if his brother saw him speaking with Hyonèku. If he did, then Desòchu was there for blood. Memories of Rutejìmo's own suffering flashed through his mind, the remembered pain of being beaten and the look on his brother's face when he kicked Rutejìmo out of the clan were the clearest.

The last time Rutejìmo and Desòchu had met, it was Gemènyo who stopped him. Rutejìmo looked down at the vase, whispering a prayer that Gemènyo was still there to watch over him. Otherwise, there would be three corpses on the desert that night.

"You don't have to look at me. You don't have to speak." Desòchu said, "Will you listen?"

Surprised at the request, Rutejìmo could only nod as he cradled his son's funeral vase. He couldn't look back to see if the expression on Desòchu's face matched his words. They were in two worlds, and he couldn't be the one to bridge them. Desòchu had made that point clear.

"I... I don't know where I ran off the path, but..." Desòchu's feet shifted on the rocks and a pebble skittered across the stone. "I was wrong about you."

Rutejìmo drew in a shuddering breath of choking smoke. He wished he could cry, he tried to, but it refused to come. He lowered his chin to rest it on the top of the funeral vase, holding it tighter in fear that Desòchu would attack and break it.

"No." Desòchu stepped closer. "I was wrong. You just... frustrated me so much. Your shikāfu with Mikáryo wasn't the only thing. You didn't change the way I thought you would. You weren't a brave fighter or a fast runner. You didn't act like a Shimusògo. I-I was supposed to cut your throat, you know that?"

Rutejìmo nodded. He had asked about it after his rite of passage.

"Of course. Gemènyo would have told you?"

Another nod.

"He was a good man and a better judge of men like you. He tried to point out that you were still running the Shimusogo Way, just... on a different trail than the rest of us."

Rutejìmo smiled bitterly. He tilted his head so his cheek rested on the rough cap of the vase and peered to the side at his brother's feet.

"Did you hesitate before you tried to get my attention earlier today? Were you afraid because you thought I was going to kill you? Even if it meant saving someone's life?"

Rutejìmo sighed before he nodded. He looked down at his wrapped hands and could still feel the ache of burned fingers and blackened skin.

"Damn it. It wasn't supposed to be like that. I... I didn't know what would happen when I," Desòchu sniffed, "said that. I thought you would... I don't know what I was thinking. But you just didn't...."

Closing his eyes, Rutejìmo took a deep breath.

"We used to joke that you wouldn't notice a sand wasp until it made a nest in your belly. I never thought I would be just as clueless to what you've become. Since you came back, before you came back, you never stopped. You came in last on every run, but you did what needed to be done. You cooked, you cleaned, you never complained. For years, you said nothing when I spoke of your slowness. And for years, I never realized you were never giving up."

Desòchu sniffed and something splattered on the rock.

Rutejìmo glanced over, keeping his eyes on the rock, and saw dark splotches of tears.

"Could you forgive me, little brother?"

Rutejìmo stared at Desòchu's feet for a long moment. Then he drew his eyes up to look directly into his brother's green eyes. He saw the tears swimming in the fading light. He didn't have the words, but he knew how to answer.

He nodded.

Desòchu reached out for him and then drew back. He looked torn and guilty. "Come back to the living, please? Just a few more months. And then, I... I need... I need to do something."

Rutejìmo nodded mutely.

Digging into his pocket, Desòchu pulled out something. He rolled it in his hand and then held it out.

Confused, Rutejìmo reached out for it.

"No, for your son."

Rutejìmo held out the vase, then opened it at Desòchu's gesture.

Desòchu dropped something into it and it rang out against the clay bottom. He stepped back and then looked back toward the valley. "A year was lost but not forgotten. May you forgive me."

He wiped his face and walked away into the darkness. It was a long walk back to the valley, over a mile, but it was the same route that Rutejìmo usually took.

Rutejìmo waited until he couldn't hear Desòchu before peering into the smaller vase. At the bottom was one of Rutejìmo's voting stones, a black rock with a white ridge. He had earned one for every year since he became a man in the clan. He would have gained an eleventh if not for becoming a banyosi-ōu for the last year.

He choked on a sob. It would be fitting that his lost year would be kept safe. Setting it down, he took a deep breath and started on his son's ashes.

It took a depressingly short time before the second vase was filled. After mouthing the prayers of the dead over his son, he headed back.

Morning was approaching by the time he climbed the last of the trail to the shrine. The two heavy vases bore down on him, but it was an honor to carry them to their resting place. The torches in the shrine burned painfully bright after the darkness outside the valley. Inside, he saw almost everyone in the clan sitting there silently and staring forward. There were tears on their faces, and many of them struggled to keep their shoulders still.

The emptiness in his heart grew when he stopped at the threshold. He wasn't allowed inside, not while he was dead, but he could finish what he started. Setting down the two vases, he let the edge scrape against the rock so someone knew he was there.

Turning around, he walked back into the darkness toward his home. The feeling of despair continued to fill him, choking off the tears and sorrow. Every footstep felt like the last of a run, heavy and plodding. He didn't know what he would find when he came home, but he prayed Mapábyo would be there. He needed her as much as she would need him.

As he came up the final curve, he saw piles heaped at the entrance of his cave. He stopped in front of them with a scuff on the ground. There were two, one on each side of the entrance. On the left, he spotted little glass flowers, figurines from Wamifuko City, and wooden carvings from beyond the desert. They were little gifts of sympathy and grief for a family who lost a child.

He frowned in confusion. A second pile didn't make sense. If he was alive, they would have just added more gifts to the same pile. The other, much smaller pile didn't have gifts of grieving. Instead, the items were white and gold, the colors of death and life. On top was one of Pidòhu's books of poetry.

"Do you know why there are two piles?" Chimípu whispered. She pushed aside the blanket and came out of the cave. She wore a simple dress and, for once, she wasn't armed. Her green eyes caught his own without flinching or looking away.

Rutejìmo shook his head. He wanted to look away from her, but something kept their eyes locked.

"You are the tender of our dead, our kojinōmi, and you saved two lives today," she whispered, "Even the dead deserve thanks when they speak that loudly."

Rutejìmo's throat squeezed painfully. He looked at her, fighting the sorrow that threatened to rip him apart.

She was looking at him with tears in her own eyes. "You spent so many years giving gifts like these to me, you know."

He thought about the little things he gave to Chimípu and the others for saving his life or running with him. The little things that made his life a joy. He never got one himself. He was never that important before.

Chimípu stepped forward and rested her hand on his elbow. "You deserve it, little brother," she whispered before kissing him on the cheek. "Go on, your love is waiting for you, and Shimusògo is calling me. She is safe for now, but hurt both in the body and the heart. No one will hear you tonight."

He listened to her walk away before entering the cave. Padding to the bedroom, he steeled himself before entering.

Mapábyo sat on the bed, her eyes red and her hand resting on her belly. She wasn't looking at him, but staring down at her stomach. Her shoulders shook and the soft pants filled the chamber. Underneath her hand, red-stained bandages crossed her belly above the hips. Her hand quivered as if she was struggling not to press down but at the same time, she was afraid of lifting her hand away.

Ignoring the grime and ashes that clung to his body, Rutejìmo crawled into the bed with her. He settled next to her and reached out for her hand. Afraid of hurting her, he held his hand over hers.

She looked up at him with tears rolling down her cheeks. "I-I see you." She took his hand and pressed it against the warmth of her belly. The bandages around his palm and the ones covering her tugged on each other, the friction of their injuries holding them together.

The dead feeling inside him shattered, and a cry ripped out of his throat.

Mapábyo grabbed him tightly with her other arm and drew her body against his. "I see you, Jìmo, and I will never stop seeing you."

He leaned into her and spoke for the first time since Gemènyo died. "I see you too, my love. And I will never stop seeing you either."

Chapter 35

His First Words

When being reborn into the clan, the first words are typically the most precious.

—Kyōti proverb

Rutejìmo walked along the ridge of a dune, the burning wind buffeting his skin. His bare feet left a ragged trail behind him, his footsteps marking the long winding trail stretching miles behind him.

He didn't look back. It didn't matter where he came from or the path he took. He started that morning by walking toward the sun, pacing in silence. He had no direction other than to follow the burning orb across the sky. When Tachìra reached his apex, Rutejìmo stopped and held his face and arms to the sun spirit until he felt the heat moving away from his upturned gaze. Now, hours later, he returned to where he started.

Rutejìmo walked naked. He knew it was part of the purification ritual, but there was a stark difference between knowing he would trek with nothing to protect him and the actual struggle to keep walking when there was nothing to shield him from the heat of Tachìra or the grit of the desert. He trembled with his effort, his body struggling without water or food for an entire day. He tried to lick his lips, but they were as dry as the rock that seared his bare feet.

He reached a large rock and leaned against it. His hand trembled violently, and he slipped on the sweat that soaked his palm. He lost his balance and thudded painfully against a sharp edge. The burn on his dark skin sent sparks of pain along his nerves.

Panting, he remained in place for a few seconds and wished he had landed in shade. Walking naked in the sun was agony and every inch of his skin felt raw and seared. The only place that wasn't burned was a black tattoo of a dépa on his left shoulder.

He found his second wind and pushed himself away. Waiting in the sun would only prolong his agony.

To his surprise, the burn hurt—but not as much as he thought it would after almost twelve solid hours with only a tattoo to protect him. Something, a sense of peace or just the realization that he was about to rejoin his clan, pushed back the agony.

Barely standing, he kept his eyes focused on the cliff entrance of Shimusogo Valley. He could almost count the steps remaining until he was once again alive.

No one would meet him outside; he knew where to go. They would be waiting at the shrine to welcome him back. It would be the first time in a year that he would be allowed to speak again.

He wasn't sure he had the courage to speak again.

For a year now, he had worked in near silence. The cloak of being there and not there had grown comfortable around him. It was a hard life, filled with helpless pain. Both he and Mapábyo struggled with their loss and with Gemènyo's death. Still, the months had trudged by and the sharp edge of grief had faded.

Rutejìmo smiled to himself and wiped the sand from his face. There was no sweat left to prickle his skin. He wasn't even sure if he could make a noise with his dry throat, he didn't dare try. The purification ritual was made in silence.

Lifting his gaze up, he watched the red crescent of the sun burn along the cliffs of the valley. It was the last thin line before he rejoined the living. With a sad smile, he held his breath and watched it slip out of sight with the briefest of green flashes.

The power of Tachìra faded and he let out his shuddering breath. The darkness brought the full weight of his mortality and weakness to bear. At the same time, he could be seen again. He wanted to cry and scream and sob. The urge to drop to his knees and stop moving rose up, but he had a quarter mile left to walk before he reached home.

Looking back up, he caught movement. On either side of the valley, two flames circled around the back areas and came around. Despite being on opposite sides of the cliffs that lined the valley, they ran in almost perfect unison. Plumes of sand rose behind the two translucent dépa. They were running in opposite directions, but he knew they would come back toward him. It was Desòchu and Chimípu and they were finally coming for him.

A twisting in his stomach caused him to falter. He watched the two warriors circle around the valley, glowing with an aura of flame and sunlight. A year ago, both had beat him nearly into unconsciousness and left him to die. But they were also the ones that stealthily gave a helping hand when he needed it, or fed him when Mapábyo couldn't help him. He couldn't touch or talk to them, but they were there, guarding and protecting him as one of the clan. And being present when the grief took him.

Rutejìmo forced himself forward. The urge to turn and run rose up, almost choking him with the desperation of flight.

This close to the valley, the home of Shimusògo, he could use his powers. He wouldn't, knowing it would be less than a minute before they caught up to him. Not to mention, his powers would wane once he reached a league from the shrine, but the two warriors could retain their speed all night long.

He felt the power from their approach, a tickling along his senses and a fluttering in his heart. It was comforting and terrifying at the same time.

With a blast of air, Desòchu and Chimípu came to a stop on either side of him. Both of their bodies burned with golden flames, and feathers danced along their skin.

Rutejìmo hesitated, unsure of what to do.

Chimípu smiled at him and turned around so she was walking next to him.

On his left, his older brother did the same. His bola thumped against his thigh from the movement.

Rutejìmo trembled between the two of them. He was naked and vulnerable. His trek across the desert left him shaking and barely able to stand. Somehow, he knew they would catch him if he fell, but he was determined to finish the walk on his own.

Together, they entered the valley. It was quiet, almost painfully so. The caves were dark, and the communal fires were banked. He looked up at the caves hoping to see someone—there was no one to see. For the first time in his life, the valley was dark.

The only light came from the far end of the valley. The shrine glowed with a hundred candles. Someone had set up torches on both sides of the path leading to the shrine. At the sight of it, he sobbed and stumbled.

Chimípu reached out for him but didn't grab him.

He glanced up to see concern in her eyes and a silent question. With a nod, he forced his aching feet down the path. The hard-packed ground and rock scraped along his abused soles, but he would make the final steps.

A day walking naked in the sand was easy compared to the simple, smooth path leading up to the shrine. He could handle it, yet as he approached he felt the pressure of attention crushing him. It was a weight that he wasn't sure he could bear. Through the opening, he spotted every adult in the clan waiting for him with their backs to him. At the far end, sitting underneath the grand statue of Shimusògo, his grandmother stared at the ground. In front of her were the two bowls that would determine his fate.

He stopped at the threshold, a moment of indecision and fear. While no one looked at him, he could feel them straining to listening. He didn't know what to expect anymore.

He scanned the backs of friends and family. They supported him in the last year: meals set outside of the cave, impromptu poetry and stories just when he lost all faith, and even sitting out in the dark to talk to the night when he happened to be nearby.

For years, he never realized how much everyone cared for him. The year of being ostracized had drawn him closer to the clan than ten years of running as a courier.

He focused on Mapábyo. Her body shifted to the side and he could see that she wanted to turn around. Flashes of her profile came into his view when she started but then forced herself to look toward the front. Her black skin shimmered in the light, reflecting light from her white dress trimmed with orange. It was her special outfit, one that she modeled for him just the night before.

Taking a deep breath, Rutejìmo stepped over the threshold of the shrine. Crossing that simple stone step felt like one world had just peeled away from him and he was entering a new one.

A shiver coursed through the room. Ahead of him, Tejíko lifted her head and focused on him for the first time in a year. "I see you, Great Shimusogo Rutejìmo." Mapábyo's private words had become the words to greet the dead among the Shimu-sògo.

He trembled, fixed to the door frame.

The rest of the clan finally turned and looked at him.

He fought the sob that rose in his throat when he saw the smiling faces.

Tears ran down Mapábyo's face as she smiled. She wrung her hands together for a long moment before lifting her gaze to him. His heart almost stopped at the sight of the shimmering in her eyes.

Rutejìmo knew he needed to say something. It wasn't part of the ritual—still he felt in his gut it was right. It was the nature of being born once again into the clan. Taking a deep breath, he stepped forward and down the narrow gap between people. He thought about his words, playing them endlessly in his head. He wanted to speak right away even though he knew he couldn't. He found solace by staring at the statue of Shimu-sògo. It gave him strength imagining the clan spirit stood next to him.

As he passed Mapábyo, he reached out and took her hand.

Mapábyo inhaled sharply and tried to pull away.

He caught her wrist.

Next to her, Hyonèku snorted with a smirk.

Kiríshi looked at him with confusion.

Mapábyo leaned over. "Jìmo," she whispered, "you're supposed to say something to everyone."

He smiled and tugged her with him, nodding his head toward the front of the shrine.

She followed, her bare feet scuffing on the rock. He stood in front of Tejíko and turned so Mapábyo and he were facing together, with Tejíko on one side and the clan on the other.

Taking a deep breath, Rutejìmo opened his mouth, but his throat froze.

Mapábyo squeezed his hands, the tears streaming down her face.

"Ma... Mapábyo. Great Shimusogo Mapábyo...." Every word, spoken as loud as he could, came out hoarse and broken. "Will you m-marry me?"

From the right, he heard a burst of noise, but Kiríshi's and Desòchu's expletive carried over everyone else. "Damn the sands!"

Hyonèku laughed and clapped. "Finally!"

Rutejìmo stared at Mapábyo, struggling with the words. He had spent months practicing them in the desert, but when it came to saying them, he could barely force the words out. He managed to get out only a few syllables before panic set in and he choked.

Mapábyo blinked through her tears and then stepped closer. As she did, she pulled her hands from his and rested them on his hips. "Y-Yes," she whispered.

He smiled and placed his own, scarred palms on her hips.

Tejíko stood up with a groan. "Boy," she said in a sharp tone. Her long braid swung free and the heavy ring at the end thudded against the ground. "You always have to do things your own way, don't you?"

Rutejìmo blushed and ducked his head. "Sorry, Great Shimusogo Tejíko. B-But," he found it easier to speak, "I will only get to say my first words twice, once when I was a babe and now. She's the most important... she is my life now."

Tejíko's scowl sent a shiver of fear coursing down his spine.

Rutejìmo gulped and stared at his grandmother. "Did I... do —"

She interrupted him by raising her hands. "Silence!"

The whispers that had started when he first spoke ended in a flash.

"Since my grandson can't be properly humble with his first words, we'll deal with the second order of business. Shall we let these two marry?"

When he heard a bowl scraping on the floor, he glanced down. Tejíko pushed the black bowl between Mapábyo and himself, centering it right at their feet. If someone agreed, they would throw one or more of their voting stones into the bowl.

He glanced at the red one, the one someone would throw a stone into if they disagreed.

Tejíko chuckled and stepped on the edge of the bowl. It flipped over. The sound of it hitting the ground sent a bolt of surprise through Rutejìmo. He had never seen anyone flip it over.

The first stone rang out at his feet.

Rutejìmo jumped at the sound and looked at Desòchu who held up his hands. Behind him, Hyonèku, Kiríshi, and Chimípu were all lining up with their hands over their stones.

Tension twisting his back, he glanced down. Instead of seeing Chimípu's normal voting stone, it was one of his black rocks with the white ridges. He threw them off the cliff months ago and assumed they were lost.

A second stone landed in the bowl, also his.

In a slow rhythm, more of his rocks were tossed into the bowl until there were nine rolling at the bottom. No one else voted, no one else spoke about his request.

"Rutejìmo?" whispered Mapábyo. She pulled her hands free and dug into her pocket. With a grin of her own, she held up her hand and spread open her fingers. With a sigh, she let it slip from her fingers and it plummeted down into the bowl.

He had one stone for every year since he became a man in his clan. A year ago, he pulled out the tenth rock from underneath his bed and added it to his bag. A year later, he still had ten, but it felt like a lifetime had passed for him.

He gave up a year of his life, but somehow, he was happier than he had ever been.

When the final stone struck the bowl, he leaned over and kissed Mapábyo.

————————— Chapter 36 —————————

Running Together

The run heals many injuries, but the scars remain forever.

—Shimusògo proverb

Shimusogo Rutejìmo chased after a bird he would never catch. He didn't feel the heat of the sun or the roughness of the desert road against his bare feet. He only felt the pulse of magic and the beat of his heart.

Next to him, Mapábyo ran in step with him. She raced neither faster or slower, but exactly the same speed. She chased the same bird across the desert, her eyes focused on the road with the euphoric smile all Shimusògo shared while running.

The world blurred past them as they ran, following the rise and fall of the road leading to Wamifuko City from Monafuma Cliffs. Their colors, orange and red, added to the boiling cloud of dust left in their wake and the flicker of translucent feathers that streamed around their bodies.

Neither said anything; they didn't have to. They ran hand-in-hand, and it was enough for a man who now spoke little and the woman who loved him. In his pack, he still kept the trappings of banyosiōu, the white outfits and the *Book of Ash*. Now everyone called him a kojinōmi except when he wore the outfit. When he wore the white fabrics, their eyes slid away and they refused to speak to him. He was the tender of the dead and a courier of Shimusògo.

He was happy.

They came to a halt at the northwest entrance of Wamifuko City, decelerating from speeds faster than human to merely running and then jogging. Their destination brought them to the gate where a familiar horse-helmed warrior waited.

"Well met. I am Gichyòbi, and I speak for Wamifūko." Gichyòbi bowed deeply when they stopped.

Rutejìmo bowed deeply.

Next to him, Mapábyo did the same.

Rutejìmo straightened and said, "I am Rutejìmo, and I speak for Shimusògo."

"You know the rules of our city?"

"Very much, good friend."

"I'm going to tell you anyway," said Gichyòbi with a wink. He continued with the rules, giving graphic detail of how anyone who used magic within the city limits would be killed. The smile on his lips belied his words, and Rutejìmo and Mapábyo joined in.

As he finished his speech, he continued, "... and I would be honored if the Great Shimusògo would join my family for dinner. I will miss our dinners together now that you'll be returning home for some time."

Mapábyo giggled softly and rested her hand on the swell of her belly. She was due in three months, and it was time to stop running until the child was born.

In a few days, Chimípu and Desòchu would be coming up to guard them for the trip back to Shimusogo Valley. Until then, they would be discreetly guarded by Gichyòbi and the Wamifūko. It wasn't a favor, but a gift from one of the many people in Rutejìmo's life.

"We would be honored," said Rutejìmo.

A thud shook the ground. He glanced to the north where four large mechanical scorpions stepped over the crowds gathering near the entrance. Their brass bodies gleamed in the setting sun but he could still see the red glow of the inhuman eyes. As they walked with their tails curled over their backs, liquid flames dripped from their stingers.

Rutejìmo turned to get a better look, his eyes dropping to the feet of the massive machines. It was impossible to see anything other than the flash of black manes and the haunches of the dark herd, but he could imagine that there were two Pabinkúe riding among the horses.

A small part of him wanted to dive into the crowd to search for Mikáryo, to see the warrior one more time. He knew he wouldn't ever find her again. She was lost to him, living her life as he lived his own. He accepted it with a pang of sadness and turned around.

Mapábyo leaned against him. "Was that her?"

Rutejìmo shook his head and looked away. "Was that who?"

"Your shikāfu?" Her green eyes searched his own.

"Of course," he said with a kiss, "she's standing right in front of me."

About D. Moonfire

D. Moonfire is the remarkable intersection of a computer nerd and a scientist. He inherited a desire for learning, endless curiosity, and a talent for being a polymath from both of his parents. Instead of focusing on a single genre, he writes stories and novels in many different settings ranging from fantasy to science fiction. He also throws in the occasional romance or forensics murder mystery to mix things up.

In addition to having a borderline unhealthy obsession with the written word, he is also a developer who loves to code as much as he loves writing.

He lives near Cedar Rapids, Iowa with his wife, numerous pet computers, and a pair of highly mobile things of the male variety.

You can see more work by D. Moonfire at his website at https://d.moonfire.us/. His fantasy world, Fedran, can be found at https://fedran.com/.

Fedran

Fedran is a world caught on the cusp of two great ages.

For centuries, the Crystal Age shaped society through the exploration of magic. Every creature had the ability to affect the world using talents and spells. The only limitation was imagination, will, and the inescapable rules of resonance. But as society grew more civilized, magic became less reliable and weaker.

When an unexpected epiphany seemingly breaks the laws of resonance, everything changed. Artifacts no longer exploded when exposed to spells, but only if they were wrapped in cocoons of steel and brass. The humble fire rune becomes the fuel for new devices, ones powered by steam and pressure. These machines herald the birth of a new age, the Industrial Age.

Now, the powers of the old age struggle against the onslaught of new technologies and an alien way of approaching magic. Either the world will adapt or it will be washed away in the relentless march of innovation.

To explore the world of Fedran, check out https://fedran.com/. There you'll find stories, novels, character write-ups and more.

License

- NonCommercial — You may not use the material for commercial purposes.
- ShareAlike — If you remix, transform, or build upon the material, you must distribute your contributions under the same license as the original.

No additional restrictions — You may not apply legal terms or technological measures that legally restrict others from doing anything the license permits.

Preferred Attribution

The preferred attribution for this novel is:

"Sand and Ash" by D. Moonfire is licensed under CC BY-NC-SA 4.0

In the above attribution, use the following links:

- Sand and Ash: https://fedran.com/sand-and-ash/
- D. Moonfire: https://d.moonfire.us/
- CC BY-NC-SA 4.0: https://creativecommons.org/licenses/by-nc-sa/4.0/

Patrons

This book is freely available on the Fedran website at https://fedran.com/sand-and-blood/. It can be reformatted for any device, shared, and even reposted on other websites (with attribution and a link to the original). If someone wants to write a fanfic or create art inspired by the book, they are allowed to do so with relatively few limitations, which are set down by the license described in the previous section.

It is hard to compete with "free" in this day and age. Releasing a book under a Creative Commons license is one way of doing that, but there are still costs associated with producing the results. There are hundreds of hours put into writing it, hiring editors to go through it, and even hosting it on a website. As economics will tell you, there is no such thing as a free lunch. Most of the time, you pay for a book before reading it. Sometimes you have a sample of a few chapters to give you a hint, other times just a blurb. Here, you get the entire piece. If you like it, please consider supporting my writing.

The cheapest way of helping is simply to talk about the book. Post opinions on social networks, write a review and put it up on Amazon or Goodreads, or give a copy to someone who might like it.

The second way of helping is to donate money. Even a dollar helps. There are quite a few ways of doing this: you can buy a print copy; the tip jar at Broken Typewriter Press (https:// broken.typewriter.press/dmoonfire/); or even consider becoming a patron. Patronage provides advance access to works-in-progress, votes on new stories and titles, and input into the world and my writing. You can read more about patrons at https://fedran.com/patrons/.

I can only hope that if you like it, you'll help me write the next one.

Thank you.

Credits

I used to do acknowledgements but then I realized there were a lot of people who went into helping me write this book, more than would comfortably fit in a few paragraphs. At the same time, I felt the need to thank them because without their help, this book would remain only in my imagination.

Alpha Readers

If it wasn't for the Noble Pen writing group, I would have never gotten that far.

- Bill H.
- Ciuin F.
- Mark H.
- Nick T.
- Tyree C.

Beta Readers

- Chandrakumar M.
- Kenneth E.

- Laura W.
- Marta B.
- Mike K.
- Stacie S.

Editors

- Blurb Bitch
- Ronda Swolley
- Shannon Ryan

Family

- Susan
- Eli
- Bruce

Colophon

Each chapter of this book was written and edited using Emacs, Atom, and LibreOffice. The files for the novel were managed in a Git repository on a private GitLab instance. Each chapter was an individual file formatted using Markdown. Information and working notes about the chapters were placed into a YAML header at the top of each chapter.

These individual chapters were combined together using a cobbled-together collection of Perl, Python, and Javascript tools that transform the results into XeLaTeX (PDF and print version), EPUB, MOBI, or Microsoft Word.

The cover was created using Inkscape. The color scheme uses eight colors of a monochromatic scale. These colors are shared among all of the Rutejìmo novels. Likewise, the "100-01" along the spine indicates this is the second published book ("01") with Rutejìmo as the main character ("100").

The font used on the cover and interior is Corda in various weights and styles.

9 781940 509167

Berrigan's Ride is a novel of love, abandonment and acceptance set primarily in Hot Spring District, Madison County, in southwestern Montana (Norris), 1866 - 1868, and a drama of symbolic healing between North and South after the Civil War.

"I must know more---even though I am reluctant to pry into your affairs." The words hung unattended in the still cool night like a lost fawn, alert, listening for a sign from the doe.

"You are raw, Kent. I don't know if you are the same man. Or will be."

Marion's sharp rebuke forced him to reorient to the one person to whom he had confessed his breakdown.

—from Berrigan's Ride

"I am impressed with how much careful work went into the manuscript. The attention to historic accuracy and detail, the poetic descriptions of landscape and flora, and the vistas and scenes. And with a style of dialogue that seemed quite 'in period.' It seemed to me there was a consistency that made it a fast and easy read.

"I think American males, in large measure, have suffered from post-war trauma throughout our history, and their families, children, and innocent bystanders have all suffered the effects. So the characters you describe—the men—from Kent to Benson—are just like the men we have always known! In short—your characters seem perfectly normal."

—Theodora Kreps, PhD (Ret.) Anthropology, Stanford University

"My great-grandmother (maternal) was the niece of Varina Howell Davis, second wife of Jeff Davis, president of the Confederacy. Varina was the sister of my great-grandmother's father. My great-grandmother's family moved to Union territory (Illinois) and fought for the Union. My great-grandfather and his brothers came from Wales, paid by the Union to come and fight for them—that was their stake in the war."

—Lilie Allen, author of poetry collections,
Bread in Your House and A Perfect Blossom

Opposite Page: Hollowtop Peak in Madison County